Pride Publishing books by Samantha Cayto

Single title
One Night in a Dungeon
Man Candy

Alien Slave Masters
The Captain's Pet
The Rebellious Pet
The Untamed Pet
The Captive Pet
The Inconvenient Pet
The Undercover Pet

Alien Blood Wars
Blood Dance
Dangerous Dance
Slave Dance

Anthologies
His Rules: Safeword
Right Here, Right Now: Never the Groom

Alien Blood Wars

STAR DANCE

SAMANTHA CAYTO

Star Dance
ISBN # 978-1-78686-383-6
©Copyright Samantha Cayto 2018
Cover Art by Cherith Vaughan ©Copyright December 2018
Interior text design by Claire Siemaszkiewicz
Pride Publishing

Published in 2018 by Pride Publishing, United Kingdom.

Pride Publishing is an imprint of Totally Entwined Group Limited.

STAR DANCE

Prologue

Scotland, April 20, 1746

"It's not safe for you to stick around."

Malcolm peered at his captain through the growing shroud of fog. "I have to. The laird has the right to know that his last remaining son now lies rotting in the bloody mud of Culloden. I don't know that there's anyone else who escaped to bring him the news."

He looked away, trying to hold in his grief until he was alone. "I owe the man that much courtesy after all he's been to me, especially when Fergus wouldn't have been part of that bloodbath if not for me."

Alex put his hand on Malcolm's shoulder. "I'm sorry. I know the MacLerie Clan treated you like family and that Fergus was as a hive brother to you."

"In all ways but one."

Fergus had been human, after all, and physical intimacy was something he couldn't give. It hadn't mattered. He'd been the first man on this wretched planet with whom Malcolm had been able to form a real friendship and who'd known about his alien nature and had not shrunk from it. That Malcolm had been unable to protect the man during the battle despite his superior strength and speed was a bitter failure that would haunt him until the end of his days — another to join one that already ate at him since the crash.

"It's more than that, though. I need to go for me. I can't do this anymore, Alex." He raised his eyes to his captain. "I simply *can't*."

He took in a deep breath and held it until his lungs burned before letting it out again. "When I refused to join Dracul's mutiny against you, I thought he'd give up his murderous plans quickly. These humans may be backward, but they don't lack courage or numbers. And yet, he hasn't. Century after century, he continues to maneuver in his quest for power. It's getting worse, not better.

"He'll never quit until he has succeeded or been killed." He shuddered with his emotions. "I'm sorry, sir, that I lack the will to keep on fighting. It's not in my nature — or perhaps it's been too much in my nature. I've fought long and hard these many centuries and more eagerly than I should have, especially this last time. I don't want to be that man anymore. Forgive me," he added, bowing his head and trying not to wish that he'd died along with Fergus.

Alex squeezed his fingers briefly before letting go. "It's all right. I understand. We started out as explorers and scientists. Despite our training, we were never meant to fight at all, never mind endlessly. Dracul has corrupted us in many ways."

A horse nickered, reminding Malcolm that they weren't alone and time was not on their side. The longer he kept Alex and the others, the greater the risk they'd be found by the Sassenach and executed — or, rather, the English soldiers would *try* to do so. They wouldn't succeed, but his brothers-in-arms weren't invincible. There was no benefit in taking the chance, not to mention that Val had rescued a pretty human boy who still looked stunned from what he'd witnessed during battle and appeared frightened to death over his uncertain fate.

"You should go, sir, please. I won't change my mind on this and can only say I'm sorry to abandon you."

Alex shot him a quick smile. "You aren't — or, at least, I don't see it that way. I appreciate your loyalty more than I can say. I can only hope you find some measure of peace here." He looked around the ever-shrouded area. "I can see why you'd love it. So like home with its rugged terrain and its cool mist."

Malcolm nodded. "I can make a good life here, sir, even if the laird tosses me out on my arse for not keeping his son safe." He paused. "Where will you go?"

Alex shrugged. Their mannerisms had become ingrained within their group over the many years they'd lived among humans. It helped them blend in but also had become second nature. "To the lowlands for the moment. Try to hide in plain sight. Maybe we'll go back to the continent in due time or even to the so-called 'new world'. America is a big and bold place — or so I've heard. A place where a person can become reborn."

"Until Dracul gets his hands on it." Malcolm couldn't keep the bitterness out of his voice.

"Wherever he goes, whatever he does, I will stop him." Alex stated it as fact, but the weariness in his tone was obvious.

Guilt ate at Malcolm, and yet, he couldn't go on. "You could stay here, sir. The Highlands are big enough for all of us to find refuge."

Alex shook his head. "No. The people here will be under siege for years to come. No need for us to add to their trouble by drawing Dracul's attention. We will be fine, and I mean it when I say that what you've done for me since our crashing here is no small thing."

But for me, we wouldn't have been marooned here at all. The confession stuck in his throat. After all these years, he still couldn't speak of it.

"I shall always be in your debt." With that, the captain turned to leave.

"Sir?" He waited until Alex looked over his shoulder. "I don't want to lose touch. I will try to find you once I've settled and get you word on what I'm doing. And if there is ever a time when you need me and no other to set Dracul back on his heels again, please don't hesitate to contact me."

"I will," Alex agreed with a nod. "Take care, Malcolm." With that, he joined the others, swung onto his horse and trotted off.

Malcolm stood watching until the last of his crewmates had been swallowed up in the mist. He waited another few minutes, absorbing how, for the first time in his entire life, he was truly alone. He briefly considered simply disappearing into the fog and living a solitary life for as long as nature and his own constitution would permit. What difference did it make now? He would never see his family or his hive again. Likely that was the last he'd see of Alex and the others, too, regardless of his recent promise.

He was no use to anyone, except he did have one last task that must be followed through. He owed Fergus' father that courtesy call. After that, who knew? It made no difference, in any event. There was no life on this planet that he could imagine living. Who could ever matter as much as Fergus had? Likely he wouldn't forge a bond that close, even with a lover—if such a man even existed. He'd never found more than a transient bed partner in all these centuries.

No, in the here and now, there was only honor. He would discharge his duty and let fate take him.

Chapter One

Dracul's Castle, 2018

Adhering stubbornly to the traditional highlander ways had its drawbacks. Malcolm MacLerie pondered that point as he knelt in the wet snow surrounding Dracul's castle. His bare knees had gone numb, but that was the worst of it. His belted plaid did well enough for the rest of his body, and he wasn't so stupid as to go without thick socks and high leather boots. Some nice, modern boxer-briefs kept the 'boys' snug, because, while tradition had its place, modern convenience couldn't be dismissed. If his friends back in the eighteenth century had been given the choice, he had no doubt they would have been devotees of Hanes.

It had been a good long while since he'd been in the thick of the war. He hadn't been able to sit out the two world wars. No one with a conscience could have. But this was the first time that Alex had called on him personally to return to the fold. Malcolm could hardly refuse, not after all Alex had been to him. And his captain had let him be for decades, giving him an opportunity to ruminate in the Highlands. Malcolm had forged a good life for himself, but he wouldn't have had any life at all if not for Alex.

So, this reconnaissance request was not much to ask. Malcolm had seen the news from Boston, in any event. He'd been halfway to contacting his old captain to offer his assistance when Alex had beat him to it. He'd been aware that Dracul had made his lair, as it were, in the same smallish part of the world as he had. But enough kilometers stood between their respective remote castles that they could have spent the rest of their centuries never crossing paths, if only Dracul would just settle the fuck down and be satisfied with the life he had.

Malcolm had found that peace, living in his beloved adopted home in the Highlands, raising salmon and producing the best single malt Scotch in the world, if he did say so himself. And speaking of which, he pulled out his flask and slugged back a wee dram to keep the cold at bay. Nothing much was going on in the castle this night anyway. His thermal-imaging scope confirmed, as it had for the last few nights, that Dracul and a few of his minions occupied the crumbling structure. At least, it looked like it was falling down from the outside. The inside was likely in fine repair, with modern amenities. He employed the same strategy in his own home to keep the curious at bay.

With the heat of the stone waning, he had no trouble pinpointing the various occupants. Most were on the lower levels, including two whose thermal signatures he identified as hybrids—Dracul's spawn, no doubt. Malcolm might have been out of the war for long periods, but he still kept up with the news. He knew the arsehole had taken a Welsh boy and turned him into a breeder. That kind of altered human created a heat signature that was different from their species or the hybrids. The hapless human was ensconced in the left tower, never leaving the one room, as far as Malcolm could determine.

And there was someone else in there as well — a purely human someone. Right at the moment, whoever he was occupied that room with the Welsh boy and Dracul, no doubt. Malcolm could only imagine that the boy — and it undoubtedly was a young male, given Dracul's predilections — wasn't there by choice. Dracul didn't make allies with humans as much as turn them into pawns and slaves.

Based on the time the figures were spending in the spot, he could only assume it was a bedroom. The pattern in which they'd come together over the many days he'd been watching left the purpose of the human obviously and nauseatingly in the category of the latter group. The boy was clearly Dracul's sex slave, a viciously horrible role that Malcolm lacked the imagination to even fathom.

"You poor, wee bastard," he muttered. "Well, we'll see about getting you out of that hellhole when we take out the fucker once and for all."

That was the plan, at least. What they would do with the boy after that was above his pay grade — and Alex's problem. Malcolm was doing his job. His surveillance was going to provide his captain with all the facts necessary for Alex to launch a direct attack. *'No more playing defense'* was how Val had put it. It tied right into Malcom's strengths, too. While he'd grown sick of fighting, spying was another matter. He could blend into the landscape and live off it, as well, for weeks on end. He might be used to sleeping in a laird's bed in a laird's home, but he hadn't forgotten his basic skills.

He'd obtained an accurate head count and mapped out the routine of the castle's inhabitants. He'd also found Dracul's bolthole, or rather, the one put in by the original owner and the tunnel it contained that would allow a secret retreat. When the time came to attack, they'd be able to use it to both enter the castle and block off the fucker's escape.

Christ, I hope this puts an end to it.

* * * *

"There now, almost finished."

Brenin gritted his teeth against the sting of Dafydd's efforts. His fellow captive had done his best every day to ease the hurts the monster had inflicted. It was sweet, but pointless. In a few hours, Dracul would be back to tear at and beat Brenin's body. The beast needed little time to recover, his appetites seemingly endless and unfailingly cruel.

Brenin had long given up any hope of respite. Not even death could be counted on, not until the monster had finished with him for good. At the rate he was going, that might not be long in coming. Since his latest efforts to do God-knew-what had failed, Dracul had become more unhinged. He vented his spleen on Brenin on a daily basis. There was barely an inch of skin that wasn't marked. Brenin's lips were almost constantly split and his head throbbed where it had taken a hard blow. He thought at least one rib was cracked. Every breath he took was agony.

But Dafydd meticulously and carefully cleaned him, and the brief respite from being covered in filth was something, he supposed. Brenin lay pliant and quiet, trying not to gain the notice of the monster across the room. He would have shut his eyes, except he worried about not being able to keep track of the imminent danger. Given how the violence had been escalating recently, he figured he would be dead within days. He both welcomed and feared it.

Dafydd tossed the bloody cloth into the bowl by the bedside then he filled a glass of water from the nearby pitcher. Before handing it to Brenin, however, he glanced quickly in Dracul's direction while he slipped his hand between the mattress and box spring. This had become the part of their daily ritual that Brenin appreciated the most. Somehow, the guy had managed to stash drugs without the monster realizing it. He plopped a pinch of powder into the glass, swirled it with his finger and held it out wordlessly for Brenin to drink.

He did so, eagerly and with his gaze averted as much as he could from the unnatural bulge of Dafydd's distended belly. It was impossible to believe that a baby grew in there, yet that was the case. It repulsed him. Somehow, Dracul had changed the boy into something both male and female. Brenin could only pray that the alien would kill him before he, too, was altered forever. Dafydd's obvious misery at his condition didn't help alleviate his disgust, either.

"Thanks," he mouthed before settling down. The drug usually made him sleep for a little while, removing the choice between vigilance and respite.

But while the pain receded to manageable levels, his eyelids didn't droop in their usual way and he didn't feel sleepy. He glanced at Dafydd, who was busy watching Dracul. Brenin wanted to ask him why the drug wasn't working as well, although he didn't dare speak out loud, of course. Maybe if he kept staring, the boy would feel his attention and turn back to him.

Dafydd didn't, though. Instead, he slipped his hand between the mattresses again, without taking his eyes off Dracul. When he pulled it back, there was a packet tucked inside his palm. The boy padded over to the fireplace where Dracul sat reading and sipping wine from his favorite golden goblet. *God, the guy is pretentious.* It was as if he were trying to emulate every ridiculous Bond villain Brenin had ever seen. The only thing missing was a fluffy, white cat.

"May I freshen your drink?" Dafydd asked in a low, silky voice.

Dracul's head snapped up and he glared at the boy. "Trying to curry favor, pet?"

Dafydd froze. He bowed his head. "Of course."

"How unlike you," the monster sneered. "Maybe carrying my son this time has made you soft." He gaze flicked over to Brenin, sending a chill down his spine. "Then again, perhaps you're already in daddy mode, trying to protect my new toy."

Dracul drained his goblet and held it out. "You shouldn't care about him, you know. He's your rival."

Dafydd crept closer and took the vessel with impressive steadiness. "For now, he's my respite." He rubbed at his side where the alien baby stretched his skin before he inched away.

The wine bottle stood on a table to one side from where Dracul sat. Dafydd maneuvered around so that his hands weren't directly in the monster's line of sight. Even at a distance, Brenin could see the boy emptying the packet he held into the glass before refilling it with wine. He did that quick finger stir, only now it was to blend something so that its drinker wouldn't notice.

Brenin dropped his gaze to the ground, fearful that whatever Dafydd was up to would be inadvertently revealed by his attention. He stared, instead, at the floor. Although he could still see Dafydd's movements, it was all bare legs and feet treading on the worn oriental rug.

"You use him too hard," Dafydd said. "You're going to kill him if you don't rein in your anger."

There was a sudden cry and Dafydd fell to his knees in front of Dracul. The monster managed to grab the goblet at the same time he fisted his 'husband's' hair, pulling him into the space between his spread legs.

"My, my, you *have* become paternal all of a sudden. If you're so concerned, you can take a turn in his place. You know what to do, slut. Now that your disgusting vomiting has come to an end, your mouth is useful again."

Brenin forced his eyes shut, unable to witness Dafydd's brutal subjugation. He couldn't block out the sounds, though, and his stomach turned, knowing how horrible it was to service the monster. He should have been grateful that it wasn't him, and on some guilty level, he was. But Dafydd was a decent mate, regardless of his motives, and Brenin cringed in sympathy.

He must have dropped off, because he came awake suddenly and fearfully by having his shoulder shaken.

"Brenin." It was Dafydd peering down at him. "Come on, mun. You've got to get up."

Benin blinked and pushed himself painfully to a sitting position. "What's going on?" He stared past the boy and saw Dracul slumped in his chair. The goblet lay on the rug. "Have you killed him?"

Dafydd rolled his eyes. "Don't be daft, mun. Drogo would never give me something that dangerous. I've only put him to sleep, like."

Brenin tried to wrap his mind around what was happening. "For what purpose?"

Dafydd tugged at his arm. "This is no time to be a chopsy boy. We don't have long."

Funny how the boy's Welsh came out now that they were essentially alone. Most of the time, his accent was muted and he spoke almost like a professor. Living with the brutal alien had changed him in more than one way, apparently. And yet Dafydd seemed older than he looked. His age was a mystery and Brenin wasn't sure he wanted to know more than he did. This whole experience was a living nightmare that he could almost believe as some kind of delusion.

He allowed himself to be pulled upright, grimacing at the stabs of pain all over and grateful for the relief the drug was giving him. "All right, then, what am I to do?"

"You're going to escape."

Brenin couldn't help but laugh at the statement. It wasn't even remotely possible. Dafydd shot him a look. "I'm not being funny. I'm going to help you get out of here before Dracul kills you."

Brenin followed the boy over to an alcove where Dracul kept a computer. It was incongruous with the ancient splendor of the rest of the room. Dafydd sat down in front of the thing and booted it up.

Pain made Brenin slow, but if Dafydd was serious about getting him away, anything was endurable. By the time he reached the alcove, the computer was up and humming. He stopped behind the chair and, putting his hand on the back, leaned on it.

"What are you playing at, mun?"

Dafydd's fingers flew over the keyboard. "I'm logging into the security system. From here, I can see where the rest of Dracul's ghouls are and set you on a safe path."

Brenin stared in fascination as a schematic of the castle appeared onscreen. It looked something like a video game. All of his time wasted on such trivial matters, as his mam would have said, came in handy as he scrutinized the information. "This is brilliant."

"There's an old escape route out of the castle and into the woods. I'm going to shut down the perimeter sensors once I judge you're at the bolthole where the tunnel starts, so that you can pass through the exit without setting off the alarms."

Brenin shook his head at the absurd words then instantly regretted it as his headache increased and his vision blurred. He froze to help it stop, and by the time he was able to view things clearly again, Dafydd was already standing.

A grimace flashed across the boy's face and he put a hand against his swollen belly. "This was supposed to be *my* plan. I've been sucking Drogo's cock for years to get pain meds. He thinks I used them to blunt the effect of Dracul's attentions, but I've been stockpiling them so I'd have enough to send the monster into sleep for a while to give me a chance to run."

He moved away and headed across the room. He motioned for Brenin to follow. "I could only guess how much would work, so we have to move quickly," he said quietly as he opened the large armoire where Dracul kept his belongings. "I have some clothing. Not much, because Dracul rarely lets me out and none of it is good for cold weather." He pulled out a shirt and jeans, socks and trainers. "It will do, though. Let me help you."

Brenin allowed himself to be dressed like a doll. It felt good to cover up after so many weeks of forced nakedness. Kneeling on the floor, Dafydd tugged the socks and trainers onto Brenin's feet—or tried to, anyway, the latter being too small.

"Damn, you'll have to make do with stockinged feet. Mind how you go, like. The stone floors in this old place are worn smooth. I've watched his computer usage, as well, under the guise of blow jobs. I can access anything I want." He stood and flashed Brenin a sad grin.

"I'll be fine, thanks. This is…unexpected. I-I don't know what to say."

"Nothing. Just get away. Dracul thought I was too stupid to understand anything. After all these centuries, he still thinks I'm a just a smudge-faced peasant that he dragged out of the mud."

"I don't understand," Brenin said with labored breath. Even this small amount of effort taxed him. "Why me and why now? You're throwing away your chance of freedom."

Dafydd clutched at his belly. "I can't go in this condition, and I know now that he intends to kill me the moment his son is free of my body." He looked at Brenin with tearful eyes. "It's too late for me. I accept that. It's not for you, though, and the way he's going, if you don't leave tonight, I'm afraid you won't last much longer."

Brenin choked back a cry. "I'm afraid of that, also," he admitted. "But he'll kill you for sure once he wakes."

"Not until Drogo can assure him of his son's safe delivery."

"He's all but mad, mun. You can't expect him to act rationally. He might kill you with the child not yet born."

Closing his eyes, Dafydd drew a deep breath. "So he ends my life all the earlier... I can't say I'll mind. I've had enough of this madness and I'd rather not give him another son to ruin." His eyes popped open again. "Come on. There's no time for talking. I'll show you the route on the computer that will lead you to the bolthole. The door inside it to the tunnel may or may not be hidden. I don't know because I've never been in it myself.

"From what I can make of the schematic, though, the tunnel will spit you out far enough into the woods that no one will spot you, even from the parapets. You're on your own from there, I'm afraid. We're high up and a good fifty kilometers from the nearest town. There's a road, of course, but I don't recommend you stick to it because it's the first place they'll look."

Brenin stopped the boy by grabbing his arm. "Come with me, then. We can take care of each other."

"No. Thanks all the same. With this spawn of his inside me, he'll come after us with a vengeance. On your own, you stand a chance of getting away without his making too much fuss."

"You know that's not true," Brenin ground out. "When has he ever been a graceful loser?"

Dafydd gave him a wan smile. "Never, but I'll buy you what time I can. Please, Brenin. Knowing you've made it out will allow me to bear what's left of my life."

Brenin wanted to argue. He couldn't imagine leaving this new friend of his to such a fate. He couldn't imagine staying to face his own hideous one, either. "Okay. And, um, thanks. I won't forget your kindness."

"Just live. That's all I ask. Leave here and run as far and as fast as you can. Your living will be my reward and your revenge."

* * * *

Malcolm walked the perimeter of the castle, careful to keep to the trees. He'd made this circuit every night to view the castle and its inhabitants from every possible angle. The thick stone labyrinth-like structure made it impossible to penetrate the entirety of it. Even with the enhanced version of imaging tech that his clever shipmate had developed, he still wasn't rocking any kind of Superman X-ray vision. His multiple visits, however, had given him a decent head count. He was surprised to find that Dracul no longer kept his full complement of mutineers surrounding him.

Of course, a few had been dispatched during the centuries-long fight, two alone in recent months over in Boston. Still, it was good to learn that when Alex gave the order to strike, they wouldn't have to bring in everyone on their side from their far-flung locations. Most of them, like Alex and the others settled in Boston, were trying to make quiet lives for themselves, just as he had. They would all come at Alex's request — again, just as he had. If they could be spared the horror of it… If he could help do that for his crewmates…all the better.

He was coming around the back of the castle and raised his scope to take a gander at what was usually a barren part, save for the kitchen. There was a young hybrid there and a couple of changed humans. He paid them little mind. All of Dracul's men had at least one enslaved boy and some, he believed, had produced offspring. They were there to guddle about, do the dirty work Dracul and his men would never lower themselves to bother with — no more than slaves, sexual and otherwise. Alex would have to figure out what to do with them afterward, as well. And those hapless humans and their offspring might prove to be another fashion of the enemy they'd have to watch out for. There was no accounting how some of them might feel after such long servitude.

A flash caught his attention. He turned to train his vision to a corner on his right. It was the human making his way down, far from the tower where he'd been imprisoned for as long as Malcolm had been watching. And he was alone, which made no sense unless...

Tossing his goggles into his backpack, Malcolm took off deeper into the forest. If he was right about what was happening, he knew the exact spot where the boy would emerge. The only problem would be the security sensors. Malcolm had found all of them the first night and, naturally, had been careful not to trip any of them, nor had he allowed himself to enter the line of sight of any of the surveillance cameras. But, if the boy came crashing out of the tunnel, he'd trip one for sure.

Except there had to be a plan... The boy couldn't have simply stumbled his way out of the tower room and through the castle to leave by the one possible avenue that wasn't being guarded by Dracul's men. He had to have had help, although the how and the why of it were unfathomable at the moment. There'd be time to learn the answers soon if he could manage to intercept the boy and get him far from here. In fact, he might prove a treasure trove of information. And whoever had orchestrated this surely knew about the sensors and…what? They'd been turned off, likely. Had to be.

With no one to mark his passage other than the creatures of the night, he used his natural speed. It felt good to cut free like that, something he dared do only on occasion in his beloved Highlands. Here and now, though, it was of necessity. Given how slowly the human had been moving, Malcolm had no doubt he would arrive at the exit first. He needed time, though, to ensure that if there was no one else taking care of it, he would knock out the sensors himself. It would blow his cover, as the Americans would say, but a chance to save this poor lad was worth any price.

He slowed down as he approached his destination and tossed his backpack against a tree. If he had to leave the thing behind, no worries. There was nothing in it that wasn't a duplicate of what he had back home, and once the boy emerged, speed would matter more than stealth. If Dracul learned of his presence, that would make the assault plan harder but not necessarily impossible.

He braced behind a neighboring tree and fixed his gaze on the tangle of undergrowth that hid the hole. Pinpricks of red from the sensors' eyes were visible from his vantage point. They were set up on smaller trees on either side of the hole, easy to miss unless one were looking for them. The beam they formed would be broken the moment the boy passed through. Except, as he stood and watched, the lights winked out.

It took a few more minutes before he finally heard the whisper of footsteps approaching. They were slow and clumsy sounding, then the branches rustled. Fingers poked out from between the leaves, then a dark head and finally the entire boy stumbled through. He would have tripped to the ground if Malcolm hadn't raced forward.

He caught the human handily and took a second to assess how little the wee thing weighed before he was forced to clamp his hand over the boy's mouth. A muffled cry of abject fear tore at Malcolm's heart, but he hardened it and tugged the human past the point where the sensors would detect them once they were turned back on.

The frightened lad struggled to free himself for a few feet before he stiffened and screamed against Malcolm's palm. Then the human went limp, dead weight, testifying that he'd passed out. Malcolm waited until he was sure he was clear of detection before turning the boy in his arms to peer into his face.

Ah, God. He was bonny — or would be if not for the cuts and bruises that marred his face. There was still plenty of pale skin to be seen and dark hair was plastered with sweat against his head. The boy's heart beat rapidly, even though he was unconscious. The pulsing at the base of his throat drew Malcolm's gaze, whether he willed it or not. There was a sweet scent to him that lay detectible under the stench of Dracul's brutalization.

The lad seemed genuinely unconscious. When Malcolm cautiously withdrew his hand, he inwardly swore at the bloody lip he found. That was his first reaction. His second was to flick his tongue over the wound to heal it shut. Sure, that had been the simple plan, but the taste of the boy was like a punch to his dick. Against all decency and logic, lust roared through his veins with a force that left him gasping.

The lad shuddered and his eyelids fluttered a bit before quieting again. Malcolm knew a moment of disappointment over not being able to tell the color of the human's eyes, but that hardly mattered. He was wasting precious time salivating over the boy's desirability. He needed to get them both out of there. He could only assume there was damage to the frail body that he couldn't see, so with as much care as he could muster, he cradled the boy in his arms.

It was awkward, yet possible, to retrieve his pack as well. No sense in tipping his hand if it could be avoided. Surveillance, at any rate, was over. The safety of this human came first. Malcolm would get him away and back home within a day. He could tend to him there, or, rather, he could have him seen to. Malcolm was no doctor. He would simply put the boy to bed and let those who knew how make him better.

As the obvious plan set into place within his head, he didn't stop to question why he pictured tucking the lad into not just any bed, but his own.

Chapter Two

Brenin woke with a cry that he muffled instantly. *Stay quiet. Don't let the monster know you're awake.* It was too late, however. He wasn't lying in some bed in a large room. Instead, he sat strapped into the front seat of a beat-up SUV that seemed particularly small, given that it was occupied by a huge man behind the wheel.

No, not a man—an alien just like the one he'd escaped. *Oh God, I failed.* He remembered it clearly now, how he'd stumbled out of the tunnel after fleeing for his life and right into the arms of another captor. The agony of his ribs had sent him down into unconsciousness, but now he was awake and all too aware that he was being driven away. The question was, to where?

"Easy, laddie," the alien said without taking his eyes off the road. "You're safe."

Brenin barked out an almost hysterical laugh at the reassurance. How could that be even remotely possible under the circumstances? He might not be with Dracul anymore, but he was with someone just as dangerous and probably as vicious. Slumped against the door, he felt particularly vulnerable. He tried to sit up. Fire licked at his side, making him grimace and drop back.

"Try not to move. You might have a broken rib or two, and until Doc McPhee has a go at you, it's best not to jar anything." The alien's mouth tightened into a straight line. "The fucker had a right go at you, didna he?"

Brenin blinked back at him, confused. The guy sounded Scottish, which made no sense. From what Dafydd had told him, he knew Dracul had spent centuries in Wales and yet he spoke as if English wasn't his mother tongue. His accent had been impossible to place because every Earth-born language was foreign to him. Either Dracul was terrible at blending in or he hadn't bothered to try. This one was different. In what way and whether that would be better or worse for Brenin remained to be seen.

"He beat and raped me every day," he said in a quiet tone that didn't betray how much it cost him to speak of the horror out loud.

The driver turned his violet eyes on him. "He'll not be doing it anymore. No one will."

The alien returned his gaze to the road. It was still pitch-black out with cloudy skies. Only the headlights revealed their path and it seemed the road was too narrow for the speed they traveled. And yet, the alien appeared at ease and Brenin didn't feel at risk of harm—not from an accident, anyway.

He looked away and out of his side window. If he went slowly, he could shift his position without a huge amount of pain. He was warm, as well, and that was something new. The castle room had been freezing, and with no clothes or covers, he'd had to become accustomed to being cold and miserable. Here, the heater blasted warmth onto him and he noticed that, in addition to the clothing Dafydd had given him, he was wrapped in a large woolen plaid. It smelled vaguely of smoke and some kind of spicy scent that he couldn't place.

He glanced at the alien and noticed for the first time that while the man wore a simple long-sleeved shirt, he also had on a kilt. It was a real one, too, not the kind tourists bought or fancy men sported to play at being a highlander. It was worn and smudgy. It rode up his right leg, exposing a large knee as the alien worked the gas pedal.

"Who are you?" Brenin dared to ask. What difference did it make if he pissed the guy off? He was either one of Dracul's minions who was taking Brenin to some hideous death or he was the next animal in line to use Brenin as a chew toy. He knew these monster aliens' ways and had already learned that being good made no difference. There was no appeasing their appetite for cruelty.

"I'd say a friend, but that would be cheeky of me. Let's say I'm an ally."

"Never," Brenin scoffed. "Pull the other one. It's got bells on."

"It's the truth, laddie. I know you don't have reason to believe me, but while Dracul and I are of the same species and we landed on your big, blue ball here together, we are enemies now."

"My name is Brenin Jones, if you're going to call me anything." He supposed 'laddie' was better than 'slut'. He was feeling peevish for sure—and rash. Perhaps somewhere down deep, he hoped to goad this creature into simply killing him once and for all.

"Well, I'd say pleased to meet you, Brenin, if not for the circumstances. I'm Malcolm MacLerie."

"You aren't, though, are you?" he snapped back. "I don't care what you wear or how you speak, you're still an alien. A monster!" He spat the last word out, leaning toward the guy, his ribs making him gasp.

"Easy, now. Dinna fash yourself." He shot Brenin another look with those violet eyes.

On Dracul, the color had been creepy, especially as they'd go blacker then red, depending on his mood. None of it had boded well for Brenin.

"I'm not going to hurt you. You have my word on it."

"Do you honestly think that means anything to me after all I've been through these last few months?" He looked away, out of the window again, blinking furiously at tears. *Damn.* He'd stopped crying long ago, knowing that signs of pain and misery only made the monster happy.

A few minutes ticked by, the only sound the noise of rubber running on the road and Brenin's harsh breathing. Then, "I was doing surveillance on the castle, looking for Dracul's warrior numbers and any security weaknesses. My thermal imaging equipment gave me a human heat signal. I knew you were his slave because that's all he does with humans."

The alien grimaced. "We would have got you out eventually, but when I saw you on the run, I intercepted you at the tunnel exit I'd found earlier. There was no choice in that. Dressed as you are, you wouldn't have lasted long out in this cold. And Dracul's goons would have found you easily enough, regardless."

Brenin rubbed his feet against the floor. His socks were still damp, although the heater was doing a decent job of drying them out. "Dafydd gave me what he had."

He licked his lips, noticing for the first time that they weren't split as they had been. Shooting a look at his captor, he wondered how that might have happened. Their saliva could close wounds. A shudder ran through him at the memory of how often the monster had drunk his blood.

The alien glanced at him sharply. "Are you cold, laddie?" He turned up the heater fan without waiting for an answer. "We'll be at this wee, out-of-the-way dock before dawn and take off for my home in my boat. Dracul will never find you."

Brenin choked back a cry and swiped at tears leaking down his cheek. "I'm not worried about him anymore, mun. It's you that scares me! How long before you do to me what he did? I don't care what you say. I know what your kind is like and I'd rather die than go through all that again."

The moment the words left his mouth, Brenin knew that he meant them. Without a second's thought, he fumbled for the door handle. At the speed they traveled, he could only hope launching himself from the SUV would be enough to end him and his misery.

The vehicle he'd rented in the sleepy fishing village wasn't big enough for Malcolm's comfort but he was grateful for the tight fit now as he lunged to keep the Welsh boy from opening the door. His unwilling passenger screamed as Malcolm's arm banged against the kid's chest of necessity. Malcolm needed to grab the handle while he maneuvered the SUV to the side of the road and braked. Once it came to a stop, he lifted his other hand from the wheel and used it to corner the boy within his embrace.

Brenin was like a wild thing, flailing against Malcolm's loose hold, trying to get the door open. It took little to contain the boy, but it was impossible to do so without hurting him. Heartbreaking tears ran down his bruised cheeks and dripped off his chin. He was hysterical with his fear and mindless with it.

"God's teeth, boy, please don't fight me. You're only going to do yourself more harm and I'm not going to let you run away. I'm trying to save you!"

The human clawed at Malcolm's arms, his efforts pitifully weak. "Just do it! Please, kill me. Snap my neck if you have to. I know you're strong enough."

Malcolm tugged the boy closer, taking him away from the door, and pressed him against his chest. "I'll do no such thing."

"Sink your bloody monster fangs in me, then. Drain me dry." As Brenin strained against his hold, his neck stretched to expose the pulse point at the base of this throat.

Malcolm doubted the human had deliberately set out to entice him in a way that Malcolm's nature made it nearly impossible to resist. He was already attracted to the pretty boy against his better judgement. The lure of sinking his fangs into that exquisite blue vein was almost overwhelming. He opened his ears to listen to how the blood and the heart raced. For a few insane moments, it was all he could focus on. His dick pressed against the confines of his smallclothes and he was damn glad to have put them on. A kilt would have done a poor job of hiding his arousal and it was the last thing the boy needed to see.

Then the sound of the sobbing snapped him back to what mattered. All the fight had gone out of Brenin liked a popped balloon. He sat pliant in Malcolm's arms with his head hanging and his shoulders shaking.

"There now, laddie," Malcolm soothed. "I've got you and in a good way. I promise that. No killing, no blood-sucking…no *nothing* you don't want me to do." He couldn't make his tongue speak of the worst of Dracul's abuse. That the bastard had used this frail boy as a fuck toy was an outrage that Malcolm would gladly avenge when the time came.

He rubbed his hand lightly up and down the boy's arm, liking that his plaid covered him. His foot remained jammed against the brake, as he hadn't had the opportunity to switch the gear into park. His leg started to ache, but he ignored it. As much as he wanted to put a greater distance between them and the castle, he didn't dare risk continuing until Brenin had calmed enough to stay in his seat.

The boy slid into Malcolm and let his head drop against his shoulder. It would have been a touching show of trust if not for his next words.

"I hurt and I'm tired of fighting. You do what you want. I won't struggle or try to run off. I just want some relief and sleep. Can I have that much?"

Malcolm placed a hand on the human's head and ran his fingers through the lank hair in the only way he knew how to give comfort. "Of course you can—the sleep, anyway. I can do nothing for the pain until I get you back home. Do you want some water, then?"

Brenin shook his head and took a shuddery breath. He felt so immensely frail, more so than most humans. He was all but skin and bones. Well, Cook would fatten him up right quick once she got her hands on him.

Aching leg or not, Dracul be damned, too. He could stay there forever with the boy in his arms. That would be stupid, though, so Malcolm forced himself to let go and help the boy sit back into his own seat. Brenin didn't fight him, his dull gaze stuck to a spot on the floor as Malcolm made sure the seatbelt was in place.

When there was no good reason to keep his hands on the boy, Malcolm returned them to the steering wheel and pulled back onto the road.

"Get some rest. We've a ways to go yet." With that, he kept his focus on the driving and not on the still, defeated boy by his side.

* * * *

Brenin woke with a start, once again disoriented and on edge until he remembered where he was. The small cabin onboard the alien's boat rocked as they sped along to only God-knew-where—a castle along the Scottish coast apparently. He hadn't been taking much notice of what his captor said. He'd been too wrung out from the crying jag to care and had wanted only to lie down and sleep.

He rolled over onto his back with a wince. His ribs still felt as if they were on fire, and that wasn't the only pain, just the worst of it. But there was nothing new plaguing him. Despite how he'd fought the alien while in the SUV, the guy hadn't beaten him—or worse. He supposed it was a matter of waiting for a better opportunity, except that seemed wrong somehow. It would have taken nothing for the beast to clock him a good one, at least, and yet he hadn't done so. He'd simply held Brenin within the circle of his massive arms, stopping him from leaving.

The opportunity to escape had passed, regardless. Unless he wanted to try jumping off the boat and drowning himself, he had no choice but to accept his fate and see what this next monster would bring. He rather doubted he'd be allowed to succeed going overboard any more than he'd been permitted to jump out of the moving vehicle. These aliens were quick as lightning and stronger than oxen. He stood no chance of gaining his freedom and any notion to the contrary had been wishful thinking. Poor Dafydd would die for nothing.

Taking a tentative breath, he felt out the possibility that his body would allow him to get up and use the en suite. His bladder was full to bursting and the bottle of water sitting on the shelf by the bed was tempting. He had a powerful thirst now that the drugs had worn off and he'd slept some. When he didn't see stars in front of his eyes, he dared to sit and swing his legs over the side. He didn't even question why he was still wrapped in the alien's plaid, nor did he consider shoving it off when he stood to stagger over to the toilet.

The wool kept him warm enough, for the cabin was chilly. He'd bet the topside was freezing. Given the way he had to brace his legs against the boat's movement, he gauged it was going at a fair clip. Add the winter temperature in with the wind and you'd have a ball-freezing time of it steering the craft. And he knew from grizzly experience that the aliens were equipped the way any human man was.

This crazy bastard wears a kilt, no less.

It seemed impossible that an alien would disguise himself as a highlander in the twenty-first century. Maybe he'd imagined the whole of it. So many recent blows to his head could have scrambled his brain.

There was only one way to know for sure and to find out what his immediate fate was going to be. He couldn't trust any of his memories, that was for certain. And while he could hide out in the cabin, he was done with being a victim.

After relieving himself and downing a fair amount of the water, he was ready to brave the outside. Gathering the plaid tightly around him, he opened the small door and stepped into a narrow hallway. A short flight of steps later, he staggered onto the windy deck. Since his capture, his hair had grown out, enough to whip around his face. He had to drag strands back behind his ears to get a good look around.

The first thing he saw was the green coast not far from where the boat sped along. The sight gave him comfort, although he wasn't sure why. Something about being out to sea would have frightened him more, although even on land, he was no closer to being free. With a hand on the railing to steady himself, he turned to look at the open cockpit behind him. There, with this long, thick legs braced, stood the man he remembered.

Not man, alien. Monster. Except he didn't look like one, not from this angle anyway. The wind whipped his kilt, exposing the backs of his knees and corded thighs. His thin cotton shirt didn't look sufficiently warm for the weather, but lots of muscular men withstood the cold better than most. His long, black hair was held back with a few braids on either side pulling the strands away from his face.

There was only a hint of a jawline and a strong, straight nose visible. He looked for all the world like an extra from *Braveheart*, although no one in their right mind would have cast him. He would have eclipsed Mel Gibson if they had. While there'd been an oily, repulsive quality to Dracul, this one presented a masculine beauty that must turn unsuspecting heads.

Not that Brenin was one. He knew all too well the vicious cruelty of the aliens. Tired of being a victim, however, he made himself approach the helm. A swell caused the boat to rise and rock, tossing him off his stride.

The alien threw out his arm and caught Brenin by the waist before he landed on his arse. "Careful, laddie. The sea is rough this time of year and I'm pushing the throttle to get us home faster."

Brenin grabbed hold of the bracing arm, even though he hated doing so. Its implacable firmness, nevertheless, made him feel safer. "It's not my home, now is it?" he said, raising his voice against the wind and giving his tone more bite than was wise, given how much this creature could hurt him. "It's my new prison."

The alien — MacLerie, he supposed he should think of him as — glanced sharply at him while he continued to steer with one able hand. "It's not that, no — neither your home nor your prison. But it is a safe place for you to rest and heal while my friends and I take care of Dracul once and for all."

Brenin blinked against the salt spray, appreciating the briskness of the open air because the plaid did keep him nice and cozy warm. "If I'm not a prisoner, why didn't you leave me back in that village where you kept this boat docked?"

MacLerie turned to give him a pointed look before replying. "And how long would it have taken, do you think, for Dracul's men to sniff you out and drag you back? I would have had to go in and rescue you before we're ready to tackle him head on, and likely we both would have died in the effort."

"Why would you bother? I'm nothing to you and it's not as if you can't find a boy of your own if that's your intent. I expect you already have one waiting in your bed." He'd intended to make an accusation, and in a sense he had, although not quite in the way he should have. It sounded disturbingly as if he were affronted at the idea. Horrified, he hurried to clarify what he really meant. "You're all monsters."

MacLerie shook his head. "Ah, laddie, what you don't know is a lot. Give me a chance to explain, to prove to you that I mean you no harm and that when it's safe to do so, I'll see that you return to your home."

It was on the tip of his tongue to reply that he had no home—hadn't for nearly a year. His father's tolerance for Brenin's gayness had ended within weeks of his mam's death. He'd been forced to leave and had resorted to living in shelters once his friends' largess had dried up as well. That was how the monster had found him, a homeless piece of trash trying to survive without even his General Certificate in his hand. No family, not enough education and no decent job prospects had made him the perfect target. He still was, truth be told.

Chop sent him staggering once more, this time against MacLerie. The man hugged him closer to his side. Brenin grabbed on to the man's waist without thinking. He met implacable hardness. But when his side collided with the guy's hip, he couldn't hold in a grunt and hiss. MacLerie somehow pulled away while holding him steady.

"Easy, there. You should go below and sit down at least. It's a wee bit bumpy out here, given how hurt you are."

Shaking his head, Brenin tightened his grip on the man. "I want to be in the fresh air, if it's all the same to you. I've been trapped inside for months." He craned his neck back to gaze at the bright blue sky. "It's glorious to be out in the sun."

"Oh, aye, I understand. Mind now that you don't overdo. And I'm that sorry if you're hungry. I don't have anything t'hand, but I called ahead and Darling will have Cook putting on a proper breakfast for when we arrive."

Darling? "You have a wife, then?" *Why did my tone turn surly again?*

MacLerie laughed, although it was genuinely joyful, not the grating gloating of Dracul. "Naw, Darling is my majordomo and a more dour man you'll never meet, even though he's half English. But he's loyal to the bone. Cook's a woman from the village and a dinnae ken her name. I've never thought to ask. She scares me a wee bit, truth be told." He flashed a smile at him and Brenin had to look away from the gleaming beauty of the man.

"I'm hungry right enough," Brenin admitted.

"Another hour or so should see us...there." He'd meant 'home' and Brenin knew it. *But he was sensitive and didn't use it for fear of rubbing me the wrong way? Is it possible that this alien is what he claims to be and not what I fear?*

Time would tell, and staring out at the white-capped water, he knew for certain that there was a still a will to live in him. He wasn't ready to end it just yet. Perhaps his sense of optimism was stupid. In a few hours, he might be trapped in another monster's bed, weeping and as miserable as he'd been for months. If so, there would always be some chance to end his life. When he'd run from Dracul, he'd done it to live. If escape proved impossible in this life, he'd achieve it in the next.

For now, he'd allow himself some small measure of hope that he was free from enslavement.

* * * *

The rest of the journey was made in relative silence and bracing enough to clear Brenin's mind from the remaining fog of the drugs Dafydd had given him. The pain wasn't unbearable, but he was looking forward to some relief once they arrived at MacLerie's home. He didn't bother to question why he remained at the man's side, either, although, if pressed, he would have said it was to keep his feet under him. It simply didn't hold the kind of fright in him that it should have. And, from the vantage point of the helm, he was able to enjoy the view.

Rolling hills along the coast turned to craggier ones. Then, as they came around a curve in the shoreline, he spotted what looked like a fishery and behind that, sitting higher up, was a brooding castle.

"That's my precious salmon farm," MacLerie said with a nod. "And beyond is the place I've lived for…well, a while now."

Soon, the man slowed the engines and pulled closer inland. They entered a small cove with a bit of a sandy beach to a dock that held a few other vessels. Some were smaller than the one they were on and one was much larger—a yacht, really—and it must have cost a pretty penny. These aliens had been on Earth long enough to amass some amount of wealth, he'd learned.

"Sorry, laddie," MacLerie said, pulling his arm away. "I'm going to need a wee bit of room to bring us in."

It took a perverse second for Brenin to make his fingers unfurl and step away. He told himself it was because he was afraid of falling. Really, he feared distancing himself from the man who he'd already become dependent on. There was an older man standing on the dock, peering at him with an expressionless, craggy face. He wore a dark suit with a vest in the same plaid Brenin still had wrapped around him. His stern demeanor reminded Brenin of the awful creatures that fawned over Dracul and did his bidding.

MacLerie pulled the boat alongside the dock with obviously practiced ease and tossed the rope coiled nearby to the man. He had to be the majordomo, Darling. Such a funny name, although Brenin would bet the lines in the man's face hadn't been made by humor. Nevertheless, the guy caught the rope handily and tied it off without any obvious effort, something he'd done plenty of times, likely. That surprised Brenin. Surely there'd be more people working such a large estate. Then again, how easily could an alien get and keep human help? Maybe the rest of the aliens were somewhere inside the castle or the outbuildings.

Hanging from rafters or lying in coffins until the sun goes down.

He wasn't sure where his sense of humor came from, given his circumstances. And he knew that no matter how much these creatures captured the legend of vampires, they didn't only come out at night or burn up in the sun. MacLerie was testament to that much. The guy didn't seem to mind being outside. He easily shut down the boat and helped his man secure it to the dock before turning to Brenin.

"Let's get you inside, laddie." He held out his hand.

"You can call me Brenin, you know."

MacLerie flashed grin. "Brenin it is, then. Come. I'll help you up." He held Brenin's hand with his big one to get him up on the side and over the narrow span to the dock. He didn't let go, however, even after Brenin's feet were both on the wooden planks.

"Take a second to get your land legs back," MacLerie said cheerily. "I know we were on the boat for only hours, but still, it was that choppy, so…" He turned to the other man. "This is Darling. Darling, this is the young Mr. Jones I told you about."

The majordomo inclined his head. "Welcome to Castle Rionnag, if I may be so bold."

Pulling the plaid tighter, Brenin said, "Thank you, I guess."

Darling looked at his master with one eyebrow raised.

"Mr. Jones is reserving judgment about us, Darling," MacLerie said rather cheerily. "And given his time with Dracul, who can blame him?"

"Indeed, sir, most unfortunate." The older man turned his steely gaze on Brenin. "I assure you, young master, this is a safe place." His sincerity and his obvious humanness did a lot to relax Brenin.

"Is Doc McPhee about, Darling?"

"Not as yet, sir. Old Mrs. Cameron down in the valley is taking her last journey and the doctor is helping to ease her way as best she can. She promised to come as soon as she is able. She did add that if matters were urgent, her medical assistant could come earlier."

MacLerie's palm slid up to the center of Brenin's back. "I don't think that will be necessary. We might give the boy some ibuprofen with his breakfast. Surely that won't hurt. What do you think, Brenin?"

It took him a moment to appreciate that he was being asked his opinion. It had been a while since that had happened. He nodded. "Um, yeah, if you please."

"That's fine, then. Let's get you up to the castle. Can you walk or would you like some help?"

Brenin briefly pictured being swept up in those brawny arms. The image frightened him, although not as much as it should. "No, thanks, I can walk."

Darling cleared his throat and looked pointedly down at Brenin's feet. "I think you'll find the crushed stone path uncomfortable, dressed as you are, sir."

Scrunching his toes, Brenin considered that observation. "I guess you're right."

MacLerie stepped into his line of vision. "I'll be as careful as I can." That was all he said before tucking his arm around Brenin's waist and behind his knees. A split-second later, he was airborne and cradled in the alien's embrace. His heart beat frantically before he could calm himself. The pressure of the fingers gripping him increased.

"I'm not going to hurt you." MacLerie's voice was as tight as his hold.

Brenin dared to look up at him from under his lashes. Those violet eyes were wide and fixed at a point around Brenin's mouth. No, at his neck, where his jugular pulsed. And a bit of pearly white showed around the man's lips. Brenin mewed in distress, memories of fangs sinking into his flesh making him fearful at an animalistic level.

"Shh, dinnae fash yourself."

Really? Was Brenin truly not supposed to worry about how he was trapped, not only in an alien's control but in his very arms? The pathetic thing was, he'd almost forgotten his precarious and morbidly bizarre situation.

"Mr. Jones?" The majordomo gently tapped his shoulder. When Brenin shifted his gaze to the man, he said, "I have been in MacLerie's employ for over fifty years now and I can assure you, he does nothing without consent. You are safe here, and may God strike me down if I let anything untoward happen to you."

Brenin blinked back at him, amazingly comforted by the old-fashioned, yet obviously earnest, vow. "Th-thank you."

"You are very welcome." The man flicked his gaze at MacLerie. "You might stop standing around with your fangs flashing if you want to prove an amiable host. *Sir.*" With that admonishment, the man turned on his heel and marched off.

MacLerie started after him, although at a slower pace. "Well, if ever I get too big for my britches, there's always Darling on hand to bring me back into line. I'm sorry, laddie-Brenin, for my lapse. My nature is not unlike Dracul's, and while I do a far better job of keeping it under control, I'm not always as strong as I'd like to be."

Brenin curled inside the plaid. "Do you drink blood?" He had to ask. It was the one thing in particular that the monster had done to him that he couldn't abide the thought of. Even the constant rapes and beatings had paled in comparison to having his vein tugged at.

"Aye, I do, yes. That's our nature, but I get my blood by the bagful normally these days. And, like Darling said, I never take what isn't given freely."

"I will never do that for you." Brenin didn't care what the consequences were for his refusal.

MacLerie kept his gaze on the path ahead. The lines around his mouth tightened. "Of course not. I've told you. You're not a prisoner and you're not my slave. You are my guest. I take nothing and expect you to give me nothing, except time to make the world safer for you and everyone else."

There was no more talking for the rest of the short journey up to the castle. They entered through a side door that looked hundreds of years old. Up close, he could see that the structure was mostly ancient stone with some weathered wood here and there. It was one of those buildings that had been expanded on over the centuries. He wondered how long MacLerie had lived there and what had happened to those that had built it in the first place, if the alien hadn't.

The master of the place didn't put Brenin down once they were inside. Instead, he carried him into a small dining room that was positively medieval. A roaring fire was lit in the large stone fireplace at one end. A plump, middle-aged women bustled about, setting food down in two places, one at the head of the table and the other to the right of it.

She looked up at their approach and smiled broadly. "Now, here is the dear lad. Come. Put him right on this chair. I've got a nice hot bowl of porridge for him. Don't make that face, laddie," she scolded good-naturedly. "You haven't tried mine yet to judge and there's a wee bit of honey in there as well, to make it go down better. And I've got some scones and bacon for later, once we're sure your poor stomach is taking to everything all right."

The woman had a point, he realized. He hadn't been given much to eat since his capture and all of his insides were a bit tender from the beatings, as well. "Thank you, ma'am," he said sincerely as MacLerie put him down beside, not on, the chair she'd indicated.

"Now, you just call me Cook. Everyone does." She smiled brightly again. Her homey appearance could have guaranteed her a spot in any period piece put on by the BBC.

Brenin slid into his seat, trying to hold back the wince that still came from any change in position. After picking up his spoon, he dipped it into the oatmeal and took a small bite. It was good, a little sweet and creamy. He smiled in gratitude.

"Good and all, then," Cook said with a firm nod. "Go on and tuck in yourself, sir. Imagine haring all the way to Wales without so much as a snack." She shook her head and tsked. "Eat your black pudding. I'll be getting that pain reliever for you, dearie," she added before leaving.

MacLerie sat in his chair and laid his napkin across his lap before picking up his cutlery. His plate was piled high with all manner of food, including the dreaded black pudding. Brenin made a face when the man cut a piece in half and stuffed it into his mouth.

The alien grinned as he chewed, then swallowed. "Don't look so horrified, Brenin. A proper Scotsman would eat this without my alien nature."

Brenin returned his attention to his bowl. "I know, mun. I just don't like it myself."

"But you do like Cook's porridge?"

"Yes, it's a proper breakfast for me right now. I wouldn't mind a scone, though."

"As Cook said, see how that sits on your stomach. No one's going to make you eat anything or do anything you don't want to here, Brenin. We'll see what the doc has to say about your injuries, and then," he added with a sigh, "as much as it pains me, I'm going to have to start asking you questions about your time with Dracul. We mean to end him, my friends and I, and I think you're the perfect person to help us succeed."

Chapter Three

"Malcolm, are you still there?"

"Yes, Captain, sorry." He leaned against the hallway wall using one bare foot to prop himself up. His head wasn't really in the game, as the Americans would say. His concentration was too absorbed by the closed door in front of him. Doc McPhee was in that room, giving Brenin an exam. Malcolm would have liked to have been there for the boy, except he understood that it was a private matter and he really had no right to gawk, however good his intention.

"Let me guess. You're pacing in agitation while waiting for the doctor to be done with the boy."

Malcolm rolled his eyes. There was a reason Alex was in command. He knew his men well. "Not as such, no, but I am standing out in the hall like an expectant father."

"These days humans go into the delivery room." A breath blew over the line. "I know you're worried. Poor kid. Dracul must have abused him terribly."

"From what little I've gleaned, aye, he did right enough. The fucker. I'm going to apologize right now, sir, for being stroppy with you when you first called about getting involved. If I hadn't been doing surveillance, the boy would never have escaped." Although Malcolm had had his fill of the war, he couldn't turn a blind eye to the havoc Dracul wreaked, especially when it occurred in his own backyard, as it were.

He rubbed his free hand down the front of his thigh and pounded the heel of his palm against it. *What the bloody hell is taking so long?*

"He's just as much a benefit to us as you were to him. To have an inside look at Dracul's scheming may prove invaluable. Are you confident that you disguised your scent well?"

Jamming his hand in the front pocket of his jeans, Malcolm pushed away from the wall and started pacing as Alex had predicted. "Well now, I would be if it had stayed a matter of my wandering about the place. Given that they could have been by the exit to the tunnel within an hour of my leaving, they might have sniffed me out under all that musky cologne I doused myself in."

"Hmm, can't be helped. Saving the boy was worth possibly losing the element of surprise. Humans may play number games with lives, but we can't start thinking that way ourselves. I need you to bring him here as soon as you're able."

Malcolm stopped and frowned. "You want us in Boston?" That hadn't been part of the plan. Alex and the others were supposed to come to him so that they could launch an attack.

"Yes. The boy changes things. We need to utilize him as a source of information as best we can. He may not be in a mental state where he'll give you everything he knows. I can't imagine he trusts you."

That was true, damn it all. He could see weariness, if not outright fear, in Brenin's eyes. It could be a long time, if ever, before he'd truly believe Malcolm meant him no harm. They didn't have a lot of time if they were going to stop Dracul before he launched more misery on the world.

"No, he doesn't," Malcolm confirmed with a grimace.

"That's why bringing him here makes sense." There was a pause. "We haven't been in touch much lately, so you probably aren't aware that Val has married a human. And, like Harry did with Lucien, he's changing his husband for breeding."

Malcolm barked out a laugh. "The fuck, you say?" He was that glad to hear of it. While he'd been mostly separated from his brethren after Culloden, he'd caught up with them and their lives from time to time. He knew Val had lost his red-haired laddie long ago in childbirth. "I'm glad of it, and I do hope he's happy."

"He is." Alex cleared his throat. "And I have entered a committed relationship with a human, although we both think marriage is premature, mostly because he's so young. He's my life, as far as I'm concerned. Emil also has a similar situation—and with someone who was abused for years."

"You've all been busy, for sure, Captain."

"We have, even as we've fought against Dracul's most recent battles. The point is these boys understand what's at stake and may prove more successful in gaining your boy's trust."

It was on the tip of Malcolm's tongue to correct Alex. *He's not* my *boy.* Then the door opened and his heart rate ticked up at the sight of the doctor. "Aye, sir, I'll get on that as soon as I can. The doc's coming out, so I'll need to see how Brenin is faring."

"Understood. One more thing, though. I've asked Willem to come join you."

Malcolm was focused on the doctor's expression, trying to read how things had gone. "Have you now?" he said, distracted. Then the meaning of Alex's words sank in. "Is that necessary, Captain? I mean, the last I'd heard, he was grieving the loss of a lover."

That was a constant pitfall for all of them — loving and losing frail and short-lived humans.

"I can pilot my plane alone." That was sort of true. He'd learned and practiced and he could get from point A to point B without too much trouble. His skill was nothing like that of Willem's, however. And Brenin's life would be on the line if he screwed up. "Thank you, sir," he added with his next breath. "I appreciate the help."

"I thought you might and Willem was more than happy to join in the *fun*. Come as soon as the boy can manage it." Alex disconnected the call.

Malcolm was already doing the same. He strode over to the middle-aged doctor, a slender woman with a mop of gray hair. "How is he?"

She gave him a tired look, reminding him that she'd been with a dying Mrs. Cameron for probably the whole night. "Not so bad as he needs a hospital, but bad enough that I hope you're planning on killing whoever is responsible."

Malcolm gave her a fierce look. "I am indeed."

"Good." She carded her fingers through her hair. "I've given him something a wee bit stronger than the ibuprofen, not that it was a bad idea, mind you," she added. "The positive news is that there's no internal bleeding that I can detect. A couple of ribs are bruised, but not broken or cracked. Rest and care are all that can be done for that. The other stuff—the contusions and the like—will heal and fade with time."

There was a hesitation and he feared there was something she wasn't telling him. "What?" he demanded.

She narrowed her gaze at him. "I don't expect I need to tell you that he's traumatized and scared out of his wits still." She gave him the once-over. "You're enough to frighten anyone, that casual sweater and jeans and those lovely bare feet notwithstanding. You still look every inch the wild highlander—and an alien one at that."

Malcolm shrugged. "Ah, well, can't be helped, can it? It's what I am, after all. What am I to do about it?"

Doc McPhee shrugged in return. "Not much, I suppose, except tread lightly and gently with that one. Keep close for the next day or two in case he needs help. I've already assured him—not that he dared ask—that he's safer here with you than anywhere else on the planet. I told him that you would never hurt him, and if you were so inclined, Darling and Cook and the whole damn village, for that matter, would be after you with pitchforks and torches—and not the kind that run on batteries. Not sure he believed me."

It saddened Malcolm more than he could say that Dracul had destroyed whatever innocence the boy might have had. "The showing of it will hopefully do the trick." He scratched at the back of his neck. "I'm going to need to take him on a wee trip to the States."

The doc raised her eyebrows. "America? Is that your idea of a *wee trip*?" She shook her head. "Whatever it is you're up to—and you know I don't want the details— I'm going to have to insist you give him a few days. Changing altitude like that isn't good for one when they're recovering from certain injuries. I don't want to risk it in case I'm wrong, about the internal damage in particular."

Waiting wasn't a good idea in case his presence had been detected. Dracul could be mounting a strike at any moment or packing up to leave his castle forever. Yet, Brenin's health had to come first. In this, Alex would have to acquiesce. "Very well. I thank you for coming so soon, especially after tending to poor Mrs. Cameron."

The doc gave him a tired smile. "Oh, now there's nothing to fash yourself about there. She went peaceful as can be, surrounded by her family. We should all end our days so." Patting his arm, she turned to go then stopped. "I'll be back tomorrow. In the meantime, he's desperate for a proper wash, but I don't want him doing it alone. You need to help him. He's weak still. And call me if you're worried about him."

"Aye, I will, and thanks again. Send me the bill for your private consult."

The woman laughed and added over her shoulder, "I always do, Malcolm MacLerie, and it's double for the house call."

He grinned at her back while shoving his phone in his pocket. Taking a fortifying breath, he knocked on the door. A few seconds ticked by before he heard a low voice bidding him to enter. He found Brenin sitting on the side of his bed with a towel wrapped around his waist. The boy watched him with those too old and too weary eyes.

Malcolm shut the door and tried not to stare at the expanse of abused flesh now visible to him. "Doc McPhee says you're wanting to bathe. A shower, is it? Or I could run a bath if you prefer."

Brenin stood with stiff movements, staring at the floor. "A bath sounds lovely, like. If you don't mind, maybe Mr. Darling can do it?" He flashed his gaze at Malcolm before lowering it again.

"It will be my pleasure to see to you myself." He cringed inwardly as that had come out sounding not quite the way he'd intended. "Darling is busy," he added, heading to the en suite before he made more of a hash of things.

He busied himself for the next few minutes filling the big tub with water warm enough to soothe without being hot enough to hurt. It was tricky. Humans had different sensibilities from his species, and despite having lived among them for a long time, he hadn't been truly intimate with one in any meaningful way. Although his friendships had been intense, they hadn't veered into such personal territory as grooming or sensitivity.

He perhaps fussed more than was necessary, but he didn't want to get it wrong. For better or worse for the both of them, he was Brenin's nursemaid for the next few days. He wasn't sure how he felt about it. Part of him wanted the time to prove he wasn't a monster. The other part was keen on getting the human to Boston where others of his kind could offer him a succor that Malcolm couldn't, no matter how much he wanted to or how hard he tried.

When he'd fussed sufficiently to approach dithering, he went back into the bedroom. Brenin hadn't moved. "There you are, laddie. I hope the temperature is to your liking. If not, you can adjust it yourself." He could have face-palmed over his own inanity. As if the human didn't understand the basics of how plumbing worked.

When Brenin didn't move, Malcolm realized that he was in the way. He stepped over toward the door to give the boy room. Hard as it was, he had to remember that Brenin's time with Dracul would make the boy skittish about the proximity of an alien. The human shuffled over to the bathroom. When he reached the point where his back showed, Malcolm had to clamp his lips shut to keep the growl from coming out. Dracul hadn't been content with beatings and rapes, he'd bitten and torn the boy's flesh, as well, and not for feeding, as there were no good veins along the shoulder blades. No, the fucker had done it for sheer sadistic pleasure.

Because it wouldn't do Brenin any good for Malcolm to harp on the obvious, he minded his tongue and watched the boy's slow, obviously painful progress. He hoped whatever the doc had given him would kick in soon. When Brenin went to shut the bathroom door, however, Malcolm spoke up.

"Best to leave it, if you will. I promised the doc I'd look after you, and if you need help, I want to hear it."

"I'll be fine, thanks all the same." Brenin issued the reassurance in a quiet, yet firm voice, although he left the door open anyway.

Too afraid to openly rebel, like as not.

Malcolm forced himself to sit on the edge of the bed, close at hand but not visible and not invading the little space the boy possessed. He winced at the sounds of Brenin struggling to get into the bath on his own. Then he closed his eyes and cringed when he realized the boy was quietly weeping as he lay in the tub. It wasn't the great, racking sobs that had overtaken him briefly the night before. This was far more heartbreaking, a measured surrender to his fear and grief while he soaked away his physical hurts.

Malcolm found himself wishing that he were only human so that his hearing wouldn't allow him to eavesdrop on Brenin's private misery but that was foolish. His otherworldly sense came with great strength and the ability to protect the young man in a way that he wouldn't be able to otherwise. Of course, if they hadn't crashed on Earth, his fellow crewmember wouldn't have brutalized the boy in the first place.

I should have plotted the course. There was barely a day that went by in which he didn't have that same thought rattling around inside his head. Nothing he could argue made any difference. His lack of seniority notwithstanding, he'd known his fellow navigator hadn't been up for the assignment he'd been given. Family influence within the hive had likely played a part. Not even the latitude given Alex to pick his own crew would have overruled the decision. Speaking of it would only lead to more guilt for his captain. *What point would that serve?*

And this habitual head-fuck of his wasn't helping current matters. He needed to keep his shite together and be the steady presence that would help Brenin. The urge to go to him, take him into his arms and soothe all the bad away was strong. It took every ounce of willpower to stay where he was and give the human his privacy. If Brenin had wanted his comfort, he would have asked for it.

Fat chance that.

A clunk caught his attention. He shot to his feet, although the sound hadn't been loud and surely not an indication that the boy was in trouble. Then he heard splashing and a grunt of frustration. It was sufficient to send him in to help. He knocked on the slightly open door, however, before stepping fully inside.

Brenin was leaning awkwardly over the side of the deep tub, swiping at a bottle that had fallen on the floor. The thing was out of reach and, fearing that the human would tumble out, Malcolm hurried over to help. He instantly regretted his actions when the boy reared back and sloshed around in the water to keep from slipping under.

Malcolm snatched the bottle off the floor and froze. "Och, I'm that sorry, laddie. I didnae mean to startle you. I only wanted to help you reach this…shampoo," he finished lamely, looking at the label.

Brenin swiped wet hair from his face. "I dropped it."

"So I see." Malcolm stood rocking on the balls of his feet, flummoxed about what to do next. He couldn't hand the shampoo over without getting closer, and given that the water was clear, there was nothing hiding the boy's body.

"The medicine is making me clumsy. I should probably get out, but I want clean hair more than anything. I haven't had a proper shower for weeks." He tugged at a hank of it. "Haven't been able to trim it since I left home, either."

"Are you wanting a haircut, then? Darling makes for a great valet. He can give you one."

Brenin looked down. "Maybe, like. Thanks. I just want to wash it now, though."

Malcolm turned the bottle over and over before he settled on the one course of action that made any sense. "How about I help you?" He flashed a grin, although Brenin wasn't looking at him.

The human said nothing long enough that he figured the answer was a no. Then, "If you wouldn't mind?" Brenin peeked up at him from under his lashes. It would have been a coy look if not for the uncertainty lurking there.

At least it's not fear I see. Progress of sorts.

"Not at all. I've had plenty of practice with my own," he added, tugging at the single braid he'd tamed his hair into after his own shower.

Brenin said nothing more. He simply sidled closer to the edge of the tub to give Malcolm easier access. The boy kept his attention on the water. Steeling himself, Malcolm padded over. He made sure to keep his own gaze on the boy's head and not farther down. The slick of soap shimmering on the water's surface did nothing to cover all that exposed skin. Malcolm didn't want to exploit the boy's position and that meant not invading his privacy any more than was absolutely necessary.

He knelt on the tile, ignoring the bit of wetness caused by the earlier splashing around. Opening the bottle's cap, he squeezed a healthy amount of shampoo into his palm before setting the bottle on the tub's edge next to the conditioner. That was all Cook's doing, the provisioning of things like a guest room that rarely was occupied. He caught a whiff of apple, which he wouldn't have tolerated in his own products, but he supposed Cook knew better what a human might like. It certainly seemed appropriate for this sweet boy to be infused with an equally sweet scent.

Och, now you're just getting maudlin.

Because Brenin had already wetted his hair, it was only a matter of reaching over and rubbing in the shampoo. Malcolm felt big and looming as he did, and while it was quick and minor, he caught how the boy jerked when he was first touched. Malcolm wanted to pull away and leave the boy be, but that would have been cowardly. The human wanted his hair clean and wasn't up to the task himself. It needed Malcolm to get it done and his own sensitivity be damned.

He worked the shampoo into the strands slowly and carefully, pausing to cup some water in one hand to make for a better lather. Brenin gradually relaxed. The set of his shoulders became less tense. He even closed his eyes. His hands, however, remained clasped against his groin. The poor boy was giving himself what little privacy he could under the circumstances.

Malcolm pressed his fingertips into the boy's scalp to scrape away the grime and add in a bit of a massage. He'd had his own hair washed by others over the years on occasion and knew how good it could feel. He smiled when a pretty little moan escaped past Brenin's lips. The boy immediately stilled and his eyes flew open.

"It's all right, laddie. I ken why you made that sound. If feels good having your scalp rubbed, yeah?"

"It does, yes. It's kind of you to take the time, but it's not necessary."

"Well, I've got nowt else to do right now."

Brenin snorted a bit. "You sound just like a Scotsman...not that it's any of my business," he added quickly.

Malcolm chuckled. "Don't worry about what you say, laddie. You cannae offend me. Besides, I take that as a compliment. I should hope I do sound like one. I've been living in the Highlands for longer than any other who counts themselves as Scots has, that's for sure."

"How...how long?"

"Since before Culloden, near three hundred years."

Brenin's lips quivered. "I knew your kind lived long."

"Aye, very long indeed. Tip your head back now."

Using one hand, Malcolm braced Brenin's neck to keep him from sliding under the water while he used his other hand to pour water over his head. It was tricky as hell because he didn't want to make the poor boy feel overwhelmed or insecure. And for damn sure he wasn't going to get shampoo in his eyes. He made short work of it in silence before helping Brenin sit up again.

Malcolm gathered the soaking wet strands into a tail and wrung it out to keep it from dripping down Brenin's face. "There now, on to the conditioner."

"There's no need, sir, thank you."

"Och now, it's no trouble at all and will make combing it out easier."

He worked the conditioner in the same as the shampoo. The process went easier, or at least he felt more relaxed about it. The human was quiet, which wasn't a surprise and shouldn't have been a problem, except Malcolm could see his lips move every once in a while as if he wanted to say something.

"You can say or ask me anything, you know. I expect you have a fair amount of questions after what you've been through."

"Only one," came the quiet reply. Brenin took a deep breath and let it out in a puff. "Am I going to become like Dafydd?" His question ended on a quiet sob and his palms pressed against his lap, making it clear what he meant.

Malcolm stilled his fingers. "Did he feed you his blood?" Brenin shook his head and Malcolm felt an overwhelming sense of relief. "Then, no, you won't."

Closing his eyes, Brenin let out another sob. "Thank God. I don't think I could have stood that. Dafydd was so miserable. It was obvious he hated the little monster growing inside him."

Malcolm worked the strands with his fingers to detangle them. "When it's done voluntarily as part of a loving relationship, it's an amazing thing."

Brenin's eyes popped open again. "Do you have that, a husband and sons?"

"No."

"Oh, okay." The boy was quiet for a few moments before asking another question. "How does it even happen, like?"

Malcolm started the process of rinsing the hair again, although this time, he did it more slowly and not bothering to tip Brenin's head back. "It's a thing that happens in my species—this changing from male to female—and our blood allows us to do it to yours."

"I think maybe in school I learned that some animals here can change sex when necessary."

"Aye, I believe so. For us, on my world, we don't have the equal gender ratio that you humans do. The queens birth a powerful amount of children but most of them are males. Of the few daughters they have, not all can reproduce on their own, and those that do birth a lot fewer offspring.

"In the old days, the queens fought for territory using their disposable sons. Sometimes the hive was overrun and the queen and her daughters were killed by the invaders. Those males that managed to escape had no way of joining another hive, as that isn't a thing for us. And, of course, they couldn't create a new one without at least one female, so nature found a way. The innate femaleness of us all could be brought out in very young males and change them. Of course, in my species, the turned males were wholly female and could produce daughters. Eventually, a new queen would be born and the hive would be replenished in earnest."

"But that's not how it works with us, like? I mean…everyone talked of Dafydd's baby as being a boy without question."

"You humans are different for sure. A changed boy seems to keep his essential maleness with a bit of the female thrown in. So far as I know, he can only contribute his Y chromosomes and produce male children, not that science is, or has ever been, my area. Harry would be able to answer your questions better."

"Harry?"

Malcolm paused in his efforts, debating how much he should share at the moment with Brenin. It didn't seem like the right time to mention the war and about going to Boston. And what would he do if the human refused to go with him? He couldn't hold him captive. That would be a repudiation of everything they'd fought for over the years.

He settled on giving just the basics. "Aye, he's one of my kind who has become a doctor, actually. He kens a lot about human physiology."

"Oh. Does he live around here, then?"

"No. He's in Boston with his husband and son. It's a true marriage and all that," he was quick to reassure him. "They've been together for a very long time, and a happier couple I've never met."

Brenin didn't respond and gave nothing away about how he was taking that news. He was silent as Malcolm finished up with the rinse. Malcolm grabbed a towel off the nearby rack and started wicking the water from the hair.

"So are you like us, then, warring all the time?" the boy asked out of nowhere.

"Not anymore, no. Eventually the queens unified under the Great Queen and her global hive. The lesser ones have sub-hives and there are many families within each one headed by a daughter who might produce a child or two. It's the queens, though, that perpetuate our species the most, and we haven't had a need for changing males for a long time. Well before my own birth, that's for certain."

"Are you invaders?"

Malcolm stilled his movements. "No. We're marooned and have been for a thousand years. Didnae that come up while you were with... Didnae you hear that before?" he amended, because he hated reminding the boy of what he so recently had escaped.

Brenin grimaced and shook his head lightly. "No. I thought..." He sighed. "I didn't think anything, actually. I only tried to survive. I assumed you intended to be here and it's a matter of who of you will succeed in taking over this world."

Malcolm took the risk of cupping the human's chin and gently turning his head so that he could look at him. Not that Brenin was helping... He kept his gaze downward. "Look at me, please, laddie." He waited for the boy to raise his beautiful brown eyes. "No one is going to conquer this world. My friends and I won't let him. We're here by mistake and all most of us want to do is live out the rest of our lives in peace."

"Can't you go home?"

"No." Admitting it pained Malcolm to the core. As much as he loved the Highlands, he would give anything to see his family, hive and world again.

"Will no one come for you?"

"They don't even know where to look. We went off course and there's no trail in space for them to follow. It was an error in judgment." *Mine.* He didn't say that, of course. There was no point other than to reassure Brenin that Earth wasn't about to be invaded by more monsters.

With a last squeeze of the hair, he reluctantly let go and stood. "There, better, eh?"

Brenin dropped his gaze again. "Yes, thank you."

"Do you want to get out and go to bed?" The mention of it caused a vision to flash through his head that he ruthlessly suppressed.

"Now, in a minute."

Malcolm grinned. "My internal Welsh translator tells me that means you need more time."

"Yes, sir."

"Och, call me Malcolm, laddie. Remember? You're a guest in this house, after all."

The boy gnawed at his lower lip. "You were going to call me Brenin. *Remember?*"

Malcolm almost laughed over his pleasure from the boy throwing his own words back at him. That was a good sign, surely. "Aye, I do. I'll give you your privacy, but call if you need help getting out of the tub."

He didn't wait for a response. Heading back into the bedroom, he started pacing. Too much nervous energy coursed through him for sitting again. There were few sounds coming from the bath. Having been washed clean, the human was likely simply lying there. The water was cooling, though. Soon it would be a detriment for the boy to remain, plus the meds might make him dangerously sleepy. He could slip under the water. He resolved to go check in a few minutes. Before he could, Brenin called out.

"Um, Malcolm? I could use some help, like, if you could."

Malcolm sped back in, slowing his movements at the last moment so as not to startle the human. "I'm here."

Seeing the boy half-risen from the water, he quickly grabbed a big, fluffy towel from a nearby wall bar. He unfolded it and held it out. It acted partially as a shield to give Brenin privacy and to keep Malcolm's inappropriate dick in check. It wasn't easy, but he managed to help the boy out while covering him at the same time. Brenin swayed when his two feet hit the bathroom floor. Malcolm was forced to wrap his arms around the boy's shoulders and waist to steady him.

"Easy. I've got you now, la— Brenin. Let's get you tucked in for the night." He forced himself to speak casually and not censor his words to accommodate his own weakness.

Instead of stiffening with the touch as he had in the past, the human actually clung to him as they shuffled carefully out of the bathroom. Malcolm counted that no-small show of trust as a victory and was careful to keep his half-hard cock from touching any part of Brenin. Thank God for jeans. Even worn ones were better at hiding his erection than a kilt would have been.

When he tried to help Brenin sit on the bed, the boy resisted. "I'm still wet, especially my hair." He licked his lips. "I don't want to ruin the sheets, like. Or the pillow."

"Don't fash yourself about that. There's probably enough bedding in this old place to populate an entire town's worth of homes."

Brenin stifled a yawn and didn't resist as Malcolm helped him to swing his legs up. Malcolm performed a magician-worthy feat of pulling the towel away while tugging the covers up sufficiently to hide the human's most private parts. They were both better off for that effort at modesty. He did, however, wipe the boy's lower legs and feet dry before covering him completely. The effort was intended to make Brenin more comfortable, the bedding be damned.

"There now." Malcolm stood back, his hands wringing the cloth he held. "Is there anything I can get you?"

Brenin ran his tongue along his upper teeth. "I forgot to brush. I didn't have much chance when I was— You know." He started to pull the covers off.

"Stay," Malcolm ordered, afraid that the boy would simply tumble out of bed, all naked and pink from his bath. "I'll get everything you need."

He hurried back into the bathroom, cursing the human race's oversensitivity to odors these days. Fortunately, everything had been properly stocked, although he had to improvise when it came to finding something for the boy to spit into. A plastic tub filled with odds and ends under the sink served the need once emptied. He juggled it, a brush with paste and a cup of water into the bedroom. He felt awkward, thinking himself a poor nursemaid, yet unable to pass the task over to Darling.

He left the bathroom light on, tipping the door so only a sliver of it would illuminate the bedroom. He found the boy lying where he'd left him and with his eyes closed. Brenin opened them, though, at Malcom's approach and did a good job on his own sitting up to tend to his oral cleaning. Whatever minor grievance Malcolm had harbored over the whole thing melted away in the face of how much the human was truly enjoying the simple opportunity of brushing his teeth.

When he'd spat out the last of his mouthful, the boy lay back and blinked sleepily up at him. "Thanks awfully. It's grand being clean again."

"It's not much, but I'm glad it helps."

He returned everything to the bathroom and took his time with it. He hoped Brenin would be fast asleep by the time he finished. No such luck. The boy was lying on his side, watching for Malcolm's return. With the way his eyelids drooped, it was a miracle he was still awake.

Malcolm stuck his hands in his front pockets. "All set, then? Do you need anything else?"

Brenin shook his head and yawned. "I'm fine. Thanks, again. You've been terribly kind."

Malcolm would have waved the remark away, except he noticed something lurking behind the sentiment. There was a wariness, he thought, in the boy's eyes. "You understand this room is for you and you alone. When I leave here, I won't be coming back unless you ask me to. In fact, if you need anything during the night, all you have to do is pull that tasseled rope by the bed there and it rings down in Darling's room. Don't hesitate to use it."

Brenin blinked rapidly. "I won't...need anything during the night, that is. If I do, I'd rather you come than your...um, what did you call him?"

"Majordomo."

"Right. Well, no offense to him. I'm sure he's a fine man, and a human at that. But I'm not so good with strange men these days and you, at least, I know." He dropped his gaze. "I mean, you've tended to me at my most vulnerable now, so..."

Malcolm tried not to read anything of importance into that statement. It was only what the boy said, a matter of the devil he knew. And, for a certainty, Malcolm was no saint, not the way his dick kept punching against his fly, as if it didn't have any more sense than God gave a goose—which, of course, it didn't, dumb thing that it was.

"I'm only down the hall, Brenin. If you need me, call my name. I'll hear you. Count on it."

Brenin tucked his hand under his pillow. He looked impossibly young and terribly vulnerable. If Malcolm hadn't been hellbent on killing Dracul before, in that instant he was.

"Thanks. I won't, but thanks all the same." He paused and his gaze flicked away a second. "Can I ask you a question?"

"Of course. Ask me anything you like."

"Why aren't you wearing your kilt?"

Och, now that was the last thing he'd expected out of the boy, and how to explain without making him uncomfortable. "Jeans are the first thing to come along in centuries that are equally comfortable, thanks to Mr. Levi Strauss. They cover me up a bit more, and well, I didn't want to be a distraction to the estimable Doc McPhee."

He hoped the lie would be taken as an attempt at humor, given that the real reason was to ease Brenin's fear of him. The more he looked like any other human, the better. Flashing less skin made sense, too.

Brenin raised his eyebrows at the explanation then giggled. The carefree and unguarded moment made him appear even younger and so adorable that Malcolm's heart skipped a beat. "Oh, you're taking the piss."

Malcolm grinned back. "Perhaps."

Brenin returned the smile for a few seconds before becoming somber again. "I was just curious is all."

"Be so as much as you like, Brenin. I'll never lie to you and no question will ever offend me. Now, off you go to sleep. I'll see you in the morning."

He made his feet move toward the door, keeping the bed and the boy within his sight until it was time to take hold of the knob and turn it. Then he turned off the overhead light and stepped out into the hall.

"Malcolm!"

He whirled around, ready to run back in.

"Thank you for saving me," Brenin called out from his bed.

"You're welcome. And you're safe here. On my life, you are."

As he closed the door, he took a few deep breaths for courage and made himself keep going, when all he wanted to do was sit right there for the whole night. But, he'd promised the human that nothing and no one would hurt him here, and that included him, most of all.

Chapter Four

"Sir, you'll kill him."

Dafydd's vision tunneled as he gasped for breath. Instinct had him fighting to live, even while he welcomed the death Dracul was handing him with his crushing fingers. He managed a grimaced smile in defiance as he glared up at his torturer.

"Sir!" Petru loomed behind Dracul then Drogo joined him. The two of them tugged at Dracul's arms to stop him. "Think of your son, sir. If you kill the slut, you kill your seed."

Dracul bared his teeth and snarled. For a second, his hold tightened more before he unclenched his fingers and let go. Dafydd gasped for air, coughing and heaving breath into his burning lungs.

Dracul huffed beside the bed as if it had been he who had been strangled. His red eyes bore into Dafydd with a hatred that he'd rarely shown, even in his most monstrous moments. No surprise there. Dafydd had deprived him of a toy and, worse, had bested Dracul at his own game — had transgressed against his very person.

"You're dead," he spat out. "When my son is liberated from your body, you will die in agony. I promise you that."

Dafydd stared back in defiance. While he lacked the breath to respond, he did his best to convey his contempt with his eyes alone. He wasn't afraid anymore. At this point, he welcomed death. Against all odds, Brenin had made it. He'd escaped the castle grounds and, based on what Petru had said, the boy still hadn't been found. Dafydd could only hope he never would be. He welcomed Dracul's fury, knowing that it had been Dafydd's own efforts that had caused it. It was pathetic, to be sure, that such a thing brought him pleasure, but such was what his life had come to.

Dracul turned to Drogo. "How did it happen?"

"Sir?"

"Don't play dumb with me," Dracul spat out the warning as he advanced on the doctor. "How was it that Dafydd could drug me? Where did he get the necessary medicine — and in such quantity?"

Ah, finally.

His haze of anger was lifting and he was working out how he'd been bested. Dafydd would have felt sorry for the doctor if the creature hadn't been cut of the same monstrous cloth. He'd used Dafydd for his own sadistic needs and had exacted a heavy price for the help.

Drogo backed up with his hands raised. "Sir, I don't know. He must have procured local plants during his outings before he was confined by you, like his anti-contraception medicine." The man's nervous gaze flashed over to Dafydd. "Your slut has ever been treacherous."

Nice try.

Dracul's steps didn't stop. "That is true, but I'm not a fool. There is no way he could have stored away and processed anything on this miserable mountainside, hidden it and poisoned my wine with it without my noticing." He shook his head slowly. "No, he had help.

"And who else would have such access and knowledge?" He sprang forward to close the gap between them. He grabbed Drogo by the neck and leaped across the room, sending them both crashing against the far wall.

"What price did you extract for your betrayal?" Dracul lifted Drogo by his throat, making the man's legs dangle and dance against the stone. "Did the slut suck your cock or did you dare put that pathetic thing into another of the holes that I alone control?"

Dracul shook the doctor and banged him against the wall in emphasis. Drogo clawed at the hand that was crushing his windpipe. The speed with which Dracul choked the life out of the other creature made Dafydd appreciate how much the monster had been reining in his strength moments ago. Then, in a blur, Dracul replaced his hand with his teeth and ripped Drogo's throat out. By the time he let go, ashes scattered around him and piled up on the floor.

There was silence in the room, the only sound being the harsh breaths of both Dafydd and Dracul. Petru made no noise at all, merely stood calmly waiting for his orders, as per usual. He really was the perfect dog to lick Dracul's hand.

"Get that piece of trash out of my bed and my sight. Take him to the tower room in the west wing. Chain him to the bed there. I'll have no more trouble from him."

"Yes, sir." Petru didn't move, however. He opened his mouth.

Dracul, who wasn't even looking at him, somehow sensed his lieutenant had more to say. "What?"

"It's just that with Drogo...gone, there is no one to deliver your son safely." Petru took a hesitant step toward his master. "I mean, from what I've seen of birth, the babe is at risk as much as the slut bearing him."

Dracul whirled around, his face contorted once more with rage. To his credit, in a way, Petru didn't cringe or even go into a defensive stance, not that he'd done anything wrong. No, that was Dracul. Dafydd laughed inside at the notion that the monster had allowed his impulses to hinder his own plans. The little creature moving inside Dafydd would likely not survive being ripped from his womb.

"We'll get another doctor," Dracul said, as if the answer were too obvious to be discussing.

"A human can't be trusted, and there is only one other of our kind qualified."

"Don't waste my time stating the obvious, Petru. Go get him."

"Horatiu won't help you, sir," Petru replied, again showing a surprising amount of courage. "He would rather die, I'm sure."

Dracul grimaced and practically stamped his feet in frustration. "Then make sure you bring leverage along with him. He has a slut and a brat of his own. Either will do. For fuck's sake, do I have to think of everything?" he added, throwing up his hands.

Petru inclined his head. "Of course, sir. A good idea."

"Of course it's a good idea!" Dracul stomped his way over to his favorite chair, grabbing the bottle of wine as he sat. He started to take a swig from the bottle before frowning at it and throwing it into the fireplace.

He sat fuming for a few seconds. "Clean up that mess," he said, jerking his thumb at the pile that was once Drogo. "Get my slut out of here then send yours to me, along with a new bottle of wine."

Petru had turned and was in the process of tugging Dafydd to a sitting position. He froze and looked over his shoulder. "Andri?"

"As if I know his name — or care. I need relief and he'll do as well as any other. Pretty, as I recall, and I expect you've trained him well."

A look crossed Petru's face. It was a mere flash before his usual stony mask slipped back into place.

You don't like that, do you? Not into sharing with your beloved master, Lap Dog?

Petru wrapped his hand around Dafydd's hair and used it to yank him to his feet. Dafydd bit back a cry, but he was perversely pleased that Drogo was dead and Petru a little bit — perhaps a lot — pissed off at losing his toy to Dracul, not that Dafydd imagined the boy would care. From what he'd seen, Andri was happy to be a slave to an alien. Maybe it was an act of desperation, a way to cope with his situation. Dafydd didn't know and he didn't have the energy to worry for him anyway. As Petru half carried, half dragged Dafydd to the door, he knew his own lot was going to get a whole lot worse before the eternal peace of death could liberate him.

* * * *

Why arent' you wearing your kilt?

Two days after the fact and Brenin replayed that dumb question in his head every hour like a clock.

What is the matter with me? No good would come from dwelling on his unfathomable lapse, and it was even crazier for him to feel a little let down every time his path crossed Malcolm's and he saw that he still wore boring, old jeans. Brenin's time with the monster must have given him permanent brain damage. That was the only answer that made sense.

He wandered down the dim hall on the third floor of the castle and tried to work up the courage to open the doors he found along the way. Darling had already told him he could go where he liked and poke around to his heart's content. And, being a boy like any other, he couldn't resist exploring the large and ancient building. It was like something out of a book, a place filled to the brim with suits of armor, huge paintings of stern people in clothing from long ago and lots and lots of rooms with furniture covered in sheets. The idea of opening up these dark rooms now that the sun had set sent a shiver up his spine. It was all a fine location for a horror movie and it came with its own monster.

No, that wasn't fair. Not really. Malcolm was an alien for sure, but he'd been nothing but kind to Brenin. He'd stared hopelessly into the eyes of true evil often in the last few months and knew that there was nothing like that dwelling in Malcolm. After the first twenty-four hours of coping with his escape, Brenin had found a measure of peace, and he'd had a clear enough head to assess his current situation. Foolish he might be, yet he felt safe and almost carefree.

Almost. Flashes of memory caught him without warning, sending him into paralyzing misery for a few minutes until he could pull himself together again. His nights were filled with bad dreams. He woke with whimpers rather than screams, a leftover defense from his captivity. Dracul hadn't been best pleased by being woken by his captive slave and had taken his anger out with a beating followed by a fucking to 'settle Brenin down'. The instinct to survive had been so strong that Brenin's mind had managed to keep him quiet, even during his worst nightmares. He wasn't sure he would ever lose that forced muteness.

In the light of day, he knew that Malcolm wouldn't fault him for the noise. The man likely would come and offer him solace. After the tender way he'd washed Brenin's hair that first night, there was little question of that. Was that what Brenin wanted, though? To have the alien come in and take Brenin in his arms and…hug him? Stroke his hair and whisper reassuring murmurs? Now that was something that made Brenin shiver for sure, and while it should have been from fear, it wasn't. His reaction disturbed him more than thoughts of ghosts and ghoulies leaping out of unused rooms.

He didn't want to think of it, and exploring the castle was as good a way as any to occupy his time. There were books aplenty in the two-story library and television, of course. A computer was available in Cook's office for him to use, as well. He wasn't, as Malcolm had promised, a prisoner. He could go outside to walk the hills and gardens if he so chose or go down to the rocky shore, so long as he told Darling where he was going. For safety's sake — or so Malcolm had said. He hadn't done so only because he didn't feel up to exposing himself to anyone other than the few people in the castle. As big as it was, the place gave him a sense of cozy safety.

As he neared the end of the hall, he paused and cocked his head. The screeching strains of a bagpipe reached his ears. "No way." But yes, it was. He caught himself grinning. It was too much, really.

There was a closed wooden door in front of him, its massive iron hinges and latch testifying that it was likely original to the castle. The sound of the pipes grew louder as he got closer to it. He stopped a couple of steps away, working up his courage to proceed. Just when he reached for the latch, the door swung open. Brenin stumbled back, his heart tumbled and his eyes popped wide.

It was only Darling. The majordomo held a silver tray under his arm. He arched one brow at Brenin. "Mr. Jones, I'm sorry to have startled you."

The man always spoke like he was on some BBC2 period piece, and the use of Brenin's last name sounded ridiculous to his ears.

Swallowing down his waning fear, he said, "No worries, Mr. Darling. I was only poking about and thought I heard bagpipes." Of course, he had. With the door open, the music came floating into the hall.

Darling sniffed. "The master often likes to play of an evening." He winced at a particularly loud, off-key note. "Obviously, not well." Then stepping to one side, he added, "If you'd like to see the tower room for yourself and believe your hearing can weather the assault, I'm sure he wouldn't mind the company."

Beyond the doorway was a twisting set of stone stairs with a rope railing attached to the outer wall. The thought of going up it was almost irresistible. "Really? It would be okay?"

"I'm certain of it," the man replied. "However," he continued before Brenin had taken a step, "be forewarned, Mr. Jones, that you will see the master as he truly is. He has tried to present a more, shall we say, human visage to you these last two days. While in his private domain, he needs only be himself."

Brenin hesitated, his foot almost raised. "Perhaps I shouldn't disturb him after all, Mr. Darling."

"That is entirely up to you. I've known the master for many decades and I can assure you that he will welcome your presence, so long as you aren't frightened by him."

Brenin licked his lips. "No, I won't be. He can't scare me, not after the horror I've lived." Saying the words out loud cemented the notion in his head. He wasn't afraid of Malcolm.

"Very well. Then I bid you good night, Mr. Jones." The majordomo left without looking back.

It took Brenin another few seconds before he went for the stairs. They were steep and worn, but the rope railing was substantial, so he didn't worry about falling. He winced a few times at the terrible music filtering down. In fact, Malcolm's bagpipe playing was so bad that it added levity to the situation and served to banish any lingering unease.

At the end of the steep climb was another wooden door that stood only partially closed. Brenin peeked through the sliver of light. Seeing nothing, he tipped it open until he spotted Malcolm looking once more like a highlander. The man paced back and forth in front of a window, his hair braided on both sides, a white linen shirt covering his broad chest and his kilt hanging in folds around his thick thighs. He wore no boots, though, leaving his legs and feet bare. There was a decided chill to the room, but if the laird of the castle felt it, he didn't show any evidence.

The man squeezed his bag and blew into his pipes with seeming ease, if not skill. As Brenin watched for a few seconds, Malcolm made his way over to a table in the corner and paused his playing to take a long swallow from a silvery cup. Malcolm's eyelids drooped and he heaved a great breath before putting his drink down again. He clasped the blowpipe to bring it to his lips once more then stopped and turned to stare at Brenin.

There was a moment, perhaps a second or two, when their gazes met. The distance between them was too great for Brenin to see into Malcolm's eyes and yet something not quite fear and not quite cold shimmied up his spine. His breath caught, and in that space of time, Brenin's head emptied of thoughts and there was a stillness to the room and himself that left him frozen to the spot. Then Malcolm smiled and the weird spell broke in favor of a different strangeness. Brenin felt shy but not unwelcome.

"Good evening, laddie. You're powerful brave to enter my lair and test your mettle when it comes to listening to my caterwauling on the pipes."

Brenin entered the room more fully, stuck his hands in his front pockets and shrugged. "It's not so bad, like."

Malcom barked out a laugh. "It's bloody awful and that, mind, is after *centuries* of practice. Fergus always said I was fooling myself if I thought I could ever master this instrument."

"Fergus?"

Malcolm's expression changed, turned in an instant from cheerful to somber. "A friend. He died long ago." Looking away, he took his cup and drank deeply this time.

Brenin came closer. "May I have some? The wine," he amended with a nod to the glass decanter on the table. He realized right away that the request was pointless, given that there were no other cups.

Malcolm's eyes flashed. "It's not wine."

"Oh?" Brenin stared more closely at the bottle and saw that the red liquid was clinging to the sides with a thickness that no wine held. "Oh!" He took a step back then made himself stop, feeling foolish. "Of course. Sorry," he added, although he wasn't sure why.

Malcolm put his cup down and moved to block Brenin's view. "No, I'm sorry. I'm sure it's upsetting to see and think about."

Now Brenin felt really bad. "You have nothing to apologize for. This is your private space and you should do what you like in it. Mr. Darling warned me not to come up unless I could deal with your true nature."

"Darling said that, did he?" When Brenin nodded, Malcolm added, "What else did he say, then?"

"Nothing, except that you wouldn't mind my intruding." In his mind, Brenin was already turning to leave, certain Malcolm wasn't happy with his presence.

"Och, he was right about that. Other than my embarrassment over my pitiful playing, I'm happy to have you here, so long as you're not frightened."

"I'm not," Brenin was quick to assure him. He glanced around the circular room. "It's proper lush here, isn't it?" He set his gaze back on Malcolm. "I mean…it's like something out of a fairy tale."

"It is, yes, although I'm old enough to remember when those stories didn't end happily."

Brenin stared down at his feet. Darling had outfitted him with nice sets of clothing that fit—jeans, sweaters — the whole lot, including new trainers. He hadn't worn anything new since before he'd left home. "I know all about that, but still, exploring the castle has been a grand time. I know you say you don't mind, but I hope that's true and not you just being polite."

"Hmm. I'm not sure anyone has accused me of being that much." Malcolm removed his bagpipes and went to set them down in a place clearly designed to hold them. "The truth is I've been hiding out in this big, drafty monstrosity for a very long time, so long that I've seen many generations of the villagers come and go."

"They don't tell on you?"

"I've gained their loyalty through the test of time. At first, I protected them against the English, who were hellbent on wiping out the Highland way of life. I saw them through famines and wars and all manner of strife. They don't all know who and what I am, but they don't ask questions and they have been surprisingly loyal, even those that leave the hills for the Lowlands and beyond. I'm blessed in that way.

"Although I'd never bring the war with Dracul to them, I've on occasion met him in battle elsewhere, despite my efforts to live a quiet life. I'm bloody glad I did on this occasion, given that you are here, safe."

"You don't like fighting." Brenin stated the obvious.

"No. What I like are the stars." His face lit up in a bright smile. "Would you like to see where I come from?"

Brenin found himself surprisingly intrigued. "Is that possible?"

"Aye, in a general sense. Come over here."

Brenin followed him across the room and over to a large window. A telescope stood in front of it, something he hadn't noticed before. It should have caught his attention right off, except Malcolm's presence loomed larger and more attention-taking than anything else. Just the thought of it gave Brenin a funny feeling in the pit of his stomach—not a bad one, only disquieting. He ignored it and focused on the telescope.

Malcolm stuck his eye against the lens and adjusted the direction then angle of the scope. "Here, laddie. Take a look." He stood aside to give Brenin room.

Slowly, shyly, but with tremendous interest, he peered into the lens. He saw a bunch of lights in some swirling pattern. "What am I looking at, like?"

"The Andromeda Galaxy. It's where my planet is located."

Intrigued, Brenin squinted. "Can I see it with this?"

"No, this instrument is not powerful enough and my home world is at the far end of about two-and-a-half-million light years away from here."

"Oh." Brenin stepped back and looked at him. "That sounds a long way off."

Malcolm grimaced. "It is."

"How did you get here? I mean, I think I learned something in school about traveling at the speed of light and such. It's impossible, innit?"

"Not if you use a wormhole."

"Go on… They really exist?"

"They do."

"How do you navigate it without getting crushed or lost?"

"With difficulty." Something passed over Malcolm's face, and for all that it was alien, it showed a human-type grief. "The navigator miscalculated and we left the wormhole too early and crashed here."

Brenin stepped closer, drawn to the guy's obvious need for comfort. "Was that you?" He couldn't say why he asked the question. He simply did because it seemed important for him to do so.

Malcolm looked away. "No, it wasn't me. Although I was — am — a navigator, it was the other one onboard who plotted that last course. You see, in a hive, there are always redundancies and a ship is manned the same way — two for each station, except there is only one captain and one first officer."

He paced away and went over to his drink. "Sorry," he said, holding the cup to his lips. "I need to finish this."

"It doesn't bother me." That was mostly true. He was careful not to watch. "If it wasn't you plotting that course, why do you feel guilty, mun?"

Malcolm looked at him with startled eyes. "Is it that obvious?"

Brenin shrugged. "To me, yes."

The alien drained his cup and refilled it. "You're the first to think so or, at least, the first to call me on it." He drank some more. There was a flash of fangs, which set Brenin's heart racing a bit until he reminded himself he was safe with this man. Malcolm wasn't a monster.

"We normally don't get to pick what our role in life is going to be. I was fortunate in that my family and hive accepted my interest in navigation. My shipmate had no such interest. We had to spend a lot of time together of necessity and he told me as much. He had no intrinsic interest in the stars. Didn't appreciate their beauty and the stories they had to tell."

Malcom returned to the telescope and pressed his eye against the lens while he swirled his cup of blood. "The irony is that I used to do this very thing back home. Only then, I was gazing at the Milky Way, intrigued and wondering what I might find there. I was disappointed when the ship I was assigned to had another destination in mind."

He straightened, drank and appeared in deep thought as he stared out of the window. "Anyway, he was senior to me. Not my place to question his scheduling or how he went about his duties." He turned to Brenin. "But I knew he wasn't up to the job. His placement had been political, not one of my captain's choices for the crew. I knew all that and said nothing."

Brenin frowned. "Was that a possibility? Saying something to your captain? I don't think a human would have. Like, I once saw one of my teachers snatch something at school. I never told because I didn't think anyone would care what I had to say and he was a good teacher, for all that."

Malcolm gave him a sad smile. "You're very perceptive. That navigator never did anything outright wrong that I could take to the captain. It was only my impression and that wasn't sufficient reason to complain. One doesn't disrupt the hive without good reason." He sighed then drained his cup. "And still I wonder what would have happened if I had expressed my concerns to the captain. I was right to worry."

Brenin took a step toward him, something unexpected and unnamable drawing him closer to this creature when he should have been putting more distance between them. He could smell the blood, and that alone should have sent him screaming.

Why am I not afraid?

"What happened to him?"

Malcolm's nostrils flared as he stared at Brenin. He didn't answer right away. Then, he abruptly turned and strode back to the table. "He, ah, didn't survive.

Most of the crew died on impact." Putting his cup down, he picked up the decanter and drank directly from it.

Instead of staying put, Brenin perversely followed him. "How many did that leave?" It occurred to him that he didn't know how many of these creatures walked the Earth.

"A couple of dozen." Replacing the decanter, Malcolm stood with his legs braced and his hands folded in front of him. "There are fewer now that we've been waging war with each other."

He sidestepped his way around Brenin and went back to the telescope. He looked at the stars again. "I've used this room as an observatory since I settled here. My equipment has changed over the years but the view hasn't. I guess some foolish part of me hopes to see a rescue coming."

"You said that wasn't possible." Brenin scuffed his toe on the stone floor and held his place. It was stupid to continue this little dance around the room – and mystifying.

"So I did – and it isn't." Pulling away again, Malcolm shook his head with a grimace. He also appeared relieved to see Brenin had remained where he was. "I'm sure they've written us off as dead and dust. They would have grieved then carried on with little thought to us again. That's life in a hive."

Brenin resisted the urge to approach him for a second or two before he started moving again. He came within a foot of the alien and made an aborted attempt at touching his arm. "I'm that sorry."

Malcolm cocked his head. "Are you now? After all my kind has put you through, you can still sympathize with me?"

Brenin's cheeks heated and he couldn't keep his gaze steady. "Why not? It wasn't you who hurt me and I know well what it's like to have no home to return to."

Malcolm reached out briefly before he snatched his hand back as if he, also, had had the urge to touch then thought better of it. "You have no place to go, then, even free from Dracul?"

Brenin shook his head. "I was living in a shelter with empty pockets. When Dracul's dog, Petru, snatched me, I was out and about to try my luck at the one thing I thought I could do to make some fast money."

"Och, laddie, no."

Brenin looked up at him and blinked back tears. "Jobs are scarce and I've got no training."

"There's always jobs that don't involve selling your body."

"Easy for you to say, living in this fine castle."

"Perhaps you're right. Who am I to give advice? I've made a rare hash of things since I stepped foot on the starship. That's for certain."

"You saved my life, so I can't agree with you there."

"Och, well…" Malcolm took a deep breath and let it out slowly. "You should leave."

Brenin blinked at him again, suddenly fearful of what it would mean to be out on his own. "I don't have anywhere to go! Can't you give me a job, like? I'm sure I can learn about salmon or whiskey-making."

Malcolm startled him by cupping his face in a move too fast to see. Brenin should have pulled away in fright, yet he stood there, staring up at the alien, feeling comforted. "I meant leave this room, laddie. Not the castle."

"Oh!" Brenin stifled a laugh. "That wasn't very wise of me."

Malcolm ran his thumb along Brenin's jaw. "You can stay as long as you like here. If you want a job, I'll give you one…when you're ready."

Brenin smiled. "Thanks."

"But you really must leave. The blood… Well, I don't have to tell you what it does to me, do I?"

Brenin's smile died and he flicked his gaze downward. Or, tried to.

"Don't, please. I can't control it and I don't want to scare you." Letting go, Malcolm turned his back on him. "Off to bed, laddie. I'll see you in the morning."

It was on the tip of Brenin's tongue to protest before he remembered that Malcolm was right. He didn't want to see how drinking the blood had aroused this man. Brenin wasn't ready for anything even remotely like a sexual encounter for all that he was beginning to feel comfortable in Malcolm's company.

He headed for the door. "Yes, you're right. Good night, then." He fled down the stairs faster than was wise. Before he reached the bottom, the shrill notes of the bagpipe met his ears. He couldn't help but smile.

.

Chapter Five

Mackie shut off the music—again—so he could demonstrate the steps.

With a groan, Demi flopped down on a nearby chair. "Come on, you guys. This is getting boring."

Mackie twirled around and leveled a killer stare at him. "I'm sorry, Demi, that we mere humans lack your alien grace and perfect timing. *We* need to practice."

"It's my fault," Jase said with a grimace. "I'm not very good at dancing."

"You're doing fine, sweetie. Better than," he added, shooting Demi a stern look. "We'll have these routines down before the club reopens, no problem. There's plenty of time. It will be a wonderful surprise for the members. And it has the added benefit of letting you dance without those men pawing over you and making Emil lose his shit."

"That's right," Quinn added and gave Jase a pat on the back. "They can shower us with money on the dance floor and we can divvy it up."

Jase hunched his shoulders. "I don't know. The kitchen will keep me pretty busy, you know, when it's finished. Dancing isn't necessary."

Demi groaned again and slid down even more in the chair. "Oh my God, can we get on with it?"

He knew he was being a brat, yet couldn't help himself. Ever since the latest round with Dracul and his part in it, he'd been a prisoner in the club. His fathers wouldn't let him step foot outside, even chaperoned. He was going stir-crazy. And it wasn't fair. Just because he'd taken the initiative and gone beyond the scope of his parents' permission, he was being treated like a felon. He had saved *lives* and yet that didn't matter because he was still only a child and shouldn't have put his own life at risk.

It was enough to make him scream and tear out his hair, except he would never do that because it was so fabulous. It was the only part of him that felt right. Everything else infuriated him. His skin was too tight and even though he was knocking Mackie's dance routine out of the park, he felt clumsy and out of sorts. His thirst for blood had increased a lot lately and the bags of blood his father gave him weren't satisfying his hunger. He would typically ask his fathers if what he was feeling was normal for a human or his other half, but he wasn't talking to them much. Every discussion seemed to devolve into an argument. Sure, that was mostly on him. Still, they had started it with this keeping him shut away shit.

He twisted to hang his head over the arm and stared upside-down at the boys on the floor. It was impossible to appreciate how these simple dance moves could be hard for them to learn instantly and execute flawlessly. It all came so easily to him. The stupid thing was that he wouldn't be able to perform. He was only killing time doing it with them. Once the club reopened, he would be stuck upstairs in the family's apartment, never joining in — always the outsider.

Suddenly, he couldn't stand it anymore. With another twist, he was upright and on his feet. "This is boring. I'm going." He stomped over to the elevator.

He could hear Jase saying he hoped it wasn't his fault and Mackie reassuring the boy that Demi was being his usual difficult self. He almost returned to them. They were as close to friends as he'd ever gotten. His childhood had been pathetically lonely. There had been no other hybrids to hang with and, of course, he had to stay away from human children. He had always been too fast and strong and everything else, along with being unable for a long time to understand why he had to pretend to be something he wasn't. Now that he did get it, it was still risky for him to hang with anyone other than those who knew his secret.

Not that he fit in with his family members' lovers and husband… He was far older than them by human standards but also younger in some ways. It was hard to relate to them and the adults treated him like he was nothing other than a kid. One man in particular came to mind, not that he was going to let Trey Duncan occupy his thoughts. The man was frustrating, although Demi had gleaned some interest in his eyes. Or maybe Demi was fooling himself.

He stomped out of the elevator and into the family living room. His fathers stood squaring off, clearly in the middle of a tense discussion. That was his fault, too. Dad was mad at Papa for involving Demi in the scheme to bring down Marius and he wasn't over it by a long shot. His normally submissive human father had been uncharacteristically confrontational with his husband. They'd been careful, as always, not to fight in front of him, yet he could tell there was friction between them.

Demi refused to feel guilty about it. He'd also become so annoyed at the both of them that he'd defaulted to calling them both 'father' and speaking to them as little as possible. Childish? Yes. He couldn't help himself. His fathers stopped talking the moment they noticed him and stood in a deceptively unified front to stare at him. Ignoring them, he walked across the living room to head for his room.

"Demi!" His dad's sharp tone had Demi's feet stopping before his brain registered the command. Such was the nature of his upbringing. He turned and waited. "Why are you dressed that way?"

Demi glanced down at his yoga pants and crop top. "I was dancing. You know, with Quinn, Mackie and Jase. Why? Is that something else I can't do? There aren't any club members around to see. My virtue remains intact." He folded his arms and glared.

Papa moved with a speed that even Demi couldn't track. The smack on his ass was unexpected and stung like a bitch. He gasped and, dropping his arms, rubbed at the sore spot. Papa was back by Dad's side before Demi could blink.

"Do not take that tone with your father. Apologize."

Demi sniffled back sudden and embarrassing tears. That was another thing he'd been doing too much of lately — crying. That part of him was very human. "I'm sorry. I wasn't doing any harm. I'm just bored."

His dad's expression softened. "Of course you are. Being cooped up inside is trying for anyone — and for a teenage boy, even more so." He huffed out a breath. "That is why I've asked Papa to take you shopping."

Demi's tears dried in a split-second. He smiled. "Really?"

"Yes, go change into something more appropriate."

"Yes, sir." The sting of his ass forgotten, Demi hurried to comply, ridiculously happy to be able to leave the club, even if it meant shopping with the father who absolutely loathed the activity and had no sense of style. Any amount of strain was worth the chance to get outdoors.

He changed quickly and conservatively into True Religion skinny black jeans and his Tom Ford cashmere-silk turtleneck that his fathers had given him as a Christmas present. He wanted to look fly for his outing without giving Dad fits. He knew when to pick his battles. He slipped his phone and wallet into his back pockets and returned to the living room.

"All set."

His dad gave him the once-over and nodded. "Very nice, Demi. I like that look better than the slutty clothes you wear when you're with the other boys."

Demi bit his tongue. He didn't like his friends being dissed like that, especially when he believed his fathers cared about the boys who had entered their familiar orbit. Not to mention the fact that while it wasn't something anyone had ever told him directly, he knew how his parents had met. His human father had been forced to whore at a hideously young age. The guy should be more sympathetic to how hard it had been for those boys before their lives with the Stelalux clan. Perhaps he was, but his determination to raise Demi properly made him harsh about the others.

"Here." His dad approached with a jacket outstretched. "Put this on. It's very cold outside."

"I know. That's why I wore this shirt. I'll be fine." God, he was hot already and couldn't wait to leave.

"It's not sufficiently warm for this time of year." Dad shook the jacket at him in mute command. Not wanting a fight that could lead to his outing being canceled, Demi allowed him to help him put on the coat. "There now… Have fun." With a quick kiss on Demi's cheek, his dad stepped aside.

"You'll want to go to Copley, I suppose," his papa said with a forced cheer.

"Yes, please." It was his favorite place to shop indoors.

"Very well. I've ordered a Lyft to pick us up outside the front of the club. We'll be back in time for dinner, my dear." He kissed Dad on the cheek with a formal stiffness that was met in kind.

As bad as Demi felt about that, he couldn't afford to dwell on things he couldn't control. So, he followed his father down to the first floor. The boys were still rehearsing and for a second, he wished he could rejoin them. But the lure of spending money on new clothes and maybe grabbing some frozen yogurt was too great. He simply waved at them as he passed and headed out on his father's heels. The Lyft came within minutes and while it was cold, Demi couldn't help removing the jacket before getting into the car.

His father eyed him. "You're feeling particularly hot these days?"

Demi folded the jacket carefully in his lap before buckling up. "Yes. Why? Is that bad?"

"No. It's normal."

Demi wanted to ask why. With the human in front able to hear every word, he didn't dare, of course, and his father was too circumspect to answer anyway. He resolved to remember to bring it up later when they were home again. In the meantime…shopping.

He hopped out of the car with an almost giddy lightness. It had been weeks since he'd seen the light of day and nothing was going to mar his enjoyment. His father slid out after him, thanking the driver. Too antsy to wait for even a few seconds, Demi took out his phone to keep his hands busy. He returned his attention to the car at the sound of his father clearing his throat. He stood in front of Demi with a look on his face like a condemned man trying to act brave.

That expression morphed in the next second, going from indulgent father to fierce warrior. His pupils turned red, and despite the fact that they were on a public sidewalk, his fangs gleamed past slightly parted lips. At the same moment, something hard poked into Demi's side and a man — no, an alien — sidled up next to Papa.

"Be good, little hybrid," a nasty voice whispered into Demi's ear, while the hard thing poked him again. "That's a gun."

The guy next to Papa leaned in. "You understand, Horatiu, that the boy's life will be forfeit before you can take a single step to save him."

Papa's eyes turned a deeper red, if that were possible. The way his chest heaved, it was obvious he struggled to contain himself. "What do you want, Petru?"

"You."

Demi froze in fright and confusion. His mind couldn't process how his lovely day had turned suddenly deadly. It had never occurred to him, either, that his alien father could be taken by surprise and outmaneuvered. He wouldn't have been, if not for his useless hybrid kid giving Dracul's goons leverage.

There was nothing he could do to help except stand there and continue to be a liability.

Except...using his thumb, he opened his phone without looking at it. With his hand down by his side, it was obvious he carried it. They'd figure it out eventually, but in the meantime, he could do something useful. There was only one number in his favorites section. He pressed that app open, or hoped he did, then, using memory alone, pulled up the contact number. It surprised him how steady his hand was. He should have been shaking. His heartbeat was jackrabbit fast, yet the rest of him was weirdly calm.

Papa took a shuddering breath. "You have me. I will not make a fuss. Let the boy go."

Petru chuckled and grinned. "Don't be stupid. He's our insurance."

God. He'd heard of this guy, like, his entire life. He'd never imagined he'd be truly this creepy. Demi wanted to punch his face in. Knowing he stood no chance of succeeding, even without a gun against his side, he continued to do the one thing possible and hoped that he was texting Trey something halfway intelligible. If nothing else, the cop would realize something was wrong. It was a long-shot, but maybe he could at least alert the others and mount a rescue.

Yeah, right. As they stood there, a big SUV pulled up, driven by another one of their kind. Petru opened the door. He took Papa by the arm and shoved him in. The guy menacing Demi pushed him forward, as well, just as Demi hit send. His one glimmer of promise was hearing the tiny swoosh to tell him his message had been sent. He tried to stick the phone back into his pocket as he allowed himself to be muscled along.

Petru saw him, however, and grabbed the phone from him.

"Uh-uh, bitch. There won't be any need for that." He tossed the thing on the ground before Demi was rammed in beside Papa and squished between him and the goon with the gun.

His father wrapped him into his arms. "I'm sorry. I thought I could protect you."

Demi had never heard such fear in his father's tone before. "It's okay."

Petru turned from his seat up front as the SUV took off. "Touching. I'm sure I don't have to explain the rules to either of you. Behave or I will let Kronid take him as his fuck toy."

"As if he could handle me," Demi sneered, fear making him idiotically suicidal, apparently.

"Demi!" His father held him tighter.

Petru laughed. "He's got more fight in him than you ever had, Horatiu. Are you sure he's yours or did our dear captain have at your slut? Or maybe it was Valeriu." With another bark of laughter, he turned to stare out of the windshield.

The car sped on, weaving in and out of traffic and leading them Demi knew not where. Rather, he did. Eventually, they were going to Dracul. There was no other explanation. The why of it was the mystery, but even that would become clear in time. He shuddered at the thought and took comfort in his father's embrace and the hope that Trey had gotten the message.

* * * *

Malcolm slapped his palm against the shower wall and leaned in. The steaming hot water beat down on his head while he worked his dick with a clenched fist and a whole lot of self-loathing. *What is the matter with me?* That was a useless question and one that he'd been asking himself for the entire night and well into morning. He'd lost count of the number of times he'd drained his balls since his encounter with Brenin in the observatory. Saying he'd emptied anything was inaccurate, as there continued to be an endless reservoir of cum and need.

He'd blamed the first urgent orgasm on the blood intake and the heady aroma of Brenin still permeating the room. The boy had barely shut the door before Malcolm had staggered to a chair and freed his hard cock from the confines of his smallclothes. Thank God he'd worn something and not let his nether bits hang free. With only the kilt on, his arousal would have been that much more noticeable. While he didn't know for sure, he believed that Brenin had been aware of this situation anyway.

Poor wee laddie, the last thing he needed was a reminder of his torture at Dracul's hands. Another alien coveting him would be terrifying. Although, if he tried, Malcolm could imagine that the human hadn't been afraid of him regardless. Hadn't Brenin come closer a time or two instead of turning and running? Perhaps he thought he had to appease Malcolm. There was nowhere for the lad to go, after all. He was completely dependent on Malcolm, the same as he had been on Dracul.

Thoughts of Brenin led to visions of him, which wasn't helping matters at all. Malcolm grimaced and grunted as he worked his cock. He pumped the shaft with punishing strokes, while his hips snapped with fervor. He didn't want to picture the human. He didn't want to imagine that instead of his fingers, it was Brenin's tight hole that he thrust into. The way the boy's jeans had hugged his arse, it wasn't hard to conjure up the delights waiting within. So small and high and tight... He could easily convince himself that he'd find a warm welcome there.

Malcolm heaved and shuddered. He pictured the way Brenin had looked at him with his rosy lips parted in a slight smile, his brown eyes wide with wonder as he listened to Malcolm speak of galaxies. There had been compassion, as well, in his expression. The human should hate everything alien and yet he'd shown genuine concern over Malcolm's sadness.

What would he look like when in passion? Malcolm had had an almost overwhelming urge to find out. He'd wanted to sweep up the boy in his arms, strip him bare and bury himself inside him until those brown eyes closed and those lips parted on cries of pleasure. Against the wall, over a chair, in his bed... It didn't matter where they would do it. All Malcolm wanted and needed was the boy to wrap his legs around Malcolm's waist and allow him to ride them both to ecstasy.

He gritted his teeth and groaned as his balls tightened and cum spurted out and over his fingers. The water washed away the evidence of his climax the moment it appeared. He curled his fingers against the tile wall and planted his feet more firmly to keep himself upright. With an ever-tighter grip, he milked his shaft until there was nothing left. There was a pain to it, like an overworked muscle, which he supposed it rather was. If he didn't let up, the thing was going to fall off.

That would be for the better. Now that he'd allowed his mind to picture what it could be like with Brenin, he wasn't sure he could manage to lock those thoughts down again. He was afraid to see the boy for fear that something of what he was thinking and feeling would show through his gaze. God knew, he'd rather cut off his dick than scare the boy.

The bathroom door opened and he abruptly let go of his aching dick and stood to face his visitor. He knew, naturally, who it was. Not only were the footfalls as familiar to him as his own, but only one person would dare to enter so. Shutting off the water, he shoved open the shower door and glared at his visitor.

"This better be good, Darling."

His majordomo glanced down at Malcolm's pesky and still semi-hard cock. "Indeed, sir, it is. I have no interest in voyeurism of any kind, yours in particular. You've had a difficult night, I imagine."

Malcolm frowned. "I'll take that as a rhetorical question and a cheeky one at that." Sudden alarm shot through him. "There's naught wrong with the laddie, is there?"

"Of course not, sir," Darling replied with a sniff. "As if I would stand here bantering if Brenin were in distress. No, he's happily eating his breakfast, as Cook went to the trouble of making laverbread."

Malcolm made a face. "Give me a proper haggis any day instead. I don't understand the Welsh palate."

"Indeed, but she's also starting in on some pannenkoeken, so I think you'll be best-pleased."

That got his attention. "Och, Willem has arrived." He shouldn't have been surprised that the guy had made haste after Alex had recruited him. The pilot wasn't one to dawdle once he'd made up his mind.

"Yes, sir, and he's brought a companion."

"Yeah?" Malcolm stepped out of the shower and grabbed a big towel. With Willem in residence, it would hopefully be easy to keep himself in check. On the other hand, now he couldn't put off asking Brenin to leave for the States sooner rather than later. "He's got another lover, does he?"

Darling retreated toward the bathroom door. "Not exactly."

Malcolm paused while rubbing the water off his chest. "Don't be inscrutable, Darling. You know it stretches my infinite patience."

"I'm sorry, sir. You are going to have to see this for yourself." With that, the man turned tail.

Malcolm stood fuming as he dried off, not liking surprises and half-mad with thoughts of Brenin...again. They'd roared back in the moment he didn't have anyone or anything else demanding his attention. Well, Willem's surprise would have to do. He stomped into his bedroom, and after throwing on his kilt and a T-shirt, he made for the door, stopped, grabbed the tightest pair of boxer-briefs he could find and raced down to the breakfast room.

He heard giggling before he reached his destination. The sound was so unexpected, he stumbled to a halt and listened. There it was again, a high-pitched expression of joy that couldn't have come from Brenin. Mystified, he continued, catching the unmistakable tenor of Willem's voice. He was commenting on Brenin's astounding bravery at eating the laverbread. And there now was the boy chuckling. Hearing it lightened Malcolm's heart as he strode into the room.

He stumbled again at the sight that greeted him. Willem was indeed there, sitting opposite Brenin. But it was the source of the original laughter that caught

Malcolm by surprise. He was absolutely gobsmacked to see a little girl with white-blonde hair pulled back in two braids next to Willem. She was smiling and laughing through her mouthful of pannenkoeken. She seemed entirely comfortable in the unfamiliar surroundings and she was clearly at complete ease with Willem. She was waving her forkful of food within a hand-span of his plate while she focused on Brenin.

"What's all this then?" Malcolm asked, finding his feet again and approaching the table.

Willem pushed his chair back. "Malcolm!" He intercepted him and gave him a thumping big hug. "It's been too long."

"Aye, it has. Good of you to lend a hand."

"The respite couldn't last forever," Willem said, pulling away. "If we can end the fucker for good, then it's worth the try."

"Agreed." He smiled at Brenin. "Gud morning to you."

Brenin's gaze dropped and there seemed to be a faint pinkness to his cheeks. "Good morning."

He wanted to stand there and stare at the boy to glean something of what he was thinking. Had he been remembering their time together the previous night? And what if he had? There was no reason to believe he thought of it fondly.

Malcolm focused on the girl instead. She was staring back at him with a frank expression and no shyness at all. "And who is this?"

Willem returned to his seat and put his hand on the girl's shoulder. "This is Annika. She's my daughter."

Malcolm didn't bother to hide his surprise. "Is she now?"

"Yes. That is to say, she's my late lover's daughter."

"I see." Malcom made his way over to his seat at the head of the table. "Welcome to my home, Annika."

"Thank you, Mr. Malcolm. I'm very pleased to be here. Willem was ever so worried about leaving me back in the Netherlands while he helps you deal with that awful Dracul. And I wanted to stay with him, naturally. You see, I never knew my mama, but Papa promised me before he died that Willem would always take very good care of me." She gave him a gap-toothed grin before stuffing more of the Dutch pancake into her wee mouth.

Malcom shot a look at Willem before saying, "Oh, aye? You speak excellent English." As if she'd been to the manor born, not a trace of an accent. "You know about Dracul, do you?"

Darling came in at that moment and placed a plate loaded with everything needed for a good Welsh breakfast, minus the laverbread, but also including the pannenkoeken. Then he poured coffee into Malcolm's cup from the pot on the sideboard before disappearing back into the kitchen. Annika's sharp blue eyes tracked the majordomo's movements. She didn't respond to Malcolm's remarks until the four of them were alone again.

"Willem says we must be careful about what we say in front of others," she intoned. "Does Mr. Darling know?"

"He does, but you're right to be circumspect."

Annika nodded while she cut a piece of sausage. "That's good. Willem said I'm to stay here while you all go Boston, so I want to be sure about what I say around those who will be taking care of me."

Brenin spoke up. "What's that then?"

Shooting Willem a stern look, Malcolm turned his attention to the boy. "Aye, we need to take a wee trip across the pond."

"Why?"

Without pausing to consider the wisdom of it, Malcolm placed his hand on top of Brenin's. "It's all right. Nothing to fash yourself over. You don't have to go if you don't want to. My captain, Alex, thinks it's best if we go to them and see what we can plan based on your knowledge of Dracul's castle."

The good news was that Brenin didn't seem to mind the touch. He didn't jerk away or even try to move his hand at all. He merely gazed at Malcolm intently. "You think I can help you?"

"Aye. You lived there for a wee while and you managed to escape, so you can maybe tell us things that I couldn't determine from my outside observation. It would help to learn about their routine or if they spoke of plans in front of you."

Brenin shifted his gaze to his plate. "I didn't hear much. There wasn't a lot of, you know, talk with me." He glanced meaningfully in Annika's direction.

Malcolm squeezed his hand in an effort at comfort. Again, Brenin didn't shy away from the contact. "Aye, I know. It's okay no matter what you have to say. Anything might help, and if nothing else, it will give you a chance to see a wee bit of America. A short holiday, if you like."

Brenin hunched his shoulders and shot him a brief smile. "That would be grand, except I don't have a passport."

"Och now, Darling can handle that problem easily enough. Don't worry."

"Really? He's handy, then, is he?"

"He is that." With a reassuring pat, Malcolm made himself let go and picked up his fork instead of clutching at the lovely warmth of Brenin's hand. "Maybe you can describe the route you took to get to the bolthole?"

Brenin also started in on his plate again. "I can do better than that. I can draw it."

* * * *

Trey hated how happy he was to be wrapping up a simple murder in which one hopped-up junkie had killed another over a quarter gram of meth. It was a sad and messy affair, but at least it was utterly human with no otherworldly components to keep him up at night. And it meant he could go home at a reasonable hour, maybe get takeout from his favorite Chinese restaurant and watch the Celtics game on TV.

"Almost done with your report?" Karl asked from his desk.

"Yeah. Not much to say. Pretty straightforward, just the way I like it."

"For a change," his partner added, clearly thinking the same as Trey had been.

His phone made its whooping sound for an incoming text. With one eye on the screen, he picked up the phone and glanced at it. He did a double-take. It was from Demi, and seeing that, his heartbeat skipped. He frowned as he tried to understand the message.

Fracuk haa ud

Trey blinked and was already rising from his chair as his brain made sense of the letters. "Karl!"

"What's up?"

Trey didn't bother to answer. Grabbing his coat, he opened his favorites app and pressed Alex's number. And what did it say about him that he had an alien on the same list as his parents? He raced for the stairs, not wanting to waste time with the elevator. Karl pounded behind him. His breathing became labored as he listened to the rings with mounting agitation.

"Come on, come on, pick up."

"Trey, what's wrong?" Karl asked.

"Sergeant, how can I help you?" Alex's calm, measured voice did nothing to alleviate Trey's worry.

"Where's Demi?" he demanded as he hit the door leading to the garage.

There was a pause. "I couldn't say. Why?"

"He just texted me. I think he's in trouble. It was jumbled but I think he was saying 'Dracul has us'. Who's *us*? Is he out with one of the other boys?"

"Not Quinn, he's right here. And Harry wouldn't let him go out without acting as his escort, regardless."

"Then the asshole has both of them. If we hurry, we can maybe find them. Save them." He was close to babbling and he dropped his key fob when he tried to take it out of his pocket.

"I've got it and I'll drive," Karl said, scooping up the fob and unlocking the car.

Too grateful for the help, Trey didn't hesitate to get in on the passenger's side. He put the phone on speaker while he buckled up. "Alex, are you still there?"

"Of course. I'm on my way to Harry's suite and Quinn's texting the others to see what they know."

Trey took a deep breath to rein in his mounting panic. "Find out where they were headed. Karl and I are leaving the station right now. We're coming to the club, but if you can get another location, we'll change course."

He jiggled his leg and worked to get his breathing in check. As fast as the aliens were, it felt like Alex was meandering to his destination. *Please let this be a sick joke.* He wanted to learn that a bored and bratty Demi was doing this only to get attention and force Trey to come for a visit.

"I'm here and putting you on speaker. Lucien, where is Demi?"

"Shopping with Harry. Why?"

The alien doctor's human husband didn't even try to hide his sudden worry. Trey could hear it in his voice. And the 'why' was the buzzword of the moment. Alex answered based on what Trey had told him.

"They went to Copley Place less than an hour ago."

"Karl."

"On it." The guy didn't hesitate to put on lights and sirens and banged a Uee sharp enough that Trey had to hold on to the grab handle.

More voices came over the connection, Quinn, Val, Mackie, Emil and Jase. Trey had no trouble distinguishing them and every single one was already at Defcon One level, testament that this wasn't some joke. Trey's stomach lurched and he had to swallow back the nausea climbing up his esophagus.

Trey forced himself to stay calm. He was a fucking cop, for God's sake. He knew how to keep it together. Raising his voice to cut through the chatter, he asked, "What entrance would they use?"

"Stuart Street," Lucien replied with enviable calm. "Demi loves Nieman-Marcus." Now, the man's voice shook.

Trey looked at his partner. "Karl."

"I heard." The man's expression was stony. His wheel skills were also unparalleled, however, and within minutes, he pulled up to the curb in front of Demi's favorite store.

Trey didn't wait for the car to come to a complete halt before he was out and scanning the area. The wind whipped open his coat. He barely remembered putting the thing on and ignored the bite of cold hitting him. Not many people were out and about. Those that were stopped and stared at him. He wanted to grab each and every one and ask if they'd seen a tall, dark-haired boy being... What? Forced into a vehicle of some sort, no doubt.

He didn't bother, though, because his attention was taken almost at once by a phone lying on the street against the curb. Two steps and he was picking it up. With an unsteady hand, he disconnected the call to the club and called Demi with his own phone. He watched with a sinking feeling in the pit of his roiling stomach as the other phone lit up.

Sergeant Hottie

Trey silenced both phones and closed his eyes. He took in deep, stinging breaths of cold air through his nose, trying to keep his shit together, when all he wanted to do was roar out his rage and frustration. That wasn't going to help Demi, though, nor was there any point in denying further that the boy meant something to him. Despite all efforts to the contrary, Demi had gotten under his skin.

Now the alien war had taken on a new meaning. It had become personal.

Chapter Six

Brenin tried not to be unnerved by Malcolm's proximity. It was hard. The guy was a looming presence, even when he was on the other side of the room. With him standing right behind Brenin's chair, he was impossible to ignore. Every fiber of Brenin's body was homed in on the sound, the smell, the vibrancy of the alien. It didn't make Brenin afraid and that was the part of all of this that was most disturbing. In the span of a few days, he'd not only become used to being around Malcolm, he'd started to welcome it.

What's wrong with me, for Christ's sake?

After everything he'd been through, he should loathe the very sight of anyone that reminded him of the monster. He should have run from this castle the moment his injuries had started to heal and his pain had abated. Doc McPhee had offered him a ride into the village, even as she'd reassured him that he was safe with Malcolm. He told himself it was a matter of money, in that he had none, and at least here he had plenty to eat, comfortable clothing and a room of his own. He wasn't buying his own bullshit, however.

The simple truth was that he felt safer with Malcolm than he had anywhere else. He felt a disconcerting tug toward him, as well. He'd spent the night dreaming of being in the tower room with the alien, and it hadn't been a nightmare, either. No, his time there had ended differently in his visions. That burgeoning arousal underneath the man's kilt had turned into an overpowering fuck on the floor as Brenin gazed up into the starry night sky. He'd awoken sweaty, tangled in his sheets and sporting his own hard-on.

That visible sign that the monster hadn't tortured the desire out of him had been scary, so much so that he'd raced to the shower and drenched himself in freezing cold water. It had killed his erection but not his images of being consumed by Malcolm. He'd dreaded seeing his host again at breakfast, worried that something of what he'd dreamed of would show in his eyes. The arrival of Willem and Annika had been a Godsend, a buffer behind which he could hide. Then Malcolm had innocently put his hand on Brenin's and his imagination had taken off again. He could still feel that touch.

But now was not the time to dwell on it. He had a task to do, an important one. His drawing had always been a private thing, something he didn't show others because he'd known his family, and even his friends, wouldn't understand it. They were laborers and damn proud of their heritage of working deep underground back in the day. Making pretty pictures on paper meant gay, and gay meant something bad. He'd hidden his talent, such as it was. It was hard to believe it could benefit the alien war.

Still, Malcolm had reacted excitedly at the news and Brenin was doing his level best to recreate the route that he'd taken. Sheet after sheet had been filled with each scene of his frightened journey. Perhaps because his emotions had been so high, he had no trouble picturing the details. Recreating them on paper was easily done.

Each time he set a piece aside, Malcolm would snatch it up and study it. The man made all kinds of murmurs before sharing them with Willem. Annika sat across the table still, drawing herself, although her pictures appeared to be of unicorns. And she was using crayons while Brenin used a fine-point pen. Still, from the glimpses he got, the little girl was very talented. There was something eerie about her. She was too adult-like and was surprisingly sanguine about the company she kept and the alien war she was embroiled in.

"These are excellent, laddie." Malcolm's voice was like a balm and his praise lifted Brenin's spirits.

He glanced over his shoulder and smiled. "I'm that glad. There's one left."

This last vignette would be tricky, as it involved what he saw as he stumbled out of the bolthole's tunnel. He didn't want to draw the truth because it would leave him possibly vulnerable, but he also wanted to help as best he could. For no other than his own personal and selfish reasons, bringing the monster down was paramount.

So, he let his fingers fly of their own accord, not fretting over what he produced, merely sketching the memory as accurately as he could. He didn't dare think of Malcolm as he did so. And when he'd laid down the last stroke, he merely sat back and let the guy figure out for himself that Brenin had finished.

There were long seconds of quiet in which the only sound was Annika's coloring and the beat of Brenin's heart. Both seemed unnaturally loud. He focused on the first and tried to ignore the second. If he allowed it, he figured he could send himself into a full-blown panic attack. Finally, Malcolm reached down to pick up the piece of paper. His coolness and scent flowed over Brenin. He took a deep breath and felt calmed.

"Is this how you see me?" Malcolm asked in a low voice.

"At the time, yes," Brenin admitted.

Willem chuckled. "It's a perfect likeness. You look every inch the wild highlander – or a demon of the woods, perhaps. It's a wonder he didn't run from you."

"He tried," Malcolm replied, his voice strained. "I wouldn't let him." His hand landed gently on Brenin's shoulder. "I'm sorry I scared you."

Brenin closed his eyes, enjoying the touch even as he struggled with the why of it. "Couldn't be helped. And I'm not scared of you anymore." Opening his eyes again, he stared over his shoulder.

Malcolm gazed back at him. His violet eyes were darker than usual. Brenin understood what that meant and he still wasn't afraid. He dropped his line of sight to the spot right in front, where Malcolm's kilt lay in folds over his crotch. There was nothing to see, not really, and still Brenin knew the guy was aroused. He could practically smell it.

Don't be daft, mun. It's only your imagination.

He'd never been a good liar, not to himself any more than to others. Worse, there was a stirring of interest in his own body. The reaction disturbed him, so he forced an image of Dracul into his mind. That did the trick. His growing arousal died and he shuddered at the memory.

Malcolm pulled his hand away and took a hasty step back, understanding in his expression. Except, he'd misunderstood, thinking it was him and his touch that had caused such a reaction. Brenin immediately wanted to reassure him on that point then decided against it. No good could come from acting on this unexpected and inconvenient attraction. There had to be some deep psychological problem in him to react as he did. After everything he'd been through, starting any kind of relationship, especially a physical one, was insane on the face of it.

"You've done well, Brenin. Alex and Val will have to study these to make our plan," he added as he gathered all of the drawings. "I dinnae have a head for strategy. That's Alex's and Val's job. And I'm sure they'll have questions for you."

"I'm happy to answer any they have," Brenin assured him. "I want to help as best I can."

Malcolm shot him a brief smile. "You're a good lad. Darling is going to take your picture and get your passport and visa done this afternoon. You can stay in Boston with the human boys that live with Alex and the rest. I'm sure they'll be happy to show you around. There's no need for you to return here while we, ah…clean up the mess in Wales."

Brenin wasn't sure how he felt about that news. On the one hand, he didn't want to ever go back to that castle of horrors. On the other, he didn't much like the idea of being separated from Malcolm, particularly given that the guy would be heading into a deadly situation.

Before he could think of a response, however, Darling came in with a mobile phone in his hand. "You have a call, sir, from Boston. I took the liberty of answering it for you, given that you didn't bother to keep the phone in sight."

Malcolm grabbed the phone. "It's not like I have pockets, now, is it?" He winked at Annika when she giggled. "Alex?" He frowned. "Wait. I want to put this on speaker. Annika, lass, why don't you let Darling take you into the kitchen? I'll bet Cook is baking up some sweets she'll let you have a taste of."

The girl stood. "You want me out of the room for the call, Mr. Malcolm? I understand." She skipped out of the room, the majordomo trailing in her wake.

Putting the phone on the table, Malcolm said, "Go ahead, Alex."

"Dracul has taken Harry and Demi."

Malcolm cursed and Willem's eyes turned flinty. "How the fuck did that happen?"

"He had them taken while they were away from the club—snatched right on the street and hustled into a vehicle. That's according to the one witness our friends on the police force could find and question."

Brenin placed one hand on his stomach, as if he could settle the sick feeling that had popped up at the news. He didn't know these people, but he knew all too well what it felt like to be kidnapped. He could easily imagine how frightened the monster's latest victims must have been.

As if sensing his distress, Malcolm sidled over and, once again, put his hand on Brenin's shoulder. He gave a quick squeeze. "When did this happen?"

"Yesterday afternoon. We've been trying to put the pieces together and hoping to find them before they took off. As near as we can tell, they've already left, using a secret airstrip or something. There's been no takeoff of a private jet from Logan Airport."

Malcolm ran the fingers of his free hand across the top of his head and tugged at one of his braids. "Damnation. You want me to go back to Wales and see what I can learn?"

The other man blew out his breath over the phone. "No. We have to assume that's where they took them, although the why of it mystifies me. Dracul must know we won't negotiate over hostages. He's been down that road before and failed. Although this time, he has one of our sons."

"He's in a panic, perhaps," Willem offered, "as well he should be. We're going to finish him. That's what he gets for staying in one place for so long."

"He might have taken off, given that Brenin escaped."

"No," Brenin heard himself say. "I'm nothing. He would never believe that I can be any kind of threat to him."

Malcolm's touch became firmer. "The more fool he, then."

Brenin leaned into the man, not bothering to contradict him. He'd known his worthlessness long before the monster had got hold of him. A thought occurred to him, suddenly, though.

"Isn't Harry the doctor, then?"

Malcolm looked at him with surprise. "Aye, he is. Why?"

The idea formed quickly and he almost didn't continue, thinking he couldn't possibly know what he was talking about. Still… "Dafydd got his drugs that helped to free me from the doctor, Drogo. What if D-Dracul realized that and killed him?" He swallowed past the bile rising in his throat at the memories that swamped him. "He has a powerfully bad temper. And he wants his son that's inside Dafydd. That much I do know. Could a human doctor be trusted or forced into safely delivering the baby?"

Malcolm shook his head slowly. "Not likely." He flashed a smile. "You're on to something there, laddie."

"Indeed," the man in Boston — Alex — said. "Thank you, Brenin, is it? We're glad to have you on our team. We look forward to seeing you."

"Aye, and he's drawn sketches of Dracul's castle as best he could based on what he remembers from his escape and his considerable skill with a pen."

"Excellent. And this theory of why Dracul took Harry and Demi will give Lucien some comfort. He's worried sick over what's happening to his family. If Dracul needs Harry for his medical skills, and he needs Demi to keep Harry quiescent, then they're safe for now, at least until the baby is born. Any idea, Brenin, on how close Dafydd is to his time of delivery?"

"No, sir," he said with a quick shake. He stared worriedly up at Malcolm. "But it's going to be soon, I think."

"Then you'd best hurry up and get here, Malcolm."

"Aye, sir. We leave tonight."

* * * *

Demi stumbled as he was shoved up the stairs, preferring to risk smashing his nose on the stone steps than remain within Kronid's grasp. Throughout the journey, the asshole had pawed Demi at every chance. Demi could still feel the putrid creature's touch. That, plus a lack of opportunity for any kind of bathing, left him feeling as if bugs were crawling all over him.

He was alive, though, and, more importantly, so was his father. Demi had been careful not to react to Kronid's assaults, keeping his breathing even and his heart rate steady. Poor Papa had spent the entire plane ride not only with his hands tied behind his back but also with a hood over his head. Despite Petru's baiting, he was clearly afraid that Papa would succeed in overtaking them. That was the only explanation for keeping him so under control. And knowing, because he could see for himself how heavily armed their captors were, not to mention that two of Dracul's other goons were piloting the plane, Demi didn't want his father to try *anything*. It would be suicide. Demi couldn't risk giving away his distress by allowing any sounds of it to filter through the hood. He had no doubt that nothing would send his father into a fit of rage faster than knowing his son was being harmed.

It wasn't anything more than juvenile groping anyway. Like now, with Demi a step above him, Kronid took the opportunity to slide his filthy fingers up the inside of Demi's leg. Disgusting and infuriating, but bearable. He gritted his teeth and twisted away while focusing on keeping his footing. At least he wasn't hooded and his hands were tied in front of him. Obviously, they didn't think he constituted much of a threat to them and, sadly, they were right. He'd resisted much of the training his father had tried to provide him with, determined that his life wouldn't be consumed by this dumb, old fight. He felt differently now, of course. After this experience, he wanted nothing more than to kill Dracul and all his men himself.

The end of the stone staircase came abruptly around the next curve. A large wooden door stood open. Papa was pushed inside and Demi hurried to join him, if for no other reason than it might put him out of Kronid's range. He blinked against the brighter light of the room. He felt, as he had since the moment he'd entered this castle, as if he'd stepped back in time – or maybe into a video game or a movie set.

His entire life, he'd lived in whatever passed for modernity at the time. This place was different. The room was circular and stood at the top of a tower. He would have found it eerily beautiful, except someone was going to die in here. If no one else, it would be the boy chained to the four-poster bed that dominated the space.

Oh God. This was the nightmare version of what his own human father had once gone through. The prisoner was naked and hugely pregnant. The sight of a male body in such a state was startling. Demi knew the basics, naturally, of how he'd come into the world. Seeing it literally laid out for his viewing made his empty stomach lurch. There was no happy father-to-be, only a pale, sunken-eyed person of indeterminate age shivering in the cold. This wasn't a matter of a loving couple bringing a child, however strange and different, into the world. This was the product of sexual slavery. There was no question about it.

The monster responsible for this horror stood by a window with his leather-clad legs braced and his massively muscled chest bare. The sides of his head were shaved and his long top hair was pulled back into a severe tail that highlighted his sharp facial features. A dead, dark stare pierced Demi, making him feel dirtier than Kronid's touch had. The monster gazed at Demi with a disturbing hunger, despite the fact that a beautiful boy clung to him. The kid was wrapped in a silk robe far too big and long for him, and his shaggy hair was striped white and black. He glared at Demi with obvious dislike. As Demi was forced farther into the room, he could see that the boy had one crystal-clear blue eye and one violet one.

The entire disturbing scene caused Demi to lose his control. His heartbeat quickened and he had to bite back a whimper as he tried to get closer to his father. In the face of this clear evil, his courage was failing him. Kronid grabbed his arm and pulled him in tightly against his chest. Then he cupped Demi's ass and chuckled softly into his ear.

"I'll keep you safe, bitch."

Demi allowed one shudder to run through him before he stiffened his resolve and his body.

Dracul gestured toward Papa. "Release him." His tone was sharp, yet also matter-of-fact, clearly someone used to being obeyed.

Petru did as told and Papa stood quietly for a few seconds as he acclimated to regaining his sight and his circulation. His gaze found Demi first. He took note of Kronid's position and his mouth thinned while his pupils turned red. Demi tried to nod in reassurance and prevent his father from doing anything stupid on his account. It must have worked because Papa moved on to glare at Dracul then look at the bedridden boy.

That sight obviously moved him as nothing else had. He swept up to the bed and laid a gentle hand on the boy's head. "Is it your time?"

The boy shook his head. "Not yet," he replied in a shaky tone.

Papa glared once more at Dracul. "This is why I'm here? Where is Drogo?"

"Gone to dust, not that it's any of your concern."

"If you expect me to help, it is," Papa retorted. Any fear he held of Dracul didn't show. Demi felt a sense of pride at his father's strength.

Dracul took a step forward, his human limpid sticking to him. "You'll do so unless you want me to feed your precious boy to my men." The guy smiled, showing his fangs. He ran his tongue over them. "He's deliciously exotic. Maybe I'll keep him for myself."

The stripe-haired human made a mewing sound. Without looking at him, Dracul casually slapped the boy's face. Far from reacting with fear or hatred, the boy fluttered his lashes and, if anything, cuddled closer.

Papa straightened, although he kept his hand on the pregnant boy's head. "You know me, Dracul. I will do everything within my power to help this boy deliver your son alive. I would have done so without the threat. But know this as well. If *my* son is hurt in any way, I'll let yours die in the womb. You have plenty of toys to play with and, I dare say, so do your men. My son is off limits and doesn't leave my sight."

Dracul said nothing for long seconds. He stared at Papa, who stared back. Then Dracul smiled like a shark who'd just taken a bite of something tasty. "So feisty these days, Horatiu. I think I like the new and improved *you*."

"Just so long as we understand each other."

"Of course. I have nothing against your sweet boy. Untie him," he ordered without bothering to look.

Kronid let go of Demi and, after pulling a knife out of his boot, slit the bonds around Demi's wrists. In his haste, he drew blood, and the grin on the guy's face told Demi it was no accident. Demi glared defiantly at him as he quickly licked his skin closed himself.

Dracul approached the bed and sneered down at the poor boy he'd impregnated. "I only want my son out alive. I don't care about the slut incubating him." His expression turned to disgust.

"Color me surprised," Papa replied. Demi had never heard his father say anything so flippant before. "But you can't have one without the other. This room is too cold and the boy obviously needs water and food, as do I and my son."

Dracul shrugged. "Do what you must. Kronid will see to your needs. He'll stand guard in here for as long as you are my guests."

"Naturally. I wouldn't expect you to be lax in your security, but tell him to keep his fucking hands off my son."

The F bomb, really? Demi was seeing a wholly new side of his father and his estimation of him was growing by the minute. Dracul barely had to gesture in their direction for Kronid to step away from Demi. As soon as he was clear, Demi raced to his father's side. He wrapped a comforting arm around Demi, who wasn't too proud to lean into the embrace.

"It will be all right," his father murmured.

"I know," he whispered back.

Dracul grunted. "I'll leave you to it. You will inform me the moment my son makes his entrance." With that final order, he sailed out of the room, dragging the striped boy with him. The kid smirked at Demi, as if he somehow had won a prize that Demi would have never wanted in a million years. When they passed a silent Petru, however, the boy avoided looking at him.

Something passed across Petru's face that Demi found intriguing, yet unreadable. Then he remembered that he didn't care what was going on in this castle of horrors.

"Stoke up the fire," Papa snapped at Kronid, with a wave at the fireplace. "Bring blankets, towels, food, a basin and plenty of water. I'll also need whatever Drogo used for a medical bag and any supplies I find missing."

When neither Kronid nor Petru moved to comply, Papa bared his fangs and roared. The sound was terrifying. It compelled the others to action, however, and once more Demi felt a sense of pride.

Now all he needed was hope. His father could keep him safe until the baby was born. After that, Demi had no illusions about his own fate. Worse, he worried that his father would be killed notwithstanding his being the only doctor left for their race. There was really only one chance that they'd be rescued.

Trey, please come for me.

* * * *

"Still awake, are you?"

Turning onto his side, Brenin watched Malcolm walk back from the cockpit. The man sat on the seat opposite from where Brenin lay and stretched his long, bare legs out in a relaxed pose.

"I can't sleep for some reason," he confessed. "I've never flown before, so that's why probably. It's kind of exciting and boring at the same time."

Malcolm chuckled. "Aye, that's as good a way of describing it as any, I suppose. Plus, it's not very late by our internal clock. But it will be even earlier when we land in Boston, which will be in about an hour. By the time we pass through customs, arrive at the club and debrief, you'll be exhausted, I expect. Sleep will come easily and you'll adjust to the new time zone right quick."

Brenin didn't say anything to challenge that assumption. Sitting up, he stretched his own legs beside Malcolm's. "I'm nervous about meeting your friends," he confessed without looking at him. "I'm used to you, and Willem's not so bad, especially with Annika around. But I'm not sure how I'm going to react to the others. I keep telling myself not to be such a baby about it."

Malcolm was a blur of movement that ended with his sitting next to Brenin. "You have every right to be leery after all you've been through." He began to reach for Brenin's hand but pulled back.

Their thighs touched, though, and when Malcolm moved his away, Brenin moved his closer. "I'm not afraid of you. Your being near or touching me, even, doesn't bother me." He glanced up at him from under his lashes. "I like it, actually, although I don't understand why."

"Well, now, you humans are awfully resilient, I've found." Malcolm reached out again and this time, he tucked strands of hair behind Brenin's ear. "It's one of the things I admire about your species."

"I can't imagine there's anything about us that would impress beings such as yourselves. I mean, you've learned how to use wormholes and travel halfway across the universe. We're barely out of diapers in comparison."

"Technologically speaking, maybe, but you've a flexibility of mind and an ability to adapt that my people could never possess. We're rigid in our ways and haven't changed in millennia. The hive structure is the same as it was back when we walked on four legs instead of two."

Brenin peeked up at him and, at the same time, slid his hand over to rest against Malcolm's thigh. "Is that how you evolved, then? I keep picturing you buzzing about like bees."

Malcolm laughed, his handsome face splitting into a broad smile. "Och, no. Our social structure is much like your insects, but we're mammals, all the same. Mostly. We certainly never flew about, although it would have been fun if we had."

"Speaking of which," Brenin ventured, "is it okay for you to be back here and not in the cockpit."

"Not to worry, laddie. Willem took to the skies as if he has wings. I'm mostly a nuisance to him up there. Besides, I like the company better back here."

Brenin dared to look at the man head on. He saw that Malcolm's pupils had turned black. His heart stuttered a bit. "You want me, don't you?" It was a stupid question because the answer was obvious and it opened up a dialogue he wasn't sure he was ready to have.

"Aye," Malcolm admitted in a low voice. "I'm sorry. I do. Not that you should fash yourself over it. I know how to keep myself under control. You're safe with me."

Brenin dipped his gaze to the man's lap and tried to see what lay under the folds of the kilt. As usual, there was nothing visible and yet, there didn't need to be. "I'm not worried." He licked his lips. "I know you're aroused and it's fine. Really, it is."

Malcolm stood abruptly. "No, it's not." He turned away. "With all you've been through, the last thing you need is my dick in your face." His shoulders shook on a deep breath. "Sorry. That was crude of me, as well. I'm usually better at keeping my thoughts and needs to myself."

Brenin stood, too. After a moment's hesitation, he placed his hand on Malcolm's back and ran his fingers down to his waist. The muscles rippled under his light touch in a way that made him feel almost powerful.

"If you'd asked me only two days ago what I wanted and needed after my time with the monster, I would have said to be alone. I figured my interest in men had been forever ruined." He ran his fingers along the waistband of the kilt before slipping one of them beneath it. "Now, I think maybe what I need is a chance to experience something positive. I don't want to be a broken thing for the rest of my life. If that happens then he's won, hasn't he?"

Malcolm twisted around, dislodging Brenin's hand, before clasping it in his own. He stared into his eyes as he lifted Brenin's fingers. "Don't speak of yourself like that. Don't think of yourself as ruined. You are by far the bravest and most desirable boy I've ever known." He brushed his lips against the inside of Brenin's wrist.

The cool, whispering feeling sent a shiver through him. His breath stuttered out and there was that odd, yet appealing, stirring of interest between his legs. "When you look at me like that, I do feel wanted."

"Because you are, too much so." Malcolm tried to release Brenin's hand.

Brenin reversed the grip to keep the connection. "What if I want *you*? What if I need you to help me banish the pain and humiliation of being the monster's slave?"

Malcom's eyes got even darker, if that were possible. "Och now, laddie, you'll be wanting someone better than me for that. Someone *human*, most like. I'm just a different monster."

Using their clasped hands, Brenin pulled them closer together. Although Malcolm was bigger and stronger, he allowed Brenin that control. "You're nothing of the kind! I know because I've been this close, closer, to one and I appreciate the difference."

Malcolm closed his eyes and sighed. "Och, Brenin, my poor, wee lad. I will turn him into dust for what he did to you. I swear I will."

Brenin could feel the warmth of his breath — the one part of the alien that wasn't always cool — and smelled the not-quite spicy undertones of his alien nature. Those things should have sent him screaming away. Instead, he got even closer and came within a hair's breadth of pressing his cheek against Malcolm's big, hard chest.

"Good. I want you to do that. God knows I do. But I'm also asking you to help me heal in a different way. Will you please show me how good it can be between two men?"

With slow movements, Malcolm drew him into a loose embrace and now Brenin did lay his head against his breastbone. He could hear the powerful beat of the man's heart. He'd known, of course, that he possessed one. Still, it was reassuring to listen to it.

Malcolm ran his hand down the back of Brenin's head. "If that's what you want, I would be honored to help you." He chuckled ruefully, the sound making his chest rumble. "Hell, laddie, it's what I literally dream of."

Brenin huffed. "Me too, actually. That's how I know it's the right thing for me to do." He dared to slide a hand down to feel for himself how much Malcolm wanted him. The hard length was easy to find. It jerked at his touch.

"I am afraid of this," he admitted, "and of the blood."

"There dinnae have to be any of that."

"Really?" He squeezed the cock as best he could through the cloth, simply because he figured he could. Malcolm's responding grunt gave him a heady feeling of power. "You can fuck without biting?"

"I can."

"That's a relief." Letting go, he pulled out of the embrace. "I'm sorry. I don't mean to be a distraction, given all that you have to do. I'm only hoping you can find time for me. You know, later, when this is all over."

Malcolm used one fingertip to lift Brenin's face by his chin. "I will give you whatever time you ask for — and more besides." With that, he placed a quick and gentle kiss on Brenin's lips. Nevertheless, the touch tingled and it continued to do so even after Malcolm returned to the cockpit.

* * * *

"They're settled in. It's become quite the party." Petru's annoyance was hard to miss. The man was usually more circumspect around Dracul, but perhaps his demeanor had more to do with seeing his slut kneeling between Dracul's legs than anything going on in the tower.

That thought pleased him. He never wanted any of his followers to get above themselves. Making use of Petru's pretty boy was serving two purposes, it seemed.

Fisting the boy's hair, he forced the slut's head down so that he took all of the shaft. The tightness of the boy's throat was delightful. He'd give Petru his due. He'd trained the human well. Dracul couldn't remember the last time he'd been serviced quite so expertly and thoroughly. He moaned, merely to watch Petru work to keep his expression neutral.

"Don't bother me with the boring details. So long as Kronid keeps my *guests* in hand and my son is safely delivered, that's all I care about. As you well know," he added with a warning glare. If Kronid fucked up, Petru understood that his head would also be on the chopping block.

"I understand my duty. *Sir.*"

Dracul rewarded that little show of insubordination by rocking his hips into the boy's mouth and holding him there until he struggled for breath. He let him up right as his pretty face started to turn red. After a few sputters, the slut continued to lavish attention on Dracul's dick with his skilled tongue without requiring any encouragement. Such a dutiful little whore.

"And what of that other irritation? Any sign of my escaped pet?"

"No, sir." Petru's gaze skittered away. "He must have disguised his scent somehow because we can't track him. Perhaps he died in the woods."

"I'm not interested in speculation. Find the boy so that I can kill him myself — or bring me his carcass." Really, it was too much to bear that some stupid cunt had managed to slip his grip. Someone had to pay, other than Drogo, and Dafydd was already dead, as far as Dracul was concerned. His ire wasn't quite satisfied, and if Petru didn't do his job, he might very well end up paying the price for that fuck-up, too.

He grinned at the guy. "Now, unless there is there anything further of importance you wish to discuss, I'm rather busy enjoying myself, as you can see."

Petru's mouth tightened. "No, sir." He spun around and left the room.

Chuckling, Dracul dragged the boy up by the hair. "That's enough of that, boy. Come sit on my lap."

The human grinned coyly, his lips shiny with spit. He required no coaxing to climb up and straddle Dracul's thighs. He fluttered his lashes as he lowered himself with practiced ease. Dracul's cock sank into the willing body smoothly. *How delightful.* The warm, welcoming tightness made for a wonderful change. Who knew that one could achieve almost as much pleasure in fucking a willing hole as from ramming into an unwilling one?

He fisted both sides of the boy's head and tilted it to expose the jugular. "You like being impaled by my cock, don't you?"

"Y-yes." The boy undulated his hips, squeezing as he rode the dick. "You fill me so completely, Master."

Oh, yes, Petru's slut knew just how to please. "Pity you're barren." As far as Dracul knew, Petru had no sons, a thing he cared little about except he always wanted more soldiers for the cause.

"That's not my fault." The boy's pouty lips turned down. "He makes me take birth control."

Dracul forced him to stay still. He peered into those strange mismatched eyes. Again, to his knowledge, no changed human had ever developed such features, nor the black striped hair. "Seriously? Why would he do such a thing?"

"I don't know, Master. I think he wanted me to stay slim and pretty for him."

"Ridiculous. There's an endless supply of fuckable boys. Sons are paramount." He'd suspected Petru was a fool, regardless of his loyalty, but this was beyond the pale. He tightened his grip enough to bring water to those weird eyes. "I bet you'd like my seed to take root, wouldn't you, slut?"

The boy moaned and squeezed his hole some more. "Yes, Master. Please. I want to give you sons. I'll give you as many as you want."

Easing his grip, he bucked his hips to get the slut moving again. "I'm sure that can be arranged."

His spirits buoyed for the first time in days, he celebrated with a fast and hard ride. At the moment of his climax, he sank his teeth into the boy's neck and drank his fill.

Chapter Seven

Malcolm was aware he garnered quite a lot of attention as he strode through the airport. There was no help for it, not unless he wanted to change out of his kilt and into jeans. He didn't — and not merely because of some stubborn adherence to a tradition that wasn't really his. No, it was to keep Brenin looking at him the way he did whenever Malcolm bared his legs. The boy liked the wild and overtly masculine appearance and that was plenty good enough for Malcolm.

He still had trouble believing it was true — couldn't really believe it, either — that he'd dared kiss the boy back on the plane or that Brenin had allowed it, not to mention that they'd essentially made a date to bed each other once the trouble with Dracul had been settled.

Dear God, did I really promise to help the boy get over his brutalization and discover what it was meant to be like between two men?

On a purely academic level, it made sense. If someone didn't show him the difference, Brenin would forever equate sex with hideous violence and degradation. He would be damaged for the rest of his life. That would be a crying shame, for sure, yet was Malcolm the right person for this serious task?

Brenin thought so and that was all that really mattered at the end of the day.

Malcolm had to believe the boy knew his own mind on this, as well. The way in which Brenin kept close to him — back at the castle, on the plane and here in the airport — certainly persuaded him that the human did. Actions spoke louder than words, or so the saying went. And it certainly seemed like it at the moment. Brenin walked so close that they were practically holding hands. In fact, Malcolm made an effort to do just that. When he clasped Brenin's hand, the boy upped the ante by entwining their fingers.

Och. Well, maybe he was simply nervous in the biggish crowd of strangers. By his own admission, the boy wasn't used to traveling. *Aye*. That was it, only looking for reassurance in a strange land. No sense in reading more into it than that. Besides, after having passed through customs, thanks to Darling's magnificently forged documents, it was time to go out and find Val. According to a text Malcolm had received in response to his when they had landed, the guy was circling the pick-up area.

They'd traveled light, as they wouldn't be staying long. At least Malcolm and Willem wouldn't. Brenin had so little that it fit easily into one small duffel. In any event, there was nothing they couldn't carry with them. No need for a dolly or the help of a skycap. All they had to do was step outside and wait for Val to arrive.

A big, black SUV approached. Malcolm knew it must be their ride even before it pulled up to the curb beside them. The passenger-side window slid down as

Malcolm and the others stepped toward it. Val leaned over, his face showing the same sternness it always had. Brenin pressed closer to Malcolm's side at the sight.

"Aren't your knees cold, Highlander?" Val drawled.

Malcolm shot his shipmate a wry grin. "Och, mun, I'm not as delicate as you." He laid his adopted accent on thick as porridge.

Val sneered. "If the cops would allow me to, I'd sit here and wait for a strong wind to lift your skirt. It's been a while since I had a peek."

"I'll be sure to mention your prurient interest to that new husband of yours."

Val shook his head. "Forget it. No flash of your junk is worth a tongue-lashing from my boy. It would only lead to my punishing him, and… On second thought, do your worst."

Malcolm laughed as he was intended to before heading to the back to store his bag and Brenin's. He heard Val greet Willem but concentrated on making sure Brenin was okay.

"I know how fierce he looks, but he's no one for you to fear. Val would lay his life on the line for you."

Brenin handed his bag over. "I'm not afraid because I'm with you. I know you won't let anyone hurt me."

The lad's trust in him was humbling. He took the risk of pulling him in for a quick kiss, amazed and pleased when Brenin permitted it. Then he brought him to the door for the second seat and handed him up.

"This is Brenin," he said as he climbed in beside him.

"Pleased to meet you," Val said through the rearview mirror. "We appreciate your help."

Brenin paused while buckling his seatbelt. "I appreciate yours."

Once Willem had got into the passenger's side, Val pulled out. During the ride to the club, he filled them in on exactly who was going to be there when they arrived. Malcolm wasn't surprised to learn that two local police officers were part of the team. Like Fergus and Darling, there were always fighting men who had accepted and supported them. The women of the group were more of a rarity, but again, Malcolm had Cook and Doc McPhee and, to varying degrees, people in the village on his side. It was good to have allies. There were always things that they couldn't do on their own. Dracul had employed the same strategy, although thankfully nearly all of them ended up on the losing side of matters and dead, to boot. If nothing else, Dracul never left loose ends.

They pulled into an alley then an underground garage. Never having been to Boston, Malcolm had no frame of reference for where they were. He had noticed Brenin peering through the window as they'd traveled through the city. He hoped the boy would enjoy his holiday here while they dealt with Dracul.

Val led them into an elevator and up a few floors until the doors opened to a lovely suite. Malcolm detected Alex's scent immediately and it sent excitement and happiness coursing through him. It had been too long since he'd last seen his captain. He admired the man and how he'd kept them alive and together for so long. More, he liked him, especially because he could have easily gone down the path that Dracul had. Instead, he'd adhered to a code of honor that didn't count on this world—except it had and did inside Alex's own mind.

There were lots of voices coming from the living space. Brenin pressed closer to him and Malcolm took the opportunity to hug him to his side. A redheaded boy flashed toward them, too quick for a human. He squealed as he launched himself into Val's arms. Wrapping his legs around the guy's waist and his arms around his neck, he peppered him with kisses.

"I missed you!"

"Don't be ridiculous, Mackie. I was gone for, like, two hours." The admonishment notwithstanding, Val hugged him in place.

The boy pouted. "Harry and Demi went out only to shop and look how that turned out."

"Oh, baby." Val pressed his lips into the boy's neck and murmured reassurances to him as he kept walking.

"He's not quite human, is he?" Brenin asked quietly.

"No," Malcolm confirmed.

The redhead's face came up. "I'm Mackie Stelalux, Val's husband. And you're safe here, Brenin."

"See there, laddie, making friends already." With a quick pat on his hip, Malcolm let go of the boy in order to greet his captain and the others more appropriately.

Alex came forward. They clasped hands and thumped backs, a ritual that they'd picked up from humans and made their own.

"It's been too long, Malcolm. You look well." Alex's gaze flicked down. "Aren't your knees cold?"

Malcolm laughed before moving to embrace Emil in similar fashion. There was a round of introductions with the human boys—pretty and shy blonds of varying shades who clearly loved Alex and Emil. Lucien he knew, although he didn't recognize the sad man who merely nodded at him from where he sat on the couch. The women were distant, assessing, capable-looking for sure, which he appreciated. The coppers were a contrast in coloring and demeanor. The fairer one barely looked up from his meal as he greeted them with a quick wave. The darker one appeared nearly as forlorn and hollowed out as Lucien. Malcolm wondered what the story was there and resolved to ask Alex if they had a moment alone.

Willem made his way around the room, then it was time for Brenin to be paraded about. The boy stood to one side of the living room entryway. His eyes were wide and his nerves obvious. Malcolm strode back to him and held out his hand. Brenin took it without hesitation. His show of trust was noticed. Malcolm could tell by the expression on everyone's faces.

"This is Brenin, and I'll be thanking you to remember that he's been in the very depths of hell these last few months and is jetlagged in the bargain. He'll need time and rest before he can answer any questions."

"No, it's all right, then," Brenin contradicted him in a firm tone and a strong voice. "I want to help bring the fucker down. I'll do whatever needs doing and now as soon as later."

Malcolm smiled. "That's my laddie. Can we at least start with a wee bit of scran?" he asked Emil.

"If you mean food, then yes, absolutely." With a sweep of his arm, the chef indicated Alex's kitchen counter. "I figured we'd do a buffet, although sheep's offal and blood sausage are not on the menu," he added with a wink.

"Och, well, we can't have everything. I'm sure it will be tidy nevertheless."

He guided Brenin to the food, even though the boy was perfectly capable of doing for himself. Now that the dam, so to speak, had broken, he didn't seem capable of not hovering over the boy and touching him in small ways. Emil had laid out typical American fare—steak, chicken, mash and veg. It all smelled heavenly and, after hours of nothing, more than welcome.

Room was made for them on the couch. Malcolm made sure that Brenin had tucked into his plate before he took the drawings of Dracul's castle from his bag. "Have a gander," he said, handing them to Alex. "Brenin's given us a partial schematic of the castle."

"It's the route I took," the boy added, "when I escaped. And I also drew some other parts based on plans Dafydd pulled up on the computer when he showed me the way to go." He focused on Malcolm's return to the couch after that. Malcolm nodded in approval before starting his own meal.

While he studied a picture, Alex paced the entrance to the room. "Dracul's boy was able to do that?" he asked without looking up.

Malcolm answered for Brenin on the assumption that he'd already taxed his comfort level. "Aye. Dracul underestimated him, for certain."

"He was never a true mate, merely a slave." This from Lucien. Everyone turned their head in his direction. "His life is forfeit, I'm sure, once Harry delivers the baby. Then Harry won't be needed anymore, either. Demi, though, will have value."

Lucien's voice caught on that last word and his eyes filled with tears. He was obviously picturing his son as Dracul's next sex slave, and why shouldn't he? It was the logical assumption, if it hadn't happened already. Although, to Malcolm's knowledge, a hybrid had yet to be changed and bred, it stood to reason that it would be easier to do than it was with a human. Demi, in fact, might become wholly female, as a member of their species would have back when drones repopulated their hive. If Dracul succeeded in turning Demi into a queen... Well, it didn't bear pondering. Dracul could populate the Earth with hundreds of his offspring within years. There was no point in raising the issue, however. Poor Lucien was grievously worried as it was and they needed to focus on the task at hand—killing Dracul once and for all.

"Oh, sweetie." It was Val's husband who went to Lucien and, sitting on the arm of the couch, hugged the man. Or, at least, he tried to. Lucien sat stiffly, unable or unwilling to accept the comfort. "We'll get them both back alive."

"Fucking A we will." This from the darker copper, Duncan.

Brenin took in a visibly shaky breath. "Dafydd saved me, even knowing his own life was on the line." He put his fork down and sat back. "After that bomber guy failed, the monster went berserk. He was taking it out on me and would have killed me if Dafydd hadn't intervened."

He stared out into the room with unfocused eyes. "Dafydd used his escape plan to help me get out." Now, he looked at Malcolm. "We can't let him die."

"We won't." Running his palm along Brenin's cheek, he added, "I promise." He really had no right to do that. Bringing down Dracul and saving Dafydd from death weren't the same thing. One was almost a certainty. The other was much iffier. Still, he couldn't stand seeing Brenin so sad. He would have said almost anything to ease his worry.

Alex went to the chair occupied by his boy, Quinn. Without missing a beat, he lifted the human up, took his place and set him on his lap. Quinn melted into the man, clearly used to the position. "I suppose it's too much to hope that we can get in the way Brenin got out."

"It would be a powerful risk. I have to assume Petru has it blocked — or perhaps merely booby-trapped. And there are surveillance cameras all around the perimeter, regardless."

"Dafydd took the one near the tunnel offline so I wouldn't be detected," Brenin offered. "They must know that by now and will have made adjustments so it doesn't happen again." Malcolm was pleased to see he'd started eating again. The boy was far too thin still.

"This Dafydd guy sounds like he's wicked smart and a good man to have on our side," Duncan remarked.

"Except, isn't he, like, ready to pop? That's got to hinder everything he does," the other cop asked. "Plus, Dracul must have him under lock and key like never before, at this point."

"You're right about that, Anderson," Val confirmed. "Stupid, Dracul is not."

"And," Lucien added, "if he's indeed near his time, he *will* be almost incapacitated. A human woman's body is designed to adjust fully to pregnancy, but it's not the same for a changed man. At least, it wasn't for me. My hips and back gave out. I was on bed rest for the last few weeks."

"It was getting hard for him to move about," Brenin concurred. "I doubt he can help us anymore."

"Nor can Harry," Emil added. "No way Dracul is giving him free rein of the castle."

"They'd be together, wouldn't they?" Quinn asked. "I mean, isn't that the most likely scenario — that Harry and Demi are locked away with Dafydd? That would make things easier for us."

Alex gave him a quick kiss. "Excellent point, dear boy. This has turned into a two-pronged mission. We still have to take out Dracul and as many of his men as we can. But we are also now mounting a rescue. We'll need to split into two groups. And," he added with a pointed look at his boy, "when I say 'we', I don't mean *you*. You boys aren't coming and this is not something we would ask our human allies to risk their own lives for."

There was an eruption of dissent. Every human boy started haranguing his husband or lover, as the case may be, about how they were coming, too. The cops joined, while the women merely shot silent glares in the men's general direction, as if not wanting to waste their breath on an argument. He suspected that they knew they'd have their way, whatever they decided to do. His kind was hard-wired to acquiesce to females.

In the end, it was Lucien who brought the whole thing to a stop by standing and clapping his hands once. The sharp sound penetrated the din and, surprisingly, had everyone shutting up.

"I am going," he said with quiet dignity. "Alex, you are the head of this family and I hold you in the highest esteem. Nevertheless, my husband and son are in danger and I will not sit here while I wait for news about their fate. I will not interfere with your attack on the castle. I know I would only be a hindrance, but I will go. Please do not mistake my submission to my husband as weakness. If you don't take me, I will find a way on my own."

Mackie jumped to his feet. "Yeah, what he said."

Val glared at his husband. "What happened to your vow to obey?"

The boy folded his arms and stared coolly back at Val. "Red."

Val rolled his eyes. "Fuck me."

Although Malcolm wasn't sure what that meant, exactly, he knew a mutiny when he saw one. This time, there was no point in fighting it. "Captain, how about we all go and the non-combatants can stay on my boat in the nearby village. It should be safe there. Although I'm going to have to get a bigger one that is also not as conspicuous as my yacht in order to accommodate this lot."

Alex didn't reply right away. Glancing around the room, he finally landed on the one person that clearly mattered the most to him. "I would have you stay safe," he said to Quinn.

"Nowhere is safe until Dracul is dead." The boy pressed his forehead against Alex's. "Please. I know I can't stick to your side the whole time, but I need to go as far as I can."

"Very well."

Alex sealed his answer with a kiss that was so tender and filled with such love that it made Malcolm's heart ache. He'd thought he could live the rest of his life without loving someone like that. He wasn't sure anymore and didn't dare look at Brenin, for fear his thoughts and emotions would show.

"That's that, then," he said instead and speared another piece of Emil's excellent steak.

"I suppose it is," Alex agreed. "However, Kitty, I'm going to ask you to stay here to keep an eye on things. Not only are the renovations still ongoing, but it's not beyond the realm of possibilities that while we're attacking Dracul, he'll be launching another disruption here."

"You got it, boss."

"Thank you. Sergeant, Detective, may I ask you to back her up as need be?"

"Sure," Anderson said. "I'm all yours," he added to Kitty. He wore an expression that conveyed a deeper meaning, which Malcolm decided was none of his business.

Duncan's answer was different. Hitching up his pants, he said, "With all due respect, no fucking way."

"Sergeant," Alex began.

"No." He ran his hand over the top of his head. "Look. This is Demi we're talking about. I know there's Dracul and the fate of my world and all that, but the moment he took the kid, he made it real personal for me." He shifted his gaze over to Lucien. "This isn't right. Believe me, I get that. He matters, though. I've got, ah...feelings for the kid. I'm going."

"Yes, you are," came Lucien's quiet reply. "Demi will be happy to see you. Whether he should be or not is something his father and I are going to have to worry about...later, once he's home safely under our roof." He sat again and stared at his knees.

Alex huffed. "Well, I suppose that's settled. Logan, what is your will on this?"

The scruffy woman sat hunched at the dining counter. She'd said nothing to date, yet had a sharp eye for what was going on. She shrugged. "Never been to Wales. Could be fun, especially if I get to blow something up."

"I'm sure that can be arranged, don't you think, Malcolm?"

"Aye," he replied with a grin.

"Wait! What are we going to do about a doctor?" Jase, the quietest of the boys, said, curled against Emil in an oversized chair. "If one of you gets hurts on the way in, Harry won't be able to help you. And what if he's injured when you do find him? Who's going to take care of the wounded?"

It was on the tip of Malcolm's tongue to say that, among his kind, death was more likely, given their physiology and how quickly their bodies disintegrated. He didn't want to upset Brenin, though. Brenin spoke up before he could, anyway.

"What about Doc McPhee?"

Malcolm shook his head. "Och, no, although it's a grand thought. She's too old to go into a deadly situation, untrained as she is. Besides, the village is remote and depends on her for its daily healthcare. I wouldn't feel right about her risking her life, either, for their sake."

Duncan said into the silence that followed, "I think I have a solution, not that anyone is going to like it any better. I'm not sure I do, but we could always ask Paz."

There was some general mumbling and grumbling over this suggestion. Malcolm glanced at Brenin and shook his head in response to the boy's unspoken question.

It was Willem who finally asked. "Who the hell is he?"

"A human," Val replied.

"A doctor," Duncan clarified. "And one that, for better or worse, knows all about you."

"He is very curious about us," Emil added. "I expect he'd jump at the chance to study us."

Malcolm was skeptical. "Is he willing to risk his life for that opportunity?"

"I'll ask him," Duncan offered. "Jase is right. Harry and, ah, Demi, might need care. We have to assume they aren't being kept in good condition."

Misery was written large on the human's face. Harry's son obviously meant a lot to him, which was strange. In all their years on Earth, Malcolm wasn't sure there'd ever been a pairing of a hybrid with a human. Not that this was a matchmaking opportunity, and how old was Harry's kid anyway? Old enough to be entering his puberty cycle, perhaps. And didn't that just add to the general difficulty of the situation?

Alex nodded. "There's no harm in your asking, I suppose. Please do so, Sergeant. Of course, nothing is going to happen unless and until we figure out a way to get into that castle."

That set them all to brooding. In the silent contemplation, Malcolm tried to urge Brenin to finish his food. The boy had been awfully quiet during the negotiations of who was going where and doing what. It occurred to Malcolm with the kind of sudden clarity that made grown men bang their heads on walls that he'd promised Brenin he could stay in Boston.

"You don't have to come back, laddie. You can still stay here."

Brenin turned his head and looked at him thoughtfully. "No, that's okay. I want to go. I always have, frankly, because I need to see an end to the monster. I only agreed to remain here so that you wouldn't worry about me."

"Och, now you don't have to be concerned about me and my feelings."

"Well, I am." He blinked and smiled. "I hope that's okay with you."

Malcolm smiled broadly, inordinately pleased that his feelings mattered to the boy. He was painfully aware that everyone in the room was listening in. "It is. Finish your food, though. You need fattening."

Brenin scooped up some potatoes and vegetables. He chewed thoughtfully. "I was just thinking about how to get in."

"Don't you worry about that."

"No, I want to. I think I have an idea — the cistern."

* * * *

Trey felt like some fifties teenager leaning against his car while waiting for Betty Lou to get out of school for the day. Being a cop had its advantages, though. He knew that Paz was taking a shift at the hospital, when he'd be done and which car was his. It made sense to hang in the freezing cold, stamping his feet and mulling over how he was going to raise the issue of the doctor going to Wales. If he looked suspicious or stupid, so be it. With a plan forming of how to invade the castle, they would be leaving Boston in a couple of days. There was no time to waste getting Paz onboard. At a minimum, the guy would surely be required to put in for some time off or something. Trey had already done it and even with the amount he'd accumulated, there still wasn't certainty that he'd be allowed to take his 'vacation'.

Fuck me, I'll quit if I have to.

Yeah, that's what it had come down to. Saving Demi had become paramount in his life. Not even the job he loved mattered more to him. He should never have let himself get in so deep with the kid. Only a few days ago, he would have continued to deny that he had. Not anymore. He'd stared into the eyes of the boy's father and all but declared his love for the boy. *Christ Jesus.* He was a mental case for thinking that he had any business wanting someone who was part alien and of dubious maturity.

It didn't matter that the Commonwealth said that a sixteen-year-old could give consent. The law wasn't the issue—a sense of right and wrong was. Demi's chronological age was probably greater than that, based on what little Trey had gleaned since becoming embroiled with the Stelalux clan. Nevertheless, his behavior so far screamed 'kid' and Trey wasn't about to take advantage of his crush for a more mature man. Not yet, anyway, and perhaps not ever. That didn't mean he could or would sit back while Demi was in the hands of a monster. The thought of it was driving Trey madder with each passing minute. He had to do something.

"Duncan?"

Shit, his head had been so far up his own ass that he'd missed the doctor coming. He turned to face him. "Yeah, sorry, Doc. Got a minute?"

Paz raised his eyebrows. "I suppose, given that whatever it is you've come about must be very important for you to stand around waiting for me. I do have a phone, you know," he added, unlocking his car.

"Yeah, this is best done in person and it's urgent."

"Come and sit inside. I can turn on the heater."

"Thanks." Trey got into the passenger side and sighed in relief when the hot air started blasting out of the console. "We need your help," he said without preamble.

"I'm listening. And I assume by 'we', you don't mean the police department?"

"Right. I'm talking about our unearthly friends." He made a whistling sound and twirled his forefinger up toward the night sky.

Paz angled his body to look at him more directly. "Well, you do know how to push my buttons. Keeping that secret is almost physically painful and my access to them has been more limited than my scientific curiosity would prefer. What is it that you need?"

Trey rubbed his hands near the vents, to marshal thoughts that should have been put into place while he'd waited for the guy. He finally spit it all out and Paz was kind enough to listen without interrupting.

Trey grimaced when he finished. "What do you say, Doc? Feel like a suicide mission to Wales?"

"You don't really think it's that, though, do you? High stakes and high risk, sure, but a doable one. A survivable one."

"What I think doesn't mean jack." Because he would walk through a wall of fire if it meant a chance to save Demi. "The others are pretty confident. Make that really confident, but then I think that's their default setting, you know? Not sure anything much rattles them."

Paz stared out of the windshield, thinking and thinking some more. Finally, "Emergency medicine is certainly something I have experience with and I do think I can be of help there. I was also in the ROTC in high school, so I've have a modicum of military training. I'm not afraid to get involved in a fight."

He looked again at Trey. "I'd be lying, though, if I didn't admit that what really intrigues me is the chance to study this man who was physiologically changed to become pregnant and deliver a baby. That is some freaky shit."

Trey sighed. "Yeah, I get that." Talking about it gave Trey uncomfortable thoughts, too. Was Demi, although a hybrid, like Dafydd in this way? Could Demi get pregnant? No, no way that train of thought led anywhere other than to the town of madness.

"Just don't be too vocal about your curiosity," he advised. "These guys are very protective of their own, especially their significant others and offspring. This Dafydd kid may be Dracul's, but he saved this other boy, Brenin. And there's something obviously between him and Malcolm and...bottom line, this has turned into a rescue mission for Dafydd as well as Harry and Demi."

"What of the baby?"

Trey sharpened his expression. "What about him?"

"He's Dracul's son and Dracul is their mortal enemy. Are they actually intending to save him, too?"

"Of course." Even as the reply left his mouth, Trey realized he hadn't thought about it. No one had said that, not in so many words. Not in any, now that he'd been forced to consider it.

"Let me make myself clear, Duncan. I'll move mountains to get the time off and go on this rescue mission with all of you, so long as it's agreed that if the intent is to kill that baby or abandon him to certain death, I won't have any part in it."

"Right. Understood. You should come by the club as soon as you're able for a skull session. We need all capable minds on the planning. You can, ah, talk with Alex to get all the reassurance you need."

"I'll get started on my time-off request tomorrow morning then head over. My next shift's not until five at night anyway." He flashed a grin. "Holy Mary, mother of God, am I really going to storm a castle with aliens? You couldn't make this shit up if you tried."

Trey dropped his head onto the back of his seat. "Tell me about it."

Chapter Eight

Malcolm was careful to open Brenin's bedroom door silently and slip in quickly so the hallway light wouldn't wake him. It hardly mattered. The en suite door was flung wide and the light inside was on. It illuminated the room sufficiently for even a human eye to see clearly. And Malcolm hadn't managed to take more than two steps toward the bed before Brenin pushed up on one arm.

"Is everything all right?" His voice was sleepy and his eyes at half-mast.

Malcolm felt a right fool for disturbing him. He'd only come to ease his own irrational worries, because the club was tight as could be, given Val's security system. Brenin didn't need protection here. He did require sleep, however, and now Malcolm had gone and woken him.

"Sorry, laddie. I didnae mean to wake you. I was only checking to see if…well…" he admitted on a huff, "I'm not sure what I thought I was doing."

Brenin slid back down. "It's fine. I'm not sorry you're here. It was hard to get to sleep alone. I don't like being in a strange place, regardless of how safe it is."

Malcolm approached the bed. "Aye, I can understand that for certain. You've been dragged about too much lately. I would say I was sorry, except your knowledge of Dracul's castle has given us the key to defeat him. We're that grateful to you and I'm that proud, as well. You've got more courage than a whole dragoon of men."

Brenin shook his head. "Naw, not really. I ran like the frightened animal I was. It was luck that had me picking up bits of information here and there and remembering all I saw on the computer."

"Dinnae do that," Malcolm said more sharply than he'd intended. He modulated his tone and his accent. "Don't dismiss yourself like that," he clarified. "You're more smart than lucky and it was a bold move to run the way you did. I've seen many a man give up in the midst of battle and wait for fate to claim him."

Although he knew better than to tempt himself, he went to sit on the edge of the bed. He reached over and carded Brenin's hair back from his face. "Has no one ever tried to convince you of your worth?"

Brenin's gaze dropped. "No. I mean, I was only that fae boy that watched the birds out of the window more than the teacher's lesson. And everyone could see I liked other boys too much."

"You had to leave home?" Malcolm's heart ached at the idea of sweet Brenin on the streets, vulnerable and ultimately an easy victim for Dracul.

Brenin nodded. "It was better all-around that I did."

"Well, I wouldn't have wished it for you, but I'm glad that I had the good fortune of having you run into my arms."

"That was the one positive thing to come from this." Brenin smiled at the admission. He gazed up with wide eyes. "Can I ask a favor of you?"

"Of course. Anything."

"Would you mind lying down with me? I don't like being in the room alone and I'm awfully tired."

Mind? Malcolm's body went on high alert at the idea. He — and it — would like nothing better, except it was the height of folly. "I don't think that's a very good idea, laddie."

Brenin's expression fell. "Oh. I understand."

Now, he felt like a miser and a coward, denying the boy his one request. "However, I did say 'anything', so scooch over."

Brenin's face lit up and he hurried to comply. To give the boy such a simple joy... Malcolm would just have to keep himself in check. Plus, there was nothing to say he couldn't stay fully clothed and on top of the covers.

After taking off his boots and socks, he climbed up to prop himself against the headboard. "There, now. How's that?"

"Um." Brenin gnawed at his lower lip, which only served to make Malcolm want to kiss him. "Aren't you going to disrobe and get under the covers?"

Malcolm had to bite back a groan. "No. I'm fine right as I am. To be honest, it would be dangerous to do so."

"Why's that?"

Malcolm scrutinized the boy's face to see if he was teasing. *Hmm, he looks serious, but can he be that naïve?* After all he'd gone through, maybe he was. Perhaps in his mind, a man was either a monster or a saint. Malcolm hated to lower the boy's impression of him.

"You're already a powerful temptation as it is, laddie. If I take off my kilt, you're going to see how much that's true, even with my modern underwear on. It's not a chastity belt, you know."

Brenin turned onto his side and tucked his arm under his head. "Yeah, I know that. I mean, I assumed that. I don't mind."

"How can you not?"

"I'm trying to put my past behind me, remember? I don't want the monster to ruin my life. Before he got his claws in me, I would have taken every liberty I could to get a look at a man like you."

The boy slithered his free hand across the covers and onto Malcom's thigh. Even with the thick fabric of the kilt guarding it, Malcolm's skin tingled at the touch. His cock had been only partially aroused but now it struggled to go to full mast. The cotton confining it was no match for its hardness.

Malcolm swallowed. "You can look and touch as much as you like. I dinnae mind, so long as it doesn't scare you." Passion thickened his voice and heightened his Scottish burr.

"Being overwhelmed and powerless frightens me. So long as I'm in control, I'd appreciate the opportunity to do some exploring."

Malcolm could only nod his assent. He forced his hands down flat on the bed, determined to let Brenin do as he wanted without interference. It might very well kill him to lie there, unmoving, a living anatomically correct doll for the boy's edification. It was a fate he'd gladly accept if it helped the human recover from his ordeal.

"You have nice feet. Strong, like."

Malcolm had to smile at that. "I dinnae believe anyone has commented on them before."

"Then they weren't paying attention." Brenin curled his fingers and scrunched up a bit of the kilt. "Your legs are lovely, too. Also strong and straight." He bunched more of the fabric in his hand. "Knees are underrated, I think."

"If you say so."

Brenin grinned up at him. "Oh, I do. Did they get cold, like your friends asked?"

Malcolm shook his head. "We have a different body temperature. It's heat we don't tolerate." He hated reminding the boy of his alien nature.

It didn't seem to bother Brenin, though, because soon Malcolm's thighs were exposed, and the kilt was practically bunched around Malcolm's waist. "This room is pretty warm."

"Aye, for your comfort."

"You must be overly warm, then, with that shirt and this heavy kilt on?" The boy touched Malcolm's bare thigh with his fingertips.

Malcolm grunted. "A wee bit."

"Take them off, why don't you?" He flicked his gaze up to meet Malcolm's. "Please?"

"Are you sure?" At the boy's nod, Malcolm stopped fighting the good fight and whisked his shirt over his head in the next instant.

With his hands on his waistband, he hesitated. Brenin answered his unspoken question by tugging at the fabric he still held. That was enough for Malcolm, because he wanted it to be. He was as keen as the boy to get naked and only the vestiges of control slowed him down.

He undid the buckle and pulled the kilt open. His dick was a visible bulge beneath the underwear and the head even poked out of the top. More self-conscious than he would have expected, he lifted his arse to tug the kilt free. Except Brenin didn't let go of his handful, so that, in the end, he held it to himself.

The boy brought a corner of the kilt up to his nose and sniffed. "It smells like you."

"Och? And what is it like, then?"

"I don't know, exactly. It's not like anything else. Spicy maybe. Uniquely you," he added quickly. "It doesn't remind me of, you know, *him*."

Malcolm let out a hard breath. "Good to know." He was back to putting his hands flush on the bed, although he wanted to cover his lap to hide his intemperate dick. Brenin had said he wanted to look and touch. He had to take the boy at his word. Trying to protect him would seem like not trusting him to make up his own mind about matters. He'd had enough of that kind of treatment. Someone had to show him respect.

Brenin went back to touching him, creeping his warm, soft fingers across Malcolm's thigh. His breath hitched at the touch and his hips didn't want to remain still.

Brenin paused in his movements. "Does this bother you?"

"In the best possible way, yes."

The very tip of Brenin's finger touched Malcolm's shaft. "You're very big."

Malcolm clenched his own fingers. "It will never be used to hurt you." His voice was suddenly rough and a powerful thirst overtook him sufficiently to make his fangs itch to come down. He held them back with effort and stayed as still as he could.

"I know that."

The boy pulled his hand back, although not completely. Instead of exploring that most dangerous part of Malcolm more, he ran his palm up Malcolm's torso. Malcolm was both relieved and disappointed. There was nothing to complain about, really. The feel of that hand on his abs, then his pecs, was delicious in its own way. It kept him aroused, that was for certain, and he imagined that the rapid beat of his heart could be felt through his chest wall.

Indeed, Brenin paused and laid his hand flat against one of Malcolm's pecs. His palm rubbed the nipple. "I don't mean to be a tease."

"You— You're not," Malcolm ground out. "Do whatever helps you or makes you happy. I dinnae mind."

Brenin curled his fingers, pressing the nails into Malcolm's flesh. "You do, though. To say otherwise is a lie, however well intentioned."

"Brenin…" He didn't know what he wanted to say.

"I think I have a way to satisfy us both, if you're game."

"Anything." He meant that. He would agree to whatever the boy suggested.

"Take care of yourself, then, and let me watch."

Malcolm frowned. "Are you saying…?"

"Yes." Brenin's tone was firm. "Get rid of these useless boxer-briefs and take yourself in hand. I want to see you palm that cock and pleasure yourself."

Malcolm would have grinned at the way the boy had expressed it, if not for the fact that this was serious business. Brenin was paving a path for his healing. It might not be one doctors would recommend—or maybe they would. He had no idea, other than he wasn't about to deny this boy anything at the moment.

Without mulling the matter over any further, Malcolm hooked his thumbs into the waistband of the underwear and yanked them down and off. He used his normal speed because he didn't have that much control. He was almost desperate to see Brenin's reaction to his fully visible erection.

Brenin's breath stuttered out. "There he is."

"Are you all right, laddie? Is it too much?"

Brenin had to fight to catch his breath. There was fear there, yes, no matter what kind of brave face he put on for Malcolm. This was *difficult*. Seeing the alien's dick spring free like that, hard, ruddier than the pale skin around it and gleaming with pre-cum, called up the worst memories of his captivity, except he kept his palm pressed against the cool pec as a reminder that he was in control. As frightened as he was on the most basic level, he still trusted Malcolm completely. He had no doubt that if he told the guy to stop, to leave, he would in a flash…literally.

He swallowed back the bile that fought to rise and shoved down the terror that worked to get out. *I am in control here.* He reminded himself of that and believed in its truth. And he took the time to stare at and study the rigid rod of flesh in Malcolm's large hand. The man's control over this part of him seemed obvious. Still, he put it to the test.

"Wrap your fingers around it." *God, where did I find the courage to issue that order?* Malcolm, of course, had led him in the right direction and given him the space to follow it.

Malcolm curled his fingers slowly around the shaft. The thing was so long and thick that even Malcolm had trouble. Brenin's hole clenched at the observation. Then he remembered that he didn't have to accommodate it. It was only something to watch and enjoy.

"Jerk it, easy-like. I want to take this slow."

"Can I look at you while I do?" Malcolm's voice was thick as porridge and a bit lower than usual.

The sound of it skittered across Brenin's skin, making it tingle. "If it pleases you."

"Och, it does."

He relaxed against the arm under his head and tucked the kilt up under his chin while Malcolm work his dick with easy strokes. The cock was a tight, satiny toy, the only movement coming at the top when the glans got squeezed. More pearly cum bubbled up from the slit. It dribbled down the length, easing Malcolm's movements with each pass. The chest beneath Brenin's hand rose and fell with increasingly quick breaths.

He glanced down at the large balls snuggled underneath the bottom of the cock. "Cup yourself," he ordered. His voice sounded strange to his ears. Strained, like.

And as Malcolm seated his other hand around his sac, Brenin's own cock finally hardened. It was a more familiar sensation than it had been only days ago. Less scary, too. This was how it was supposed to be — two men who wanted each other having a bit of fun in bed. If he were truly brave, he'd reach inside his underwear and do to himself what Malcolm did at his command.

He wasn't that brave, though, or, rather to Malcolm's earlier statement, he wasn't ready to go that far. For now, it was enough to have control over Malcolm's pleasure. He wanted to see the man come, to confirm what he already knew intellectually—that seeing it would bring him pleasure, as well.

"Do it faster. Make yourself come, whatever it takes."

Malcolm didn't need to be told twice. He picked up speed as he worked his dick with a brutal pace. He clenched around the balls he held. The grip made his knuckles even whiter, if that were possible. His breathing became like that of a locomotive.

"Help me!"

Brenin glanced up in surprise. Coal-black eyes stared back at him and a gleam of white showed past the lips. "Please…with my nipple. Pinch it…hard!"

Brenin didn't hesitate. He was nearly desperate to see this through, whatever it took. Sliding his hand down a few inches, he grabbed the hard nipple between his thumb and forefinger. He squeezed with all his might, trusting Malcolm to know his own limits.

He almost missed the moment of climax, it came so fast. With a roar, Malcolm doubled over as cum burst out of the tip of his cock. The musky scent of semen erupted, as well, hitting Brenin's nostrils. It might have made him sick with the visceral memory, except he stuffed the kilt into his nose and inhaled deeply. Yes, this was the smell that made him feel safe. It reminded him that he was with Malcolm and Malcolm was his savior.

Malcolm was also now his lover.

* * * *

"That's it. Squeeze with gentle pressure."

Brenin did as instructed and this time, the bullet hit closer to the bullseye. Putting the gun down, he jerked the headphones off and blew out a breath. "I think that's it for me. This is all worst-case scenario and now that I know I can more or less hit my target, I'm done with practicing. I don't much like these things," he added with a nod toward the gun.

He also didn't like being taught how to load and shoot a weapon by Mackie, not that he had anything against the guy. It was only that he wasn't Malcolm, and that was a mark against everyone this morning. After that spectacularly enlightening and liberating event with the man in bed and a night spent curled against his reassuring presence, Brenin had woken alone. Achingly hard and alone, rather. He'd tossed one off, using the scent clinging to the kilt as a goose to his arousal. An intense orgasm had ripped through him, leaving him panting and sweaty and more at peace than he'd felt in…forever.

In its own bizarre way, the experience had been the most normal thing he'd done since leaving home. It had left him calm and certain and hopeful, so much so that he'd wanted to keep a part of it with him the whole day. After showering, he'd dressed in jeans and a sweater, then wrapped the kilt around his waist. It was ridiculously long on him, almost ankle length, even with his folding part of it over the band. Still, wearing it gave him a sense of power and kept a connection between him and his lover that he needed. It was an anchor in a strange environment. It didn't matter how safe and welcoming the club and its inhabitants were. This was just one more place that wasn't his to call his own. He'd been on the streets, in a shelter, held captive in one castle and cossetted in another. He was tired of feeling adrift and as inexplicable as it was, somehow in a short few days, Malcolm had come to represent *home* to him.

With his peaceful state of mind, freshly washed body and grounded sense of being, he'd left the bedroom with confidence in search of breakfast. The only missing element was Malcolm himself. Brenin would have liked to have shared that moment with him. But Malcolm was nowhere to be found until Mackie had brought Brenin down to this locked room beneath the club.

Target practice had been the goal. All the boys had received basic self-defense lessons, as well as training in various weapons use. Brenin saw the wisdom in it, but even after all he'd been through, he didn't have a warrior's heart. He'd kill if necessary, yes. Fear of being brutalized again would drive him to it easily enough. He just didn't want to be in the position and was glad the aliens hadn't given in to the idea of the boys joining in the assault on Dracul's castle.

His gaze skittered over to the side of the long room, where Malcolm stood with the other men, poring over a digital map and no doubt discussing their plans. He couldn't hear what they said and didn't much care. He only wanted — no, needed — to catch sight of Malcolm every once in a while to maintain that secure feeling.

Except for his long dark hair braided back from his face, the man looked like any other of the modern age, dressed as he was in the same basic clothes as Brenin and everyone else in the room. Brenin didn't like that, though. He wanted his highlander back. Of course, that would mean giving him his kilt. That could only happen if the man came to him, because the group of aliens was giving off an intense and private vibe. Brenin didn't dare disturb it. He wasn't sure of his welcome, either. Malcolm had barely glanced at him and that had been the one time when he'd entered the room.

"It's hard, I know," Mackie remarked as he picked up the gun and removed the clip.

Brenin shifted his attention to the boy. "You seem comfortable handling them."

"I didn't mean the weapons." Mackie tossed his head in the direction of the men. "When they're together like that, knowing what we do about them, it feels like we're always on the outside and don't dare intrude."

Brenin was surprised at the observation. "Is it that obvious I want to be over there instead of here?"

Mackie gave him a sly grin. "Natch. Your face is an open book, sweetie. Plus," he added while he put everything back into place, "I'm you, so I know how you feel."

Brenin shook his head. "No offense, but you're not even remotely like me."

"Oh, no?" Mackie cocked a hip. "You left home because staying there and being gay wasn't an option. You were either close to selling yourself to make money, or you'd already taken that plunge before Dracul forced you to use your body to survive."

The boy moved to face the group across the room. "You want him, although the fact that you do is confusing. He's a blood-sucking alien. You should be running away, screaming. Instead, you want to get closer." He slanted his gaze toward Brenin. "How am I doing so far?"

Brenin barked out a laugh. The sound had Malcolm's head coming up. He looked at Brenin briefly before returning his attention to the rest of his group.

"You're bloody brilliant. Go on."

"Okay, so the biggest problem by far is that, even though you know — you absolutely *know* — he wants you, too, he's not taking anything. He's avoiding you, pushing you away either physically or figuratively. And that's the most confusing part of this whole fucked-up thing. Why is he doing *that*?"

Brenin let the rhetorical question hang in the air for a few seconds before responding. "What's the answer, then? You seem to have it figured out."

Mackie giggled. And that caused Val to look over the same as Malcolm had. This man, though, shot his husband a sexy smile that held a lot of promise. The sight of it caused a sense of jealously to spark in Brenin. *Ridiculous!* He tamped it down.

"Sweetie, I don't. I just kept crashing against the gate of resistance until he let me in. All I can advise is that you do the same. Their strength is astounding, but they do have weaknesses and loving their boys is one of them. We've got at least twenty-four hours before Operation Bring Fucking Dracul Down begins in earnest. Take the opportunities you get to batter against whatever noble intentions Malcolm is using to remain distant.

"Just not now. They need time and space to plan something that won't get them killed. You and I are a distraction. Come on. Let's go back upstairs."

Reluctant as he was to leave Malcolm, he understood the wisdom of Mackie's observation. He permitted the boy to usher him out and back up to the main floor. He wasn't sure where they were headed until Mackie led him into a big room with the stages and dance floor. Brenin hadn't caught more than a glimpse of this space. It had left him wide-eyed with wonder. What a great nightclub this must make when it was open for business.

Mackie waved at the tall woman who was silently polishing the long, wooden bar. "Hi, Kitty. Would you please put on my playlist?"

"Sure thing."

As Brenin followed Mackie farther into the room, jazz was replaced with hip-hop. Mackie kicked off his trainers and leaped onto the nearest stage. He began to gyrate his hips like they were on ball-bearings then grabbed the pole.

Brenin went to sit on one of the plush chairs surrounding the dance floor and relaxed into the cushions as Mackie executed a series of acrobatic feats using the pole and an unexpected amount of physical power.

He's not quite human.

The speed and grace of the boy were amazing, exquisitely beautiful. Brenin was envious, as well as enthralled. He could have that. He could *be* that. All he had to do was allow Malcolm to feed him blood and his body would change like Mackie's had. Like Dafydd's had, he reminded himself. That was the dark side to all of this. To become pregnant and bear a child when his body wasn't designed to do so... Was it really something he was willing to do in order to achieve near immortality and superhuman abilities? He was gay, yes, but not transgender. Every part of him identified as a boy. Could he accept a fundamental change the way Lucien had out of love?

Wait. What am I thinking? Since when did love have anything to do with it? He'd accepted last night that he and Malcolm had become lovers. That was a physical state of being, not an emotional one — except the more he allowed that emotional concept to rattle around in his head, the less absurd or frightening it seemed.

"Hey, no fair, Mackie. Play something the rest of us can dance to." Quinn came in with Jase at his side. Both boys were dressed for exercising, with skin-tight yoga pants and sleeveless tees that barely covered their flat stomachs.

Hanging out at the top of the pole as if it were no more effort than lounging in a chair, Mackie laughed. "Kitty, sweetie, can you please change the music to toddler level?" He slid down to the stage.

A few seconds later, Ed Sheeran's *Shape of You* started. Being held by Dracul meant being cut off from the rest of the world, but Brenin had caught some stuff through the television that the monster had watched. Sometimes, when they were alone, Brenin and Dafydd had been able to amuse themselves with the box, too.

The upbeat song made it impossible for him to stay still. He nodded to the beat and tapped his fingers and toes as he watched the three boys go through a routine that started on the floor and quickly took to the pole. Quinn and Jase didn't have Mackie's otherworldly skill, but they had their own enviable grace and rhythm. Each of them used the upright piece of metal like an extension of their own body. They spun around with their feet leaving the ground then stuck their landings and twerked their tight asses in a blur of sexy movement that caused Brenin to laugh out loud.

Up they went, their lean, yet strong, arm muscles bunching with the strain of holding their entire weight. At the top, Mackie held himself straight out, perpendicular to the floor. Brenin gasped and leaned forward in awe. Then Mackie split his legs in a wide V before twirling around and wrapping himself around the pole like a snake. Brenin couldn't help but clap at the show then stopped abruptly when he realized the boy had collapsed at the bottom and was weeping into his arm.

He raced over and reached him before the other boys did. "What is it, mun? Have you hurt yourself?" Mackie shook his head, yet continued to sob. Brenin looked helplessly at the others.

Quinn pulled Mackie into his arms. "It's okay, sweetie. We're here for you."

"I don't understand what's happening," Brenin said to no one in particular. "Should I get Val?"

"No!" Mackie peered out from Quinn's embrace with a tear-streaked face. "Don't bother him. I'm just being stupid."

"About?"

"Demi." Mackie's face crumpled. "I'm so worried about the brat. He should be here, annoying the shit out of us. Instead, he's suffering God-knows-what." Mackie sniffled and shuddered. "No, I know what could be happening." He stared into Brenin's eyes. "You know exactly what he might be enduring."

Brenin fell flat on his arse, a sick feeling welling up inside him. "I do, yes."

"Jase, too. Right?" Mackie asked, directing his question to the boy behind Brenin.

"Yeah," came the quiet reply.

"But," Brenin sputtered, "didn't everyone agree last night that so long as Dafydd hasn't delivered, the monster won't hurt Demi in order to keep his hold over the doctor?"

Mackie wiped his nose on his sleeve. "They want Lucien to believe that so he won't worry as much. Think about it, though. You know Dracul better than any of us. When has he ever been cowed by anyone else? Isn't it more likely he's given Harry a simple ultimatum—deliver my son or watch me kill yours?

"And why wouldn't Harry make the choice of letting his son get raped in exchange for helping Dafydd? At least he'd still be alive, and whether Harry helps or not, Dracul can always do whatever he wants to Demi." He shook his head. "No, Dracul has all the leverage and we can only hope to get Demi out alive, not unharmed."

Brenin shuddered. "You're right. Of course you are." He hadn't liked thinking about it much, but in the face of the obvious, he couldn't deny it. "The monster isn't one to let his appetites go unappeased. That's why they took me, because Dafydd was too sick to *service* him."

"He can survive this," Jase said fiercely. "I did. You did, too, Brenin. And Demi is stronger than we give him credit for. Whatever happens, this doesn't have to be something that defines him for the rest of his life."

"Jase is right," Quinn agreed with a grim look. "I can't say I truly understand what any of you have gone through, but I do know this. Demi isn't merely a brat. By the blood in his veins, he's a warrior." He shot them a wry grin. "He might even save himself and his father before the rescue mission starts."

Mackie giggled, his tears drying up. "You're right. If nothing else, he's probably annoying them all to death."

The other boys laughed. Brenin didn't. He couldn't. His mind was back in the dank castle that was always cold, always nightmarish. Demi was a stranger to him, not a friend like with the others. And yet, he felt for him, worried about what misery the boy was experiencing at that very moment.

Chapter Nine

"Come on, a little bit more, please. You need the fluids." Demi pressed the paper cup against Dafydd's lips to make him drink the rest of the water.

The boy—no, man, really—did, even though his demeanor was one of someone who had given up. He allowed Demi to bully him into anything. The fight, if he'd ever had any, had gone out of him entirely. When he was done, Demi crushed the cup and tossed it over the side of the bed. Mother Earth be damned. They weren't allowed glasses or even mugs, nothing that could be broken into a weapon. And there was no wastebasket, either, so rubbish was piling up in one corner. Every now and again, one of the silent human slaves would come in to clean up.

Whatever. Demi had more important concerns. Helping his father keep Dafydd alive and comfortable was the main one. The baby inside him was the only thing giving everyone relative safety. If it died before being born or during, Papa would be killed outright and Demi's life would become something not worth living. He was old enough to understand that and Papa hadn't tried to sugarcoat it for him, either.

He carefully lay Dafydd's head down from where he'd been supporting it with the crook of his arm. Demi needed to climb onto the bed to do so, given that Dafydd's outside arm was manacled to the bedpost. *God, is that really necessary?* Of course not. It was merely one of Dracul's many cruelties. The other was having Kronid stay in the very room with them, as if the narrow windows weren't sufficient to ensure they remained. Not even Demi could squeeze through them, and if he did, the fall was so high that he didn't think he could survive. Dafydd certainly wouldn't, not that they would leave him behind.

"I don't know why you bother to be so kind to me," Dafydd said in a quiet voice.

Demi slid down beside him in order to talk more privately, not that Kronid couldn't hear everything they said, regardless. The smallness of the room coupled with his alien hearing meant nothing was secret. Although the guy was mostly engrossed with his phone, when he wasn't stalking Demi with his eyes, that was.

"Why shouldn't I?" he replied. "I think I might want to be a doctor like my father, and I've got nothing against you anyway."

Dafydd turned his gaze toward him. "Don't you, then? I'm the reason you're here."

"No, Dracul is the reason I'm here."

"Same difference."

"Not to me." A ripple under the blanket where it draped over Dafydd's abdomen caught his attention. "Does it hurt?"

Dafydd placed his hand on top of the mound. "No. Not now. Not yet. Everything else does, though."

"I can ask my father to give you something." He started to rise.

"Don't even try. Dracul won't allow him to have medicine stronger than what he's already dosed me with. It hardly matters, anyway. Soon my pain will be gone forever."

"You shouldn't think that. We won't let anything happen to you. My father knows what he's doing."

A smile ghosted across Dafydd's lips. "You are so young. I was once like you. Centuries ago, I still clung to hope. Hard to believe," he added with a shake of his head.

Demi reined in his irritation. "Staying positive does not make me naïve."

"You're right. I'm that sorry, but I'm done fighting my fate. My life is forfeit, no matter how successful your father is in bringing Dracul's next evil spawn into the world."

Demi resisted the urge to dispute that assertion. With Kronid's avid ears in the room, he didn't want to tell Dafydd that a rescue was, without question, being mounted. Any time now, Alex and the others would invade this castle and save them. Dracul's hubris would bring an end to him. He couldn't conceive that his location was known by his enemies or that they could override his security systems. His overconfidence would be his downfall.

Instead, Demi tried to focus on something both positive and safe for discussion. "I know it must be hard, but don't you feel any affection for your son? He's living inside you, after all. There must be some connection between the two of you."

Dafydd's face turned stony. "Other than his sucking the life out of me? No, we don't share a *connection*. Like the twins, he will be wholly Dracul's."

"You don't know that."

"I do."

Demi tried a different tack, a personal one. He didn't dwell on his own nature very often because he still grappled with it. He had mixed feelings about what it meant to be a 'hybrid' — two species in one body that didn't fit in either of his fathers' worlds. The one thing he was sure about was that he didn't regret being the child of two loving and honorable parents.

"Then it must upset you terribly to have me by your side, touching you, helping you."

Dafydd shot a surprised look at him. "I didn't mean that. I'm not disturbed by you. I appreciate your caring."

"Even though I'm a hybrid like your own sons?"

"Please. I'm not in the mood for a philosophical lecture."

"Sorry. I'm only trying to make the point that there's a nurture component here. My nature notwithstanding, I was raised to be decent, to follow the rules and not take advantage of those that are not as smart or strong or capable as I am."

He flicked his gaze over to Kronid, who naturally picked up on the split-second attention and took advantage by licking his lips at Demi. "Just as some of the crew that crashed here took a dark path while the rest adhered to the morally right one, this son doesn't have to end up like the others." He let his hatred show through to Kronid before ignoring him again.

Dafydd sighed. "I understand what you're saying and appreciate your effort, but I can't love this thing.

Dracul has beaten any kind feelings I ever had out of me. I just want it out of me and the peace that my death will bring."

Demi dared to put his hand on Dafydd's arm. "It's okay. I understand. Why don't you try to get some sleep? Night's falling, for whatever that's worth. My internal clock is all screwed up and I think I'll try to rest, as well."

Even as he closed his eyes, though, he pictured Trey kicking open the door and scooping him up from this waking nightmare. That happy thought allowed him to relax and forget the predator in the room.

* * * *

"Are you trying to avoid me, laddie?"

Brenin stowed his meager pack in the luggage compartment and tried to act indifferent to Malcolm's presence. He also tried to shrug off the effect the man's breath had as it played across his skin, raising the fine hairs and goosebumps.

"I would have thought it was the other way around." He shrugged and moved on.

Malcolm blocked his path. "I'm sorry if I haven't paid enough attention to you today."

Brenin crossed his arms. "Oh, no. You're not going to turn this into my being clingy or something. I understand that you've been busy with your war planning and all. It just seems to me that you've been careful to keep your distance. At least, you did this morning. I'm simply returning the favor—steering clear so that I won't bother you."

Heat flared in Malcolm's eyes. "Your very existence disturbs me, if I'm to be honest here."

That confession melted any resolve Brenin had cultivated, caused it to evaporate even while they stood in the aisle of Alex's massive private plane and others moved around them getting ready to take off.

"If by that you mean you've been giving me space so that I don't freak out over what we did last night, you needn't. I'm fine. I'm working on being fine," he amended when doubt crept into Malcolm's face.

The guy nodded. "That's honest, at least, and I want that from you. The last thing I could live with is hurting you." With that confession made, he leaned in and took Brenin's lips in a soft, yet lingering kiss that only brushed the surface, even as it felt like a claiming.

"There's a stateroom in the back, guys," Val said as he hurried past them.

"Come here." Taking Brenin's hand, Malcolm pulled him aside and sat him down in one of the two wide, stuffed chairs nearby. Then he sat in the other, still holding on to him.

"There's not going to be too much time for us to talk or be alone from here on out. We fly straight back to Scotland and to my home. From there, we'll gear up. I already have Darling acquiring what we need that I don't already possess."

"Didn't we bring the arsenal from Alex's place?"

"No. We could fly in literally under the radar, but we prefer to stick to the humans' rules whenever we can. We go through customs the same as we did in Boston. Everything will be aboveboard until we head for Wales. Darling's already secured an old fishing trawler that will give us more room and less notice. We'll be armed for every eventuality, make no mistake."

"Okay, then. I get that we have to focus on the mission, as it were. I'd still like to spend whatever time I can with you."

Malcolm stroked one finger down Brenin's cheek. "As would I, laddie. We've got a few hours' flying time to be sure. We can take advantage of the stateroom anytime you'd like."

Brenin's cheeks heated up at the thought. "Aren't you needed in the cockpit?"

"Och, no, not all the time. This behemoth of Alex's requires his and Willem's deft touch. I've already laid in the flight plan. My job is mostly done."

"Oh." Shyness stole over him, however. If they went to the back of the plane, everybody would realize what they were doing. Or, at least, they would be imagining all kinds of things. Brenin himself didn't know what he wanted from Malcolm right now.

"I wouldn't want to take Alex and Quinn's bed from them."

"I doubt they'd mind. There's plenty of places hereabouts for couples to grab some time together."

Brenin glanced around with wide eyes. The plane was spacious and luxurious, to be sure, but there were not a lot of doors. "No real privacy, though, is there?"

Malcolm winced. "We're not like humans. We don't have the same need for that. And I expect the boys have got used to being out in the open."

Brenin didn't need to be told that. His time with the monster had informed him of many things. Being fucked in front of others had been the norm. No one in the castle of horrors had thought anything of talking to their master while he tortured Brenin with his cock.

"They're all going to want to wring as much intimacy out of the hours they have left with each other," Malcolm added.

Because they might die. Malcolm didn't say that. He didn't have to. Nor did he have to highlight one other thing the aliens needed from their boys. "They're going to drink, too, aren't they?"

Malcolm nodded, although he couldn't hold his gaze on Brenin. "Aye. It's best. The blood helps with strength and endurance."

"Then you'll need some, too," he said with sudden clarity.

"Aye, but that's not your concern."

"How isn't it?" Brenin felt affronted, which was ridiculous. The bloodsucking had become the worst of his experiences.

"Emil has stocked a supply in the galley. I'll heat it up before we arrive."

"But is that sufficient? I mean, isn't it better for you to drink right from the source, like?" Even as the words came tripping out of his mouth, he wondered if he'd lost his mind. The mere thought of giving his vein to someone — anyone — made him sick.

Malcolm squeezed his hand. "You aren't to worry about this. Do you hear me, laddie? Emil's supply will do me right enough."

"Okay, yes." He nodded.

"Now, buckle up. We're about ready to taxi and I need to go see if Alex and Willem require my assistance for the takeoff. I'll be back as soon as we're airborne, regardless."

Brenin nodded again and did as he'd been told. This was only the second time he'd been on a plane and, while Willem's had been smaller, he wasn't sure he'd enjoy lifting into the air any more this time than the last.

"Mind if I sit here?" The human doctor, Paz, came up and pointed to the seat across from him.

"Not at all, sir."

The man chuckled. "Please, call me Ric." He buckled in and stretched out his legs. "I must confess I'm not a fan of this mode of transportation. I understand the aerodynamics of it, but it still feels unnatural."

Brenin clenched the armrests when the plane lurched forward. "I know what you mean."

"I can give you something for the anxiety if you'd like. I stocked up my own prescription and, while I know it's not strictly legal to give you some of mine, I *am* a doctor."

"I'm okay. Thanks all the same."

"Well, let me know if you change your mind." Ric stared out of the window at the darkened runway. "I supposed I'd be more anxious if I could actually believe this is all real."

"Yeah, I know what you mean by that, as well." Brenin stared at the man. "Can I ask you something?"

"Sure." The handsome doctor gave him his full attention.

"Why are you doing this? It's not your fight and you could end up killed." The man, after all, was going to enter the castle with the warriors and the cop, not hang out in the relative safety of the boat.

Ric shrugged. "Scientific curiosity and the opportunity, if and when the presence of these aliens in our world becomes known, of having the inside scoop. I'm sorry if you thought I had nobler reasons."

"No, that's fine. It doesn't matter why you're doing it so long as you're on our side."

Samantha Cayto

"Please, don't worry on that score. I've seen up close what that fucker Dracul has done to humans. I want him dealt with, once and for all." He turned his gaze back to the window as the plane revved up. "I just hope my *abuela* back in Columbia will forgive me the sin of lying to get time off. I told the hospital she was dying. It was the quickest way to catch this bus."

The plane rose, the sensation causing Brenin's heart rate to kick up, but not as much as the sight of Malcolm coming down the aisle toward him did. His calm demeanor soothed Brenin and the ready smile he sent his way made Brenin's breath catch in his throat.

"Your pardon, doctor," Malcolm said, stepping over the man's leg. "All right, then, laddie?" he asked as he retook his seat.

"Yes." He nodded and relaxed into his comfy chair. "I don't expect commercial flights are this grand, are they?"

"Doubtful." Malcolm stretched his legs beside Ric's and took hold of Brenin's hand. He gave the doctor a shark smile, all teeth and no warmth.

It was a minor show of jealousy, but it pleased Brenin all the same. "Do you want your kilt?" He'd been wearing it the whole day. Now that he and Malcolm were together, it occurred to him he should give it back.

Malcolm gave him one of those heated looks again. "I prefer it on you."

Brenin gasped in delight. Before he could think of a pithy reply, though, music filled the cabin. He looked around. The other boys were getting up. Jase and Emil headed for the galley, undoubtedly to put out a buffet, even though they'd all eaten a few hours before. One thing Brenin had noted about the aliens was that they had huge appetites.

Mackie popped over. He tugged on Brenin's arm. "Come on and dance."

Quinn was already shimmying up and down Alex, who had come into the cabin. The big, stern leader of the group was laughing in obvious delight and affection at his lover's antics. Jase kept bumping his ass into Emil as they laid the food out.

Mackie was doing a slow version of a twerk in Val's direction. "Brenin! No one can sit while *Sit Next to Me* is playing."

The beat was irresistible. Knowing that these last few hours might be all that any of them would have with one another, he let go of his inhibitions. After unbuckling, he stood up and let the music take over his body.

He shook his hips while standing next to his chair at first. Then, lifting his hands over his head, he moved away, improvising steps the way he used to do long ago when things had been simpler if not happier. Mackie sidled up to him and, grabbing him by the waist, bumped hips. He did some steps back and forth with one foot and the other. Brenin watched for a while before joining in. They moved in tandem, turning at Mackie's indication. Quinn and Jase were doing the same.

They were putting on a show for their men. And although the presence of the woman, Lucien and the two human men meant they weren't truly dancing to an audience of lovers and husbands, the familial atmosphere was impossible to ignore or resist. He let himself get lost in the music and the movement. He felt...liberated.

Mackie released him and moved to form a line. The others fell into step, Brenin included, although he had no clue as to what they were doing. It didn't matter. When the chorography had him turning in Malcolm's direction, he saw not mere heat in the man's eyes, but a molten look that would have incinerated Brenin if he'd held it for more than a second.

Flushed, aroused, confused and a bit frightened at his own feelings and reaction, he twirled away and concentrated on keeping in sync with the other boys. *Later.* There would be time for him to explore perhaps for one last time what his attraction to this alien really meant.

* * * *

Malcolm carried the sleeping Brenin through the cabin to the stateroom. By unspoken agreement, it was theirs for the rest of the journey. No one else wanted or even needed it the way they did, because Brenin deserved the privacy that the closed-off space afforded him.

Willem was happily watching his flashing lights in the cockpit. Paz and Duncan were dozing on each of the long couches in the main cabin — or, at least, they had their eyes closed. They might have simply been avoiding the goings-on around them. Logan had stuck to one corner on her own since the beginning, ignoring them all, as had Lucien. The man wore his grief like a shroud and yet he said nothing, made no complaint.

Alex, Val and Emil each had their boy in a delicate position in various parts of the open space. With the lights on low, it wasn't as if anyone could see much of what was happening, at least by a human's ocular standard. As he went about gathering Brenin and carrying him down the aisle, Malcolm had no trouble seeing the couplings.

He tried not to be envious, because that was a human emotion—one that he'd learned he wasn't immune to, despite it being uncharacteristic of a hive mentality. It was good for the group that each of the warriors had his fangs and his cock sunk deep into their mates. It would relax them and power them up in equal measure. That was just what their mission required. He would find his own strength in the blood Emil had stored for him. Once he'd settled Brenin in, naturally. The boy didn't need to see that and with him putting on a marvelous show then curling up in Malcolm's lap, there'd been no chance earlier to feed.

Alex gazed at him over Quinn's neck. The boy straddled his lover, his naked arse riding Alex's dick while Alex took his jugular. There was a flash of concern in that stare, a question of whether everything was all right. Malcolm gave his captain a nod of reassurance as he passed.

He didn't bother turning a light on in the stateroom. His eyesight didn't need it and it would have woken Brenin. Instead, he sealed them in by shutting the door and lowered the boy onto the narrow bed. Brenin sighed and smacked his lips. Poor lad, his internal clock must be all screwed up from the back and forth.

Quickly and as gently as he could, he stripped the boy in the hopes of making him more comfortable. He hadn't seen much of him since the bath, but even in the dark, he could make out the scars and bruises that remained. It reminded him that only a few days had passed since the boy had been in Dracul's brutal embrace. Being human, his ability to heal was much slower. And yet, Brenin hadn't complained once of being sore or needing care. He was that brave.

Malcolm had left the kilt until last, having maneuvered the jeans off already. It seemed too heavy, however, so he reached down to unbuckle it. Brenin murmured dissent and batted his hands away.

Malcolm smiled. "All right, laddie. Have it your way."

"Hmm. Join me."

He hadn't meant to wake him, wasn't sure he had, given that Brenin's breathing continued to be deep and steady. There was no resisting the invitation, either. He tore off his own clothing, except for his smallclothes, and lay down on the bed. Brenin didn't hesitate to roll into him and he threw an arm across Malcolm's stomach.

Malcolm gave in to the desire he'd been harboring all day and touched every spot he could reach, albeit lightly. So soft and silky his boy was. And yes, he knew he shouldn't be thinking of Brenin in such possessive terms. He couldn't help himself. Brenin had gone from obligation to heart's desire in the span of a few days. The capper had been the time they'd spent the previous night in bed. When Brenin had fearlessly explored Malcolm's body before commanding it, Malcolm had lost any resolve he'd had to keep his emotional distance from the boy. Being here with him, caressing him, was a purely selfish act and he couldn't bring himself to stop.

Brenin slid his leg over Malcolm's. His knee came up to brush against Malcolm's stiff cock. He bit back a groan until it happened again…and again.

He's doing it on purpose.

"You're awake, are you, and keen to play games?"

"Uh-huh." Brenin curled closer. "I've been thinking of this all day."

Malcolm's dick twitched at the confession. "Have you now?" His voice strangled with the effort to be coherent.

"Is that bad of me?"

"I'm hardly in a position to complain." He moaned long and low when Brenin replaced his knee with his hand. He snaked it under the waistband of Malcolm's boxer-briefs and clasped the dick waiting there with his slender, warm fingers.

At the same time, Brenin pressed his pelvis against Malcolm's hip. "You make me hard."

Malcolm panted as the boy ran his fingers up and down the shaft, putting enough pressure on it to coax Malcolm's climax. He gritted his teeth to keep himself in check and gripped the covers with one fist.

"Is that a bad thing?" he had to ask, ever mindful of how recently Brenin had been raped.

"No, it's kind of a miraculous one. I'm that glad of it." He rolled his hips in a clear effort to stimulate himself. "I'm afraid, though, that I'm about to come in your kilt. I hope you don't mind."

"Christ!" Malcolm uttered the curse in a low voice, but the force of his orgasm had him rearing up nevertheless.

Brenin kept with him. Instead of letting him go in disgust, he held on, milking the dick with clumsy, yet sure strokes. Malcolm's cum coated both Brenin's hand and Malcolm's abdomen and had him shuddering into Brenin's still humping body. With a muted cry, the boy clenched the shaft hard enough to make Malcolm wince. He ignored the pain and, rolling over, captured Brenin's lips in a deep kiss.

Always before, he'd been careful to keep it light. This time, he pressed his tongue inside the boy's mouth and explored it with the fervor of a man dying of thirst and desperate to suck every crevice dry. Brenin lay quiescent at first, other than his hips still bucking. Then his tongue shyly chased Malcolm's. For a few heady seconds, they kissed each other with an electrifying passion that Malcolm had never known before.

Then, it all changed in a split-second. Brenin whimpered and pushed at him. Malcolm rolled away, parting their lips, releasing any hold on him. "I'm sorry. Did I scare you?" He lay flat on his back, unmoving and trying to convey a complete lack of menace.

"No," Brenin replied with a shaky voice that tore at Malcolm's heart. "It was my memories that did."

That should have been the end of it. Malcolm would have risen and let the boy be, except, in the next instant, Brenin was sitting up and slinging one leg over Malcolm's lap, straddling him.

Malcolm fisted his hands so as not to touch him. "What are you doing?"

"Taking control. It works best when I do that." His breath remained unsteady and he shook a bit.

"You don't have to prove anything."

"Yes, I do—to myself."

"Don't push it. There's no timetable for you to recover from your ordeal. I'm not one to speak of this, but I bet Doc McPhee could help you with that."

"I know. She told me there are places I can go for counseling and whatnot, but I can never tell the truth, the whole of it, to anyone. I'm not sure that's for me, anyway. We Welsh are a stubborn and stoic lot—or maybe that's only my family. This," he added with a pat on Malcolm's bare chest, "seems to do the trick. I know you can overpower me, but the illusion of dominance appears to be enough. Can I kiss you?"

The question caught Malcolm by surprise for about a second. "Of course."

Brenin didn't at first, at least not in the traditional sense. He started by leaning over and licking a stripe across one of Malcolm's nipples. Then he swirled his tongue around the hard nub in tight circles. The teasing attention made Malcolm harden again.

Brenin lifted his head. "You like that?"

"Aye, you know well I do." He didn't dare buck his hips in emphasis for fear of alarming Brenin.

He needn't have worried. The boy wiggled his arse in a delightfully erotic way, notwithstanding that with the kilt and the Hanes, there was a fair amount of clothing between them.

Brenin solved that problem, too. As he returned to laving and nipping at Malcolm's nipples, Brenin managed to tug the kilt away and slide the underwear down to expose Malcolm's cock. Now, they touched flesh to flesh. It was electrifying. Another climax built without effort or direct touch. By the time Brenin pressed his tongue against Malcolm's lips, Malcolm was nearly done.

But he held on to his control this time. Brenin deserved slow and, more, he needed help with his own burgeoning arousal. The boy's small, slender dick rubbed against Malcolm's in a steadily growing erection. Malcolm wanted so badly to take it in hand. It took more strength of will than he'd ever summoned before to resist that temptation.

Once again, Brenin showed amazing courage by wrapping his hand around both shafts — or, rather, he tried to. It was too much for him to handle and, when he used both hands, he started to lose his balance. Malcolm took the chance to steady him by grabbing his shoulder. When Brenin didn't flinch or pull away, Malcolm took it as a sign that it was all right.

With his sweet boy claiming his breath and those shy, but clever fingers jerking him, he fell into a second orgasm that was no less intense than the first. His balls tightened and his dick jerked as cum pulsed out. Malcolm groaned deep inside Brenin's mouth and curled his toes to keep from tightening his grip. He would rather his insides explode than hurt the boy or make him afraid again.

He did anyway—not with his hand, but with his teeth. The surge of pleasure that shook his core caused his fangs to punch down without warning. He realized what he'd done only because Brenin yelped and pulled back. Forcing his eyes open, Malcolm saw the boy lick his nicked lip. A spot of blood welled up right away. The sight of it nearly caused Malcolm to lose his shite.

The thirst came over him with agonizing intensity. He had to drop his hand before he crushed Brenin's shoulder. He took it out on the bedding instead, clawing at it, twisting it. Throwing his head back, he vocalized his need with guttural growls. His body shook as if in the throes of a seizure, with his heels bouncing against the bed. All the while, he silently pleaded with Brenin to get off. *Go away*. He didn't want to scare the boy or show him this side of his nature. It was too much like Dracul's.

Brenin didn't leave. Instead, he rode the storm. "Malcolm? Malcolm? Take my vein." The shocking words caused him to lower his chin. Brenin held up his wrist. "Take it!"

Malcolm could only shake his head in denial. He would not do it. It was too much to force upon the boy. This fit would pass. It was only thirst, nothing fatal, no matter how painful it was at the moment.

Brenin, thank God, finally got the message and rolled off him. There was a light from the attached head, maybe. Some rummaging around. Then Brenin was back, climbing up, straddling Malcolm once more. The scent of blood caught hold. Not a bead of it, but a trickle.

It was sufficient to take hold of Malcolm's attention and his control. When Brenin pressed his bloody wrist against Malcolm's lips, his fangs descended and he latched on to the vein.

Och God, the sweetness of it. Exquisite. Warm and salty. It slid down his dry throat and eased the ache. His head felt instantly heavy and he knew it had been too long since he'd fed, really fed. Microwaved blood in a fancy goblet was a poor substitute for the real thing.

He collapsed into the pillow, letting the languid pleasure cause his muscles to go lax, even while his cock punched up again. Brenin stayed with him, somehow positioning himself to grab both their cocks once more while his wrist remained caught by Malcolm's teeth.

"Everything okay in here, guys?" Val's voice.

Malcolm couldn't bring himself to let go of the vein long enough to answer. Apparently, he didn't need to.

"Oops, sorry."

"There now, see? Even your friends trust you to be careful with me. Take what you need and I'll do the rest."

Brenin's meaning became apparent in the next instance when he started moving the hand holding the dicks. There was no gentle caress this time, however. The boy jerked their shafts with vigor. That effort, coupled with the blood filling his mouth and coating his throat, sent Malcolm spasming. More importantly, Brenin came, too, at the same time. Over the scent of the blood, Malcolm caught the smell of the boy's cum. His cock pulsed against Malcolm's own.

It was all too much. His senses went on overload. For a few seconds, he believed he'd actually swooned, like some Victorian miss with a too-tight corset. When he came to his senses, though, he retracted his fangs and licked the punctures closed. He knew he should do more. Brenin needed tending to. Surely the boy was freaked out—in need of water, at the very least.

"Are you all right, laddie?" he panted out, the best he could do at the moment.

By way of answer, Brenin kissed his cheek. "Hush now. I'm fine. You worry too much, Malcolm MacLerie."

The boy rustled about, the upshot of it being that he lay on his side curled into Malcolm's. The kilt covered Malcolm's middle and he hoped Brenin's as well. He would check himself if he could only get his eyelids to open.

"I'm afraid your kilt is soiled now from the both of us."

Malcolm smiled. "I shall never wash it again."

"What will you wear, then?"

"I have others."

"Good. I like the idea of your being dressed like a wild highlander when you invade the monster's lair. *My* highlander," he added with a loud yawn before he rested his head on Malcolm's chest.

He found the strength to wrap one arm around the boy. *My boy...and* his *highlander.* Och, he liked the sound of all that a might too much.

Fuck me. I've fallen in love.

Chapter Ten

"Darling, I'm home. Did you miss me?"

"With every breath I took, sir," the prim and proper butler-type intoned.

Christ Jesus, it's like I'm in some Masterpiece Theater *program.* Trey was too under-slept and overwrought to find much humor in anything, however. And whereas the old castle nestled in the faraway hills of Scotland would normally have intrigued him, at the moment it just represented one more thing to hold them up. He wanted to get going, find Demi, kill as many fuckers as he could and go home.

"This is amazing." Paz uttered the remark as he spun around the foyer, taking in everything around him. "That's an actual suit of armor." He pointed to one corner.

Yup, lots of nifty keen things. But there was only one Trey was interested in seeing. "Where's your armament room, MacLerie?"

Before the guy could answer, a pretty blonde-haired girl skipped in and over to Willem. "You're back!" She launched herself into his arms and he brought her up for a hug.

Alex, Val and Emil went suddenly still, shooting looks at one another. Whatever was going on, their surprise was both obvious and intriguing. Or it would have been if Trey's mind wasn't totally focused on rescuing Demi.

Willem, the most sedate of any of the aliens Trey had ever met, set the girl on her feet before saying, "This is Annika. She's my adopted daughter."

"Indeed," Alex responded. "We are pleased to meet you, I'm sure. I am Alex," he added as he perused her with a narrow-eyed gaze.

The girl's face lit up. "Oh, captain. It's an honor, sir." Then she opened her mouth wide and let out a multi-toned screech that made Trey's ears practically bleed.

Every human winced, in fact, and started to put up their hands before the sound ceased. Then there was silence until Annika looked back at Willem.

"Did I say that correctly?"

Willem didn't appear too happy with the matter, but he gave her a curt nod and a brief smile. "Yes, that was very well done."

Trey was about to ask by what standards, before he flashed on the obvious. *That is their language, the aliens' native tongue.* Like cats fighting, someone had once remarked, and that wasn't off base. How had that horrible sound come out of a human child? Not even Demi spoke it, at least not to Trey's knowledge. Then again, what did he really know about the boy, other than he was a pain in Trey's rear that had ended up lodged under his skin.

"Willem, I think you and I need to have a little chat," Alex said.

"Agreed, sir, although later, please—when there's more time and less anxiety over Harry and Demi."

"Hmm," Alex seemed to agree.

"I'm very sorry, captain, if I've caused you any alarm." The girl walked all the way up to Alex. "I assure you your secrets are safe with me. My papa loved Willem and so do I. Before he died, Papa made me promise to take good care of Willem. And that's what I do," she added with a firm nod.

"Of that, I have no doubt," Alex answered with equal solemnity and not a trace of irony or indulgence. "We do have serious business to attend to now, however. I'm sure you'll understand when I ask that you not distract him and stay safely with Malcolm's staff."

"Yes, sir." With that, she gave Willem another hug.

Before she left, however, Lucien stepped out from the back of the crowd. The guy had been eerily quiet the whole trip. "Annika, I am Lucien. Would you please take me to the kitchen? I should like to make myself useful."

Holding out her hand, she said, "Of course, Mr. Lucien. I should be happy to." Lucien accepted the help and allowed her to lead him back the way she'd come.

"What an odd child," Paz whispered.

"Yeah," Trey agreed, which was saying something, because his bar for weird was really high these days.

But at least they wasted no more time. With little fanfare, they split up. Brenin led the boys in one direction while the men and Logan followed Malcolm down a hallway. He took them to a room in what centuries ago must have been part of a dungeon. It was about a half a football field in length and loaded with so much weaponry of such varying types that Trey was momentarily stunned.

"Fucking A," Logan spoke for the first time in hours. "Now, this is what I'm talking about. Anything off limits?" she called out to Malcolm.

"Well, now, I don't think you'll be needing the bazooka or the flamethrower, but help yourself, lassie."

"You don't know me very well," she muttered as she made a beeline for those very things. Trey couldn't be sure, but he thought she caressed them before moving on to her specialty…explosives.

Trey went for his own comfort zone, preferring an easy-to-carry nine-millimeter to something more cumbersome like a rifle. There was a shocking array of choices. He picked up a few and tried them for grip and balance before going with the Glock. It was what he was used to in his service revolver, after all, and in the heat of the battle to come, he wanted to be wholly comfortable with his weapon.

In addition to back-up clips, he would require a vest, zip ties in case civilians needed to be kept under control, flash grenades maybe and a knife or two. Glancing around, he could see that none of that was going to be a problem.

Paz came up. "I don't know how to choose." He scratched the back of his neck. "I might have oversold my ROTC training. I've never actually fired a pistol, only a rifle."

Trey rolled his eyes. "Great. I guess you need a crash course in shooting."

Paz winced. "Sorry."

"Hey, MacLerie, you got a firing range?"

"Next room over," the man replied as he and Alex perused what looked like large swords.

Grabbing his piece and an extra clip, Trey beckoned to the doctor. "Come on."

"All right," Paz replied, although his focus was on the alien-turned-Scotsman. "He's not honestly going to fight using a claymore, is he?"

"Fuck if I know." But, yeah, he did kind of and he'd given up trying to figure these aliens out. Anything that worked was fine with him, too, no matter how bizarre.

Hang in there, Demi. We're coming.

* * * *

"They can't be very happy," Jase remarked, "swimming around in circles all day."

Brenin put his chin on his hand as he stared down at the salmon. "Cook said that Malcolm's fishery is smaller than most, so they're not as crowded. I guess fancy restaurants in lowland cities pay a lot more for them because they're such high quality." He worried the faint scar at his wrist as he spoke.

Jase grabbed his hand. "He fed off you?"

"Yes." Brenin pulled away. "At my insistence."

"Are you sure?"

"Absolutely." He went back to leaning on the fishery fence. "We were fooling about, *you know*. Anyway, he nicked my lip with his fang then went into this seizure, like. I offered my vein and he refused. So, I found scissors in the loo, cut myself and made him drink."

"Being fed from must have been harder for you than the sex was," Jase remarked quietly. "I can't say for sure because all of my rapists were human."

Horrified, Brenin straightened. "There was more than one?" When Jase nodded, Brenin couldn't keep from asking, "How did you ever recover from it?"

"I haven't, not completely. I probably never will in the sense that it's a part of me. I can't change the past or forget it. I don't want to, but I also won't allow it to dictate how I handle my present or my future."

"You love Emil." It wasn't a question, although he was keen to hear the why of it.

"I do. I shouldn't if I think about it. After what men did to me, I should have trouble bonding with anyone, let alone an alien, of all people. Then again, maybe that's what makes it easier. Emil is unlike anyone else in my experience. When he touches me, I don't remember the others.

"His skin is cool for one thing. His eyes change color and, when he sinks his fangs into me, all it does is make me come harder. Sorry," he added with a quick glance. "Does hearing that upset you?"

Brenin shook his head. "No. It makes sense, too. I can't claim that he's different. Malcolm feels and looks just like the monster—and yet, he isn't. I know that bone deep. I guess I don't trust myself. Maybe I've just pushed everything so far down that it's waiting to pop out when I least expect it.

"I did, actually, start to panic last night. When Malcolm covered me with his body and kissed me, it was lovely at first—the kiss, that is. I've never experienced the like before. Then, I was all of a sudden swamped with memories of being pinned down. I started to struggle."

"What did Malcolm do?"

"Got up, mun. Like the Flash, he was. And he let me sit on him, control what happened. That works for me and he doesn't seem to mind."

"That's why you're okay with him. He isn't a monster and you know it. Give yourself time, Brenin, and also give yourself trust. You know what you're doing."

"Hey!" Mackie called out as he and Quinn raced up from the dock. "You should see the trawler. It's hideous and as old as dirt. No one will think anything's happening when we pull up in it."

He stopped and grinned at them both before glancing down at the fishery. "Ooh, salmon. My favorite fish. Think we'll have time to eat before we go?"

Quinn laughed. "God, Mackie, we just ate a few hours ago."

The other boy shrugged. "What can I say, I've gotten my appetite back because tonight we're rescuing Demi."

* * * *

"Is it time or not?" Dracul's patience was at an end. Petru's briefings were proving more and more useless, so he needed to see for himself what was happening.

Horatiu glared back at him with obvious disdain and arrogance. Dracul couldn't wait to wipe that look off the man's face for good. "You know it's not that simple. The signs are there, but if I take the babe out too soon, he will die — the child, that is. I understand you care nothing about the father."

On the bed, the slut in question writhed in obvious pain. Normally that would have been entertaining. With his son's life on the line, he couldn't afford to enjoy it. He clenched his fingers, making the next vessel for his seed mew in distress. That was a pretty sound, especially as the cunt seemed to like the pain. *Go figure.* Humans were ridiculous creatures under the best of circumstances.

"I understand well the dangers of the birth, otherwise I would have had Drogo cut the boy out of that useless lump days ago—before they both dared to defy me. Don't think you can, as well. Safely deliver my son this night or yours will be choking on my cock for breakfast."

His point made, he stormed out of the room and back to his own. Such was his anger that he didn't make it there before he needed to find relief. The alcove at the bottom of the stairs did nicely. Slamming the striped-haired slut against the wall, he tore the robe from the boy's body and resolved to keep the chit naked from that point on.

Dracul liberated his dick and rammed it into the always-welcoming hole. Far from trying to avoid him, the cunt pressed his ass backward and clenched—satisfying in many ways, lacking in others. The resistance was part of the pleasure, although, at that moment, he needed fast relief.

He pounded into the boy with a snap of his hips that made the slut groan and quiver. "That's it, Master. Take out your frustrations on me. Forget about that room. I will give you so many sons that you'll never miss any other."

Dracul twisted the striped hair in his fist and pulled the head back. "I can never have enough." Shoving his dick in as far as it would go, he bit the exposed neck with a force designed to hurt.

The boy shuddered and groaned, coming from the abuse alone. And so did Dracul. A perfect match at last.

* * * *

"Please be careful."

Malcolm peered down into Brenin's worried eyes. "Always, laddie. Always. And you stay here. I cannae concentrate on what I have to do if I'm worried about you."

"We'll stay right here on the boat, I promise you that. Nothing will get us to leave." He glanced down and said, "I'm glad you're wearing a kilt."

"Cheeky boy."

Malcolm nodded once, as certain as he could be that his boy would keep his promise. *His boy*. It was getting easier to think that. He closed his duffel and hefted it over one shoulder. The rest of the men — and Logan — were also ready, each carrying their own bag of tricks. Each was armed, too, except the doctor, who'd decided that guns weren't for him after all. But he had a knife sheathed on his belt and Doc McPhee had fitted him with an array of medicines and instruments that he'd never have got through customs.

They were as ready as they ever were going to be. There was only one last thing to do, to his way of thinking. He pulled out a bottle of his own Scotch and, after popping it open, took a slug. The burn felt good and it was like it had been back in the old days before going into battle. He passed the bottle to Alex, who took his dram before giving it to Val. Willem came next, then Emil. But he passed over Logan by some unspoken agreement and gave it to Duncan instead. While the cop didn't flinch, the doctor shook his head.

"All right, then," Malcolm said, taking and recapping the bottle. "We're off."

The goodbyes had been done in advance, so they left the boys and Lucien behind without further ado. Darling had arranged a large SUV for the trek up to the castle. It was a tight fit with the eight of them and all their gear. No one grumbled. They were all too focused on the mission. Malcolm was painfully aware that he could die that night. For the last thousand years, that possibility hadn't worried him over much. Now, he had something to lose — Brenin. Or, more to the point, he worried what would happen to the boy if this battle ended badly. He couldn't stand the idea of Brenin being alone in the world again or, worse, at Dracul's mercy.

Well, he just couldn't allow that to happen and that was that.

Willem was as good a driver as he was a pilot. He brought them within a kilometer of the castle in record time. They finished the journey on foot, with Malcolm leading the way. He knew the area as well as anyone could after a few days of surveillance. He'd figured out the range of Dracul's security and had already established the perfect vantage points to screen the castle. Alone, he did so while the others waited in a huddled group in the forest.

His goal was easier this time. He only needed to find where Harry and the others were being kept, so the rescue party would know where to go as soon as he let them in. He found them on the first try, because an educated guess had him looking at the towers. The heat signatures told mostly a good story.

"They're all together," he said without preamble once he returned to the group. "Harry and his boy are in a tower room with Dafydd."

"Are you sure?" the cop asked.

"Aye." He tamped down his irritation at the interruption. He understood how important it was to Duncan to learn that Demi wasn't with Dracul. "There is a guard, though."

Duncan swore. "Dracul?"

"No. One of his men, no doubt."

"How can you know?"

Once again, Malcolm made allowances. "Not only would Dracul never stoop to do such a job himself, I checked his room before coming back here. He's there with another changed human. I'll be careful, as careful as I can, to keep him out of the fray when I take on Dracul."

That had been the deal that he'd struck with Alex. Although everyone had treated this as a joint mission in which whoever got the chance to take out Dracul would, there had also been an unspoken assumption that it would be Alex's honor if possible. Malcolm had asked Alex to step aside as the senior man. The basis of his request had been that Dracul's brutality of Brenin had become an issue of personal honor for Malcolm. For him, it was a matter of family and Alex had understood.

Alex clapped him on the shoulder. "Good work, Malcolm. Now, on to the cistern."

This bit was trickier because they only had the most general sense of where the water that caught in the underground cavern might flow out again. They made some educated guesses based on what information Brenin had been able to give them. It took too long by Malcolm's estimation. Finally, though, a trickle of water turned into a small stream that led into the side of the hill.

Val pushed to the head of the group. "I'll check it out." His knowledge of security transcended Malcolm's own, so he was happy enough to sit this one out.

A while later, a wet Val returned. "It's not monitored."

"You're sure of that?" Malcolm asked, amazed that access could be that easy.

Val gave him a pointed glare before saying, "Yes, but that's not surprising, actually." He frowned. "They don't expect anyone can find it, let alone wiggle through because it's too damn small for any of our kind to push through. I went in a way to make sure we had the right spot. The opening is large, then around the time it is completely underwater, it narrows to impossibly small."

"Fuck!" Malcolm responded for all of them.

"Logan might manage it," Val said.

They all looked at her. She stared at the ground, shaking her head. "I, um, don't like small spaces. I can't… Sorry." She shook all over as she uttered the apology.

"It's okay," Emil said, putting his arm around her. "You don't have to explain."

"What about Paz, here?" Malcolm asked. The human was slender, like Logan, although a little taller.

He put up his hands. "You say it's underwater? I can't swim very well. A few feet I might manage, but anything more and I'm likely to drown before I could reach the cistern."

They sat there silently, contemplating how their careful plans were falling to shite. There had to be another way.

"Maybe one of the—" Willem started to say.

Malcolm looked up sharply. "No."

"You have a better idea? We need someone smaller and we have a boatload full of 'smaller' to call on."

"They're just boys. Would you send Annika?" Malcolm was being irrational, but he knew right down to his bones that if they went and asked, the one who would fit the bill would be his boy.

Willem glared. "She's a child. We call them boys, but they're *adults*."

"Enough!" Alex's quiet voice was no less commanding. "Malcolm, you, Willem and I will return and see if any of the boys have the skill to make the journey. Who knows? Perhaps Lucien can do it."

"Aye, right." He was certain that wouldn't be the case. "Except, that water is like to be freezing this time of year. If a human is to go in, he'll need a dry suit."

"We passed a dive shop in the village," Duncan offered. "Drop me off there and I'll, um…liberate one."

"Perfect. Let's go. Night isn't going to last forever." With that friendly reminder, Alex took off.

The others and Malcolm followed, his stomach a churning pool of dread.

* * * *

Mackie and Lucien both became alert while the rest of them continued to mope and worry. "They're coming back," the red-haired boy said before racing up on the deck.

"It's too soon," Brenin warned, even as he followed. Concern morphed into relief when he saw Malcolm step out of the SUV. Whatever was going on, at least he was safe for now.

Alex ushered everyone back inside, although Malcolm managed to sneak in a quick kiss to Brenin's upturned face before doing so. "How good a swimmer are you?" he asked.

"Very," Brenin replied, confused over the question. "I was on the team back in school."

"Bugger me. Of course you were," Malcolm muttered, but he also offered a shaky smile as they joined the others.

"We need someone smaller than us to enter the cistern, as it turns out," Alex was saying.

Ah, so that's it. Poor Malcolm. He must be having all kinds of fits over the prospect of me getting into harm's way. For himself, though, Brenin was glad of it. Hanging around while the men did the dirty work hadn't sat well with him from the beginning. No matter how Malcolm might feel, Brenin was a man, as well. Young and naïve and still dealing with the trauma of his capture, but a grown-up nevertheless. He might not be a soldier, but he wanted to fight. He had a feeling it would go a long way toward his healing.

"That would be me," he said before any of the others could speak up. "Unless one of you was in the running for the Olympics, I'm the one to go." The others looked at him as if he had three heads, so that was that.

Alex gave him a brief nod and a smile. "Excellent. We would be in a bind if you couldn't. Are you sure you're willing to do it? It's all right if you say no. That castle is a terrible place for you."

"I want to do it," he replied. He directed his next statement to Malcolm. "I need to do it, mind. You understand?"

"Aye, I do." He tucked some of Brenin's hair behind his ear. The man seemed to like doing that and Brenin liked it in return.

"What's the plan, then?"

"We'll tell you the way," Alex said. "Duncan is getting you a dry suit, because the water will be frigid for a human. We'll meet him outside." He started to go. Quinn stopped him.

"Alex, wait. Brenin's joining the fight and we're not?"

Alex frowned at his lover. "We only need Brenin for the swimming part."

"Which ends in the castle part," Quinn retorted. "If Brenin's joining the fight, then so are we."

"What he said," Mackie added with his usual snark, arms folded and a determined look.

"Emil will be pissed," Jase observed. "But seems to me that we would be the perfect third group in this assault. I mean, everyone has kind of glossed over the humans, changed or not, that are captive in there. Someone's got to deal with them. They can't stay there once Logan's explosives start going off. And who better to speak to them in a way that is sympathetic and in terms they can understand than us?" He waved his hand to encompass the humans in the cabin.

"It does rather fit into the revised plans, sir," Malcolm said.

Alex sighed. "Emil and Val both will be apoplectic if I show up with you boys. I'm going to have a mutiny on my hands if I do. They won't want to proceed if you're going to be in danger."

Lucien stepped up. "Please, Alex, what Jase says is true. These boys can be helpful in your fight. Don't underestimate them because they are mere humans. And don't let your love for Quinn cloud your judgment. You can't wrap him up and keep him safe from everything. I thought I could do that with Demi and look how wrong I was. I'll stay with the boat. Someone should."

Alex nodded once. "You all make fair points and we're wasting time."

With that, he grabbed Quinn's hand and bolted out of the cabin. It took another second for everyone else to realize that they'd won the argument. Brenin and Malcolm let Mackie and Jase go first before following.

At the doorway, Brenin paused long enough to look over his shoulder at Lucien. "We'll bring them back to you. I promise."

Everyone piled into the SUV, a tight fit, but it allowed Brenin to sit close to Malcolm. Willem sat behind the wheel, eyes wide for a moment before he started the engine. He pulled away from the dock and stopped about a block away. The reason became apparent when Duncan sprinted across the road with a bag in his hand.

The copper squeezed into the SUV, paused, then, shaking his head, buckled up. "This isn't going to go over well, but I can't say I'm surprised."

That was the last anyone said, other than Malcolm, who laid out the revised plan for Brenin to access the cistern. "Are you okay with it?" he asked Brenin.

"Sure. It will be dead easy." His false bravado faltered in the next instant because he leaned against the man, drawing what strength he could for the ordeal to come.

"Keep going, Willem," Alex said when the man started to pull over at the edge of the woods. "The boys can't make the trek as fast as we can and we don't want Brenin tired by the time he arrives."

"It's riskier," the driver replied, even as he kept going.

"Not by much," Malcolm said. "I've done a lot of surveillance, don't forget. I saw no cameras by the road. I was only being extra-cautious before. Like Alex said, Brenin needs all his energy for the swim." He squeezed Brenin's hand.

Proverbial butterflies wreaked havoc with Brenin's stomach for the rest of the journey. The closer he got to the castle, the more the memories of his ordeal threatened to overwhelm him. He used Malcolm's touch as a way to ground himself and pictured how wonderful it would feel once the monster was dead. His direct contribution to that eventuality would go a long way toward putting it all behind him. His damsel in distress persona was about to become the instrument of revenge.

They finally exited the SUV and the physical act of walking helped with the jitters. The rest of their group was huddled in a small hollow and sheltered by large trees. The expressions on their faces when they saw the boys creeping up to join them were priceless. A mixture of surprise, anger and simply 'holy fuck', when it came to the doctor, served to distract Brenin even more.

Alex held out his hand before anyone could speak. "We don't have time to discuss this turn of events in committee. I'll give you the *revised*, revised plan once Brenin is off."

That shut everyone up, although Emil gave Jase a brutally hard hug and Val swatted Mackie's arse before doing the same.

Duncan opened the bag he carried. "Here's the suit and I grabbed a diving knife, too."

Malcolm took both from him. "Bless you, Sergeant."

"I, ah…had to guess on the size and ended up taking one from the women's rack. I also left some money on the counter because I'm a cop and these things are expensive."

Malcolm was already helping Brenin strip down. "Looks a good fit and I'll reimburse you the cost."

"Nah, not necessary. My point was that I didn't like the idea of a small business being cheated out of their stock."

"Admirable."

Malcolm's attention really wasn't on the conversation, Brenin realized. The man's face was extra-grim and his hands appeared a little shaky. Brenin didn't remark on it, though. He figured this was a weakness that the man rarely showed and it humbled Brenin to know it was on his account. It made him even more determined to succeed.

As he was outfitted for his journey, the others adjusted to the new plan. First Duncan, then Logan and finally the doctor stripped off the Kevlar vests each of them had been wearing and silently handed them over to the boys. Or, rather, they gave them to the boys' significant others, who muscled them onto their boys, whether they wanted them to or not.

"There, now." Malcolm patted Brenin's shoulders, checking the dry suit's fit. Then he took the knife from Duncan and tucked it into the pocket on the side. The last thing he added was a tiny homing beacon. He'd shown it to Brenin on the way over. Once Brenin had reached the cistern, he was to activate it, so that the others would know he'd made it and the next phase of the operation could begin.

"That should do it, laddie. Ready?" he asked, grabbing his torch.

Not trusting his voice at the moment, Brenin merely nodded. He followed Malcolm up the slope to where a trickle of water turned into a shallow stream and into an overgrown hole in the side of mountain. Malcolm shoved aside the vegetation growing there and ushered Brenin into the dark. It didn't stay that way for long, however. Malcolm quickly followed and turned on his torch to give them a beam of light to follow.

The dank space made Brenin's nose twitch and the roots growing from all around them made walking hard. He focused on the illumination and hooked his fingers around Malcom's waistband for stability. The space was so narrow that they had to walk single file. He would have much preferred to be safely tucked under his lover's arm. This wasn't a walk in the woods, however. It was a mission and he needed to keep his *nerve* and do what only he could for the greater good. If he succeeded, he would have helped eliminate a threat to the entire world.

As the water level rose, the tunnel narrowed. At a certain point, Malcolm squeezed Brenin in front of him. A turn in the bend revealed why.

"Here's as far as I can go, laddie." At this point, the water was up to Brenin's thighs and he was glad for the dry suit. Malcolm's kilt was sodden and wrapped around the man's legs. He held out the torch. "You're going to need this. It's waterproof."

Brenin took it. "Right." The gloves Duncan had taken were flexible, so it was easy to get a good grip on the thing. He used it to highlight the slit in the tunnel he'd have to squeeze through. "It's going to be a tight fit, mind, given how much you've fattened me up."

He was trying to lighten the moment. Instead, he made his own eyes water with emotion and, next thing he knew, Malcolm was hugging him. "You have a care, now. Don't take any unnecessary chances."

"I won't. I want to survive. I have something to live for now." It was chancy for sure, but he needed to be brave in all things. "I love you, Malcolm." He buried his face into the man's chest and hugged him with all the strength he had.

"Och, laddie, you stole my line."

Brenin lifted his head. "Really?"

Malcolm nodded. "Aye. I didnae want to distract you with something as heavy as my feelings right at the moment. Now that you've said it, though, I can admit my own." He kissed him, then, the kind that stole Brenin's breath at the very moment he needed all of it.

Brenin didn't mind. He used the opportunity to borrow some of Malcolm's courage by inhaling his scent. Then, sensing he would have to be the one to end things, he broke away. Without another word, he plunged forward.

The narrow opening was only the half of it. The tunnel didn't widen appreciably after that for quite a distance. All the while, the water rose until only his head was above it, and he bounced along the floor on the balls of his feet. When he needed to go underwater, he took two deep breaths and let them out. On the third, he went under and clawed his way sideways along the tunnel.

The space mercifully opened sufficiently for him to swim horizontally instead. He could go faster that way, and there was no good estimate of how far it was to the cistern. His limit on holding his breath was seventy-five meters. Not bad for an amateur swimmer, but it also meant he had to estimate how far he'd gone so that he could turn around when and if necessary.

He wasted no time shooting through the tunnel. It was easy, this. He'd always liked the peace and liberating feeling that came from swimming, especially underwater where there was nothing to see or feel other than its cocooning embrace.

This was no sanitized pool, though. The tunnel was icky, in a horror movie kind of way. He half-expected eyes to stare back at him as he flashed the beam of light in front of him or hands to reach out from the slimy dirt walls. If he allowed himself to think about it too hard, he'd freak out. He couldn't let that happen. Besides, the mud turned to metal quickly. The sight gave him heart. He'd obviously entered the part where the cistern had been created. He was almost at his destination.

A few meters more and his heart sank. The monster hadn't been so stupid as to leave an entry to his fortress. A metal mesh grate barred his way. Swimming up to it, Brenin showed the light around the edges of the bar. It was a kind of door with hinges on one side and a padlock on the other. Brenin wrapped the fingers of his free hand around the grate and tugged. He pulled with all his might, trying various points — the lock and even the hinges. Nothing gave. The thing was slimy, and clearly old, yet it wasn't compromised and held fast. Beyond the barrier, he could see the cistern. He was so close to his goal.

A burn in Brenin's lungs told him his time was running out. He had to get back to Malcolm so they could figure out a way for him to get past this roadblock. Reluctantly, he turned around in the tight space and took off back the way he'd come. A wave of dizziness washed over him and the urge to breathe became overwhelming. He'd come farther than he'd realized. Or no, he'd judged his capacity based on the boy he used to be — fit, well-fed, in perfect health. He wasn't that boy anymore, hadn't been for months now.

It was going to be a close call as to whether he could reach air before his lungs gave out. He would do it, though. He had to because Malcolm, who loved him, was waiting on the other side.

* * * *

It was taking too long. Malcolm braced himself against the dirt wall and tried to push away his worry. *Not possible.* The beacon in his hand remained silent. Brenin hadn't reached the cistern. It had only been a few minutes since he'd let the boy go, the hardest thing he'd ever done. Not even watching the life leave Fergus' eyes had taken such a toll on Malcolm's emotions. He loved Brenin and, miraculously, the boy loved him back. Perhaps it was only circumstantial and, after this hard work was finished, Brenin would realize his love was only gratitude. If that were the case, it would kill Malcolm to let him go. He would do it, though, because Brenin alive was all that really mattered.

How long can a human go without breathing? A couple of minutes, maybe longer for a good underwater swimmer. But was Brenin even that, still? He'd been a prisoner for months. The boy wasn't in good shape. *Damn it to hell.* Malcolm knew that and had still let him go? Yes, for the greater good, he had.

Fuck that.

He whipped off his sweater and kilt. Kicked off boots and socks, then, shoving the beacon into his smallclothes, he charged the narrow opening. It was merely dirt and roots and it was only his skin to lose. He pressed against the constriction, scraping every inch of himself. He could feel his flesh turning to dust. His nose broke against a jutting rock. The taste of his own blood fueled his efforts. All the while, he hoped to feel the beacon go off, and when it didn't, he redoubled his efforts, grunting with the pain, yet determined to reach Brenin, no matter the cost.

The mountain was an unforgiving bitch. She pressed him, making it impossible for him to go far. The tunnel was filled with water at the point he started to flail against the impediment. Holding his breath was nothing. His lungs could hold a lot and naturally suppressed the carbon dioxide. But his fucking body was too damn big to squeeze through.

He peered into the murk. *Brenin!*

Like that, the boy appeared, a ghostly apparition that was obviously in distress. Malcolm shot his hand out as far as his arm could reach. Brenin managed to clasp it. Malcolm yanked him forward before releasing his hand to grab the back of his head. Pressing their lips together, Malcolm opened his mouth. He used his tongue to force Brenin to do the same, then breathed into him.

The boy, bless him, caught on quick and inhaled. As he gave his love the very breath in his lungs, Malcolm clawed his way back. Having done nearly as much damage to the tunnel walls as they had done to him, retreat was quicker. He had Brenin at a point where he could lift his head above the water in seconds—long, long ones that nearly stopped Malcolm's heart from fear. He didn't lose the sense of terror until Brenin gulped in a great breath on his own. Malcolm wasted no time on his relief. Instead, he muscled them both out. When they reached the entryway, he collapsed on the floor and pulled Brenin onto his lap.

They sat there shaking for long minutes, saying nothing and everything at the same time. It was Brenin, in the end, who showed the greater courage by pushing away from Malcolm's embrace and explaining what had happened.

Malcolm listened then wrapped his kilt around the boy. "I'll be back in a moment."

He returned to the group, who sat silently where he'd left them. "Who has the bolt-cutters?"

Logan pulled the tool out and handed it to him. He nodded his thanks and turned to leave. He caught Alex's gaze and wanted nothing more than to rail at the man for everything Brenin was going through. That would have been foolish, he knew. This wasn't Alex's fault, none of it. It was Malcolm's because it all started a thousand Earth years ago when Malcolm hadn't done the right thing and warned his captain that his chief navigator wasn't up to the job.

Tonight he'd rectify that mistake.

Chapter Eleven

Brenin figured that many people might think him awfully brave to plunge back into that tunnel after nearly drowning. To his way of thinking, it was Malcolm who'd shown the most courage. He'd let Brenin do it. The price he'd paid emotionally had been written across his face. He'd said nothing, actually, as he'd handed the bolt-cutters over. His handsome face and magnificent body were battered and scarred from his Herculean effort to reach Brenin. If he hadn't done it, Brenin was pretty sure he would have drowned. It had been that close.

But there was no point in dwelling on it. This time, he made it through. As he hoisted himself onto the ledge around the cistern, he took a moment to appreciate the beauty of the place. It was ancient and someone had taken care to add art to something that was functional. The water that dripped down from the roof when it rained ended its journey in a space that pleased the eye. He was likely one of only a few who would ever see it.

He stopped his wool-gathering and pulled out the beacon. Pressing the button was immensely satisfying because he could picture the relief Malcolm felt seeing that Brenin was safe. Well, he'd made it into the castle, at least. Saying that he was safe was a bit of a stretch. The mission was far from over.

He stripped off the dry suit and his underwear. He'd given this part of the plan some thought. If he was going to try to blend into the kitchen staff as one of them, being naked made the most sense. He'd seen very little of those other boys, only those who cleaned the monster's personal lair. They'd been either naked or wearing short, rough kilts. As hard as it was for him to strip off his clothing and his dignity, it was practical. So was leaving the knife behind. There was nowhere to hide it on his person, and really, he doubted he could use it effectively to fight off any of the guards.

Because the castle's inhabitants drew from the cistern for all their water needs, the kitchen was right above it. That made sense and worked perfectly into the plans. He found an ancient stone staircase leading up. It was dusty and full of cobwebs. He powered through his natural disgust for all of it and eventually reached a point at which he gauged he'd gone up an entire floor level. Slowing his steps, he creeped around the last curve until he found himself in front of a door.

It had rusty hinges and a latch handle, testament to its age and disuse. Of course, the water was drawn through pipes. There was no need for anyone to actually go down to the cistern. Nevertheless, he had no way of knowing whether he'd walk directly into the kitchen or somewhere more remote. He pressed his ear to the door and, hearing nothing, went ahead and pulled on the latch.

He winced at the squeak it made and opened it only so much as needed to slip through. He found himself in darkness but, of course, he had left the torch with the knife. It took a few seconds for his eyes to adjust to the gloom. It was a storage room and, beyond that, he found a hallway that lead to the kitchen.

His heart beat double time and his palms went clammy. This was it. Either he succeeded in going out into the back courtyard unimpeded or the slaves milling about would all stop, point their fingers at him and screech out a warning.

Okay, he was being silly. This wasn't a remake of *Invasion of the Body Snatchers*. If he kept his head bowed, likely none of them would recognize him. He'd been face-down in the monster's crotch or on the bed any time they'd come into the room. Few, if any, of the guards had seen him, either. Even if he were recognized, the worst that would happen was he'd be dragged up to Dracul. If that was the outcome, he was already prepared to confess he'd been hiding inside the castle all along. Malcolm and the others would find another way in. He had to have faith in that.

Hunching his shoulders, he bent over, picked up some random nearby bag and shuffled into the kitchen. Being night, there were only a couple of boys about. One was on his knees servicing a guard, so neither of them paid any attention. Brenin could feel the other boy's gaze on him for a few seconds, but it came to nothing. He was able to go straight to the back door, open it and step outside.

He scanned the area before heading to the spot Malcolm had shown him where the surveillance camera was stationed. He could see it easily enough once he'd arrived, so he had no trouble blocking it with his body. Whatever guard manned the security room would see only a dumb human fussing with a bag. Brenin made sure, as well, to place his privates in the frame of the camera in the hope of being a distraction. It sickened him to do it, but nothing compared to keeping Malcolm safe.

A couple of flashes in the corner of his eye told him that his lover and Val had entered the kitchen. Now, Brenin just had to wait until the others confirmed the coast was clear. It didn't take long. They emerged from the woods. Dropping the bag, Brenin joined them. He had to blink back tears of relief when he entered the kitchen and saw Malcolm taping one of the boys' mouths shut. The other was already rendered mute and they both had their hands zip-tied behind their back. An empty pile of clothing and a bit of dust lay where the guard had only recently been feeding his dick to one of the slaves.

While Quinn and the other boys went to soothe and guide the humans into one corner, Brenin went to his man. Malcolm greeted him with a quick kiss and a broad smile.

"I'm that proud of you, Brenin, my lad. The rest is up to me and the others. You stay put at the spot we've delegated. No place is safe, but at least it's out of the way of every exit. Under no circumstances are you to confront anyone. Understand?"

"Aye." He gave him a cheeky grin.

"Good lad. And here… Put this on. You've been awfully brave running around in your altogether. This will keep you warm."

Malcolm had pulled out Benin's clothing, except he also had a kilt in his hands. It was just like the one he was wearing, except smaller. He handed it to Brenin with an unusual uncertainty in his eyes. "I'd intended to give this to you when this was over. Now seems a better time."

"I'll be proud to wear it," Brenin said, conveying, he hoped, all of his love and respect for the man and understanding how momentous it was to wear someone's plaid.

"Right, then," Malcolm said with a nod. "Let's finish this."

* * * *

"It won't be long now. The brat will be born, the slut will die and your father's cooperation will no longer be necessary. Then you'll be all mine. Dracul has promised."

Demi rammed his elbow into Kronid's gut, smiling in satisfaction when the guy grunted. His bravado didn't last long, however. Kronid grabbed Demi by the hair and yanked his head back.

"You'll need disciplining. I look forward to that, *too*, cunt." The asshole clamped his teeth around Demi's earlobe and scraped.

"Demi!" His father's voice rang out over Dafydd's pitiful moaning. "I need you here. Now!"

Kronid had no choice but to release him and Demi wasn't embarrassed to flee to the relative safety of his father's side. He trembled as fear threatened to overtake his optimism. Dafydd's time had come and yet rescue hadn't. It wasn't worry about himself that was overwhelming him, so much as the sure knowledge that, even if Dracul intended to keep Demi's father alive, the moment Demi was thrown to

Kronid for his amusement, Papa would die trying to stop it.

Oh, God, how can I face that loss? What would he say to his human father when they were reunited? He must be able to stop this horror from happening. His strength and cunning should be useful to him finally, but they weren't. He had no idea what to do and the impotence of his situation caused tears to leak down his face. He wiped at them, hating this human show of weakness.

His father gathered him close. "Take heart and stay out of his way. This is going to get ugly. I want you to sit here by the window. I need to know you are within reach if I'm going to manage. Understand?"

Demi nodded and did as his father had asked. He fought to bring himself under control and all the while he couldn't help asking, *Trey, where are you?*

* * * *

"Stay here until I secure the room." Trey breathed the order into Paz's ear, keeping his voice as low as possible. He knew enough about these aliens to worry that the thick wood of the door and the stone walls wouldn't be able to hide his words from whoever was inside.

He used his free arm to press the doctor to one side in case his meaning hadn't been clear and he studied the latch as he did so. It was the same kind of old iron one that he'd seen on other doors. There was no visible lock, which meant either it would open or it was bolted on the inside. Malcolm's surveillance had determined that there were two full-blooded aliens inside. That was assuming nothing had changed in the last couple of hours. Odds were that one was Harry and, while logic had always dictated that the doctor had been abducted to deliver Dracul's son, any indication that Harry was still alive eased Trey's worry. Those alien heat signatures along with one 'changed' human and one hybrid told him that he had only one of Dracul's goons to deal with—and also that Demi was still alive. That belief was what had given Trey the courage to enter into this alien's lair and lead Paz up the incredibly creepy staircase to the tower room. It was as if every horror movie he'd ever seen had come to life.

He prayed, as well, that the one guard was too confident in the castle's security to have bothered to lock himself in with his captives. There was one way to find out for sure. If he got it wrong, it put Demi and the others at risk—greater than what they were in already. *God.* If he allowed himself to think of the boy, he'd never be able to act. His fear would paralyze him. He couldn't allow that to happen. Demi was counting on him. Everyone was and he'd begged to be brought along with the promise of being a help, not a hindrance. He needed to call on every ounce of training he possessed.

Without allowing another single thought, he lifted the latch and threw himself into the room with his gun drawn. At least three startled faces turned in his direction. He focused on only one. Dracul's man reached for a pistol on his belt, but Trey was already firing his own. That had been his plan from the beginning—find and kill. He did it without hesitation, double pops straight to the alien's chest, then he swept the room for more hostiles as the guy shattered into dust.

Fortunately the space was small, dominated by a four-poster bed on which a hugely pregnant young man lay. One of his hands was chained and he writhed in obvious pain. Harry stood on the far side, smiling at Trey. And Demi — thank God — was sitting on the edge of a nearby window, staring at him with wide eyes.

Trey stepped inside, waving at Paz. "It's clear. Come on."

He shut the door behind the doctor and now he did bolt it to keep others out. In the movies, silencers made gunshots sound like quiet pops. The reality was that they still made one hell of a loud sound. He couldn't afford to have any of Dracul's men come storming in. Fortunately, the lock might have been simple, but it looked sturdy. That was good given that, other than the bed, there was nothing big and heavy in the room he could slide over to block the door.

He shouldered his weapon as he turned. "We stick tight until the fight is over. Humph!" He staggered as Demi flew into him and hugged him so hard Trey worried the boy would crack one of his ribs.

"I knew you'd come," Demi said, his voice muffled against Trey's shirt.

He allowed himself a moment of pure selfishness. Wrapping his arm around the boy, he returned the hold and took deep, calming breaths. *Demi is alive*. Whatever else had happened, the boy was here, standing, sufficiently unharmed to run to him and clutch him as if he'd never let go. He gave them both a few guilt-free seconds to revel in the depth of their clearly mutual affection. He knew in those few moments that whatever hope he'd harbored of resisting the allure of this half-alien boy, who was somehow too young and too old for him at the same time, was gone. Someday, somehow, Demi would be his and God help him.

"What is going on here?"

Paz's incredulous question broke the spell. Reluctantly, Trey disentangled himself from Demi, although he couldn't quite let go of the boy entirely yet. He looked at Harry. "This is Dracul's, um…husband, right?"

Harry grimaced. "This is his slave, the forced incubator for his next son, yes. Dafydd."

At that moment, the pregnant boy lifted his sweaty head and cried out. The chain attached to his wrist rattled. Paz swore and rushed forward. He put his medical bag on the floor and held Dafydd by the shoulders as pain clearly caused them to shake.

"Easy, now. I've got you. You're going to be fine."

Dafydd lifted his pinched face. "I'm going to die!"

"No, sir," Paz replied vehemently. "Not on my watch." He stared back at Trey. "Can you get this manacle off him? Jesus, like this isn't difficult enough as it is."

Trey nodded and tossed Demi a quick, reassuring smile as he let go of the boy and stepped up to the bed. "I can help there, yeah." He had his lock-picking tools with him and it took nothing to free the Welsh boy's reddened wrist.

As soon as he was free, Dafydd clutched at his swollen belly with both hands. There were no bedcovers to speak of except a balled-up blanket on the floor, so his unnatural body was on full display. It was fascinating in a kind of bizarre way, except Trey had to appreciate the process because that was how Demi had come into the world.

Paz whipped off his jacket and folded it up, then placed it behind Dafydd's head as he helped the boy lie down again. "What's the plan here, Dr. Stelalux?" He glanced at Harry while he rolled up his sleeves.

"Harry will do and there is only one thing for it now. The baby needs to come out."

"Right." Paz nodded once. "C-section. You know how to get it done?"

"Yes, Demi is proof that I can perform it successfully, except I don't have what I need, I'm afraid."

"What?" Paz craned his neck around the room. "Is there an operating theater somewhere in the castle that we need to get to because there's shit-all in here?" He shook his head. "Sorry, stupid question. This is it, but where's the anesthesia, the plasma and blood supply?"

Dafydd let out a bitter laugh. "You think I'm supposed to survive this? My life is forfeit. It's the baby you're going to save, if you want Dracul to unleash another monster on this world."

Paz cringed, then his eyes went wide. "What?"

"It's true," Harry confirmed. "Dracul brought me here only to save his son. He doesn't want Dafydd to live."

"Yeah?" Paz's lips thinned. "Well, tough shit, because he's going to." He scooped up his bag and placed it on the side of the bed. "First things first."

Trey knew that, with the aid of Doc McPhee, Paz had packed a lot of emergency medical supplies for any wounded that might need his help. The man loaded up a syringe and held it over Dafydd.

"Sir, is there any reason you know of why I can't give you a shot of morphine?"

When Dafydd looked up at him with wide eyes and shook his head, Paz quickly swiped an injection site on the boy's naked flank. The doctor administered the shot and the effect was immediate. The Welshman's face relaxed and, in that moment, Trey could truly appreciate his ethereal beauty.

"There," Paz said, putting the syringe away. "That should buy us time. I'm type O negative, so I can act as a blood donor. We'll do a direct transfusion. It will be tricky, but if you can act quickly, I should be able to handle giving him enough to cover his blood loss."

"No, that won't work," Harry replied. "He's changed. Your purely human blood won't sustain him. His body at best will find it unnourishing and it could even kill him when introduced directly into his vein instead of through his digestive system."

Paz paused in his process of pulling all manner of tubes and needles from his bag. "Damn it. Then who can donate?"

"Me." Harry's shirtsleeves were already rolled up.

Paz shook his head. "Oh, no. It can't be you because I can't do the C-section. I mean, sure, I did one once in my obstetrics rotation, but that was on a woman. I have no idea how to perform one in a situation like this."

A visible shudder ran through Harry. "It is very tricky, that's true. We have little choice, however, if we are to save Dafydd as well as the child."

Dafydd giggled eerily, the drug making him unnaturally happy. "Let me die. I'm ready."

"We've already covered that, sir," Paz ground out. "You are *not* dying." It was amazing, really, how well the doctor was keeping his shit together in the situation. He looked at Harry. "What's Plan B?"

Trey felt like collapsing in the corner and sucking his thumb and he'd had months to acclimate to the weirdness of these aliens' goings-on.

"There is no other source of blood that Dafydd can tolerate," Harry was saying, "except…"

Aw shit!

"Mine," Demi said, going over to his father. "I can be the blood source, can't I?"

"Yes," his father agreed with a weariness that conveyed how much he loathed the idea. "But it's dangerous. You might lose too much." He placed his hand on his son's cheek. "I can't risk your dying."

"Don't!" Dafydd called out, even as his body twisted with his muted labor pains. "Don't risk your life for me, Demi. That's more kindness than I deserve. We've talked about this, remember? I don't want to live."

"I have to! And so do you." The boy didn't wait for a response. Tearing off his shirt, he crawled onto the bed and lay down next to the Welsh boy. "I want to do this, Papa. Please, I know you can syphon my blood without killing me. I trust you." He held up his arm. "You need the radial artery, right?"

"You *have* been reading up on those medical sites, haven't you?" Harry sighed. "We'll have to be quick about this. I'll need you to both assist in the operation and take care of the babe once he's out," he added to Paz.

"Understood." Paz wasted no time prepping first Demi's wrist then Dafydd's inner elbow for the transfusion.

Harry reached inside Paz's bag and took out a bottle of clear fluid. He squeezed some into his palm and started wiping his hands together. Trey stood around like the fifth wheel that he was, watching Demi lie there with a determined look on his too-young face. *I can't risk your dying*, Harry had said. Yeah, well, neither could he. He tugged off his jacket and tossed it on the floor.

"Harry, how about I feed Demi during the transfusion? I mean, he can drink blood from my vein, right? Wouldn't that help him replenish what he's losing, even if it's a little bit?"

The older alien looked over his shoulder. His gaze narrowed for a few uncomfortable moments before he smiled. "Yes, he can and it would. It's an excellent idea. Thank you, Sergeant."

"Wait, what?" Demi started to sit up. Paz pushed him back down none too gently. Demi shook his head at Trey as he climbed up beside him. "You shouldn't. I've never fed from a living source. I might take too much."

Trey ran a finger down the boy's cheek, pushing aside a few strands of hair. "I trust you," he said, throwing the boy's words back at him.

With his heart suddenly racing, he brought his wrist over Demi's mouth, turning it to expose the inside. He kept his gaze firmly on the boy's eyes and smiled in encouragement. He focused his attention on the pretty violet pupils, the one thing in particular that told him this wasn't a mere human. Then Demi parted his rosy lips and bright, white fangs twinkled. The sight of them made Trey's heartbeat stumble, but he swallowed down his fear.

All around him there was a flurry of activity as Paz set up the transfusion and Harry prepped Dafydd for the surgery as best he could with what little he had. Still, Trey kept his attention on Demi, willing him to do the same in reverse and not look at how the dicey efforts were playing out. There was only a minor wince in the boy's eyes as the needle went into his wrist and Trey resolved to be as strong when it was his turn.

"Now, if you please, Duncan." Harry's calm voice made it easy to comply.

Trey moved his wrist closer to Demi's mouth, right against those fangs. He held back a yelp and a grimace as pain lanced through the tight skin. Then, an exquisite feeling stole over him. He was both calm and – dear, sweet baby Jesus – aroused. The rhythmic tugging at his vein, the look of pleasure clouding Demi's eyes, was like a spark to Trey's dick. He went instantly, embarrassingly and alarmingly hard.

The beat of his heart pounded loudly in his ears, muting everything around him. The sounds of Harry and Paz racing through the operation barely registered. Through the haze of his arousal, he caught sight of a splash of red. He smelled the metallic scent of blood, but it was nothing compared to the heady aroma of Demi. They were linked in a beautiful and disturbing way that would have scared the crap out of him if he hadn't been so completely lost in the suddenly inky blackness of Demi's eyes.

In those few minutes as Demi drank his blood, Trey knew he was completely fucked. Strangely, he wasn't worried in the least.

There was the angry cry of a newborn yanked from the quiet safety of his womb-home. The startling sound pulled him from his trance. Trey looked away from Demi to see Paz carry the squalling, bloody boy over to a small table covered in towels and other baby stuff. Dracul had at least provided something for his son's birth.

Dafydd lay limp, staring at the ceiling. For a moment, Trey feared he was dead, until his hand twitched. Harry stood between the boy's spread legs, working furiously. Trey cringed and blinked as the man extracted something that looked like an eggplant covered in gore. Harry tossed it on the floor before grabbing a medical stapler. His fingers were a blur after that, as he closed Dafydd's body.

A wave of dizziness forced Trey to close his eyes. "Shit," he croaked out. "Think I'm going to…"

"Demi, let go. Now!" Harry barked out.

The connection to the boy broke, as Demi retracted his fangs then lapped at Trey's wrist. Trey missed the contact, even as he was relieved at getting control back over his body. Something landed on his stomach. He clutched at it instinctively, even as he popped open his eyes.

"Take care of him while I end the transfusion." The order came from Paz and the 'him' was the baby.

Dracul's son mewled and squirmed and rubbed his tiny fists against his face like any other baby would. It was impossible not to instantly want to take care of him. Trey placed both of his hands on the bundle and patted him gently.

"Hey, kid, welcome to the world."

A split-second later, he realized to whom he was talking. His discussion days ago with Paz came to the fore. The doctor had been adamant about saving this child. Now, he had to consider that taking care of this baby wasn't necessarily the best thing for Earth and humanity. It was as if he were in the moral dilemma of holding a newborn Hitler. Except, no, it wasn't like that at all. This little boy was another Demi, a hybrid that could be raised to be either good or evil. Hopefully Dracul was already dead, but regardless, he wasn't ever going to get his hand on this son to twist as he had the other two.

"It is done," Harry said, wiping his hands as best he could on a small towel. "With the right care, Dafydd will be fine and I've given him a hysterectomy the way I did my dear Lucien. He will never have to bear any more children."

Trey sat up gingerly, clutching the baby to his chest. "Is that what he wanted?"

"He wanted to die, but yes, he was clear on not wanting to do this ever again. Now, he won't have to. The transformation happens only once. Without the uterus he grew in his youth, he will be unable to breed more sons for any of our kind."

Paz came over and shook out a large towel. "Here. This isn't much but it's clean, unlike the blanket, and will cover him a little while we carry him out of here. Let's pack up the formula over there so that we can feed his son. I doubt Dafydd will be in any condition to do so." He frowned. "*Can* he lactate?"

"Of course," Harry replied, gathering up what he could and stuffing it into Paz's bag. "But he won't nurse the baby, I'm sure. He doesn't want this child. He made that very clear as well."

Dafydd said nothing on his own behalf. With his eyes closed and his body lax, he was obviously unconscious. That reminded Trey of Demi. He refocused his gaze on Demi and saw him awake, yet sleepy-looking.

"You okay, kid?"

Demi gave him a tired smile. "I'm fine. You taste...sweet," he added.

Trey rolled his eyes. He knew nonsense when he heard it. Blood was salty. "Is he telling me the truth?" he asked the boy's father. "About his condition, I mean," he clarified.

Harry nodded. "He is, but he's also weak. He's going to need to be carried."

"I can walk," Demi protested, rising. His body betrayed him, however, when he slumped back down.

Trey stood on slightly weakened legs. "Here," he said, thrusting the baby at Harry. "You take this one and I'll get Demi."

Harry opened his mouth then shut it again. Nodding, he took the baby. Trey had just started to gather Demi into his arms when a pounding on the door had him reaching for his weapon.

"Duncan? It's Val. Open up. Time to book out of here."

Chapter Twelve

Malcolm crept up the tower stairs with his beloved claymore gripped in both hands. He'd encountered precious few of Dracul's men, which was a blessing but a disappointment, too. In his mind, he wanted to slaughter them all. Traitors, murderers and, worst of all, men who'd stood by while Brenin had been forced into sexual slavery to satisfy their twisted master's needs. No fate was too bad for them to suffer. But he'd have to be satisfied with Alex and the others dealing with them. He had to focus on the main event.

As he rounded the last bend in the circular staircase, he saw light and heard grunting and groaning. Dracul's hubris had made him vulnerable. His door was open and Malcolm had a clear line of sight to the fucker. He was mounting his latest slave on the bed, pounding into him from behind and oblivious to how his fate was creeping up to meet him.

This was the best outcome possible. Naked as he was, Dracul couldn't pull a gun out of somewhere. Malcolm had a nine-millimeter strapped to his thigh because he wasn't stupid. He still hoped that this final battle could be fought old-style. He and Dracul had one thing in common. They both preferred the sword to a gun—a point of honor for Malcolm and another example of Dracul's excessive pride. He couldn't conceive of someone, a mere human in particular, winning against him, under any circumstances.

Malcolm deliberately made a noise to be noticed. The boy on all fours squeaked when he saw him. Dracul shoved the kid away and staggered to his feet in the next instant. His face showed how his thoughts ran from 'how the fuck?' to 'how dare you?' Yeah, that was the thing about Dracul. He wasn't scared of failure, only annoyed at the intrusion.

"I thought you'd been smart enough to sit out the war," he sneered with his hands fisted on his waist.

"More fool me," Malcolm admitted. "I thought I could. You've been instrumental in changing my mind. You couldn't leave it alone, could you? Fabulous wealth and your own wee fiefdom here in Wales weren't sufficient. You had to keep trying to take over the world. It ends now and at the point of my sword."

No fear showed in Dracul. The guy had gigantic balls, that was for certain. "Of course, I could always count on you to stay mired in the past. Why didn't you take off my head while I was distracted? This slut does a marvelous job of keeping my attention, I must say."

"This is a battle, not an execution."

Dracul rolled his eyes. "Honor? How dreary...and stupid. I will best you, naturally."

Malcolm bared his teeth. "You can try." He tossed his head to the far wall. "Go and get your sword, but know that if you reach for a gun, I've got one on me. Killing you with a bullet will be less satisfying for me, but you'll be dead either way."

"I don't need a pistol to finish you."

Dracul strutted over to the wall and pulled his sword off. It was heavier than Malcolm's claymore, an English design. No matter. They were evenly matched regardless.

Patience not being one of Dracul's strengths, he sprang for Malcolm seconds later. The steel blades clashed with a ringing sound that brought back memories. In fact, it allowed Malcolm to resurrect his sword skill with ease. Practicing with Darling had kept his edge. Thoughts of how he'd fought side by side with Fergus gave him heart.

He danced around the room with Dracul, neither of them gaining ground. Neither of them ceded it, either. They knocked over furniture and slipped on the rugs under their feet. They both started to huff from the exertion. This wasn't going to be any easy kill. Malcolm didn't want it to be. The longer he made the fucker suffer, the more he felt as if he'd avenged Brenin.

Then with a feint he'd learned from his dear, dead friend, Malcolm drew first blood. A gash of crimson welled up on Dracul's arm before raining down in ash. Dracul hissed and pulled away from Malcolm's range.

Coward.

There was little time for feeling the pleasure in his minor success, however. With a screech, the boy Dracul had been fucking launched himself at Malcolm. The boy's attack came as a surprise. Malcolm wasn't able to block it before the human raked his nails down Malcolm's cheek. *Och.* Well, it wasn't as if he weren't scarred already from his time in the tunnel. He shoved the boy away and he landed with a howl against the wall. The momentary distraction gave Dracul a chance to attack.

He went for Malcolm's leg, which was a mistake, as the kilt absorbed most of the blow. Malcolm staggered out of the way, twirled and lashed out. His strike hit truer, lacerating Dracul's lower back and sending him flying forward. Dracul allowed the momentum to take him to the doorway. As he reached it, another figured loomed up from the stairs—Petru. Dracul's lackey held a pistol in his outstretched hand.

"Kill him!" Dracul screamed the order as he skidded to a halt. So much for honor, of which, naturally, the arsehole had none.

Malcolm was reaching for his own gun, when Petru surprised them both. Instead of aiming at Malcolm, the man's gaze skittered to one side, to a point beyond Malcolm, before returning to Dracul. For a moment, it appeared as if he were going to shoot the man he'd followed for centuries. Shock registered on Dracul's face, as he obviously thought the same thing.

For a few tense seconds, Petru kept his weapon pointed at Dracul. Malcolm found himself silently egging the man to pull the trigger and also wanting him to leave so that the kill could be his. Finally, Petru backed away and kept going down the stairs.

Dracul wasted no time in following his former right-hand man, although he turned in the opposite direction, running up the stairs. Malcolm followed him, all the way to the top and onto the parapet. Dracul nearly took his head off when he popped through the door. The whoosh caught Malcolm's attention just in time. He ducked, rolled and came up swinging.

Then it was all about the clash of steel. With the wind whipping around them, Malcolm and Dracul waged a battle worthy of the old days. For thousands of years, humans had fought one another in this very fashion. It was both old and new to them, their own kind having given up such petty fighting long before humanity had started walking upright.

It was satisfying on a primitive level for Malcolm, regardless. Every time he hit Dracul's sword or body, it was to avenge Brenin. He wanted this man, this monster, to hurt the way Malcolm's precious boy had. Every drop of blood spilled was in sacrifice to Brenin's ordeal.

He cornered Dracul against the outer wall. They were both winded and slowing. But Dracul was more so, testament to how soft he'd become — or maybe Malcolm's fury was more powerful than Dracul's sense of self-preservation. On that note, Malcolm whirled around and, uttering his best highlander scream, threw every ounce of power he possessed into his next blow. Dracul's sword winged away.

Now he had the bastard. He paced slowly forward, the point of his sword getting closer to Dracul's neck. "Poor, wretched Dafydd wasn't enough for you. You had to brutalize another one. Brenin didn't deserve what you did to him. No one does, but he's mine now, so you die for that alone."

Surprise made Dracul's eyes go wide. Then he grinned in a way that made Malcolm's blood boil. "At least I die knowing what happened to the slut. I underestimated him. But enjoy him, by all means. I did. And every time you take him, you'll know that I had him first."

Malcolm screamed again, this time in their own tongue, using every invective available. He charged to deliver the killing blow. When he swung, though, all he hit was air. Dracul had catapulted himself over the edge and disappeared into the night.

Racing over, Malcolm peered down, expecting to see a pile of dust on the ground below. Instead, he realized that Dracul had gone down one of the rainwater catches. It was a narrow well that undoubtedly led to the cistern. Traces of blood turned to ash before his very eyes, testament to how Dracul's body must have been torn by the stone walls.

"Cowardly fucker."

Malcolm raced back into the castle, down the stairs and into the kitchen. He caught his boy's scent and followed it into a storage room and eventually to the cistern. He was careful to sniff out any signs of Dracul before entering the moist cavern. There was nothing to see there except still water and a small pile of Brenin's things. He gathered them up and scanned the water keenly. A full sweep of the perimeter showed no signs. The only logical assumption was that Dracul had died coming down the shaft.

Malcolm felt cheated, which was stupid. The fucker was dead, and that was all that mattered.

He returned to the kitchen. He found Alex and Logan there. They both turned with guns raised until they saw it was him. "He's dead," was all he said. No need to illuminate who he meant.

Alex nodded once. "That's a relief."

"Is there anyone left?"

"No. We've eliminated eight and no sign of any others. If they're hiding somewhere here, Logan's charges will likely take care of them."

"They will destroy the cache of arms," Logan said. "Not sure anything will bring down this structure."

"We'll take what we can get," Alex replied. "We'll meet you out with the others."

Logan gave him a two-fingered salute. "I'll be waiting for your signal to blow it, sir." She left them alone.

Malcolm was still catching his breath and bringing down his adrenaline. "There should have been more."

"I agree. Not all of them were billeted here, obviously. I'm not sure what threat they'll be without Dracul to lead them. You're positive he's dead? I know that's a stupid question..."

"No, it's not." Malcolm explained what happened.

Alex huffed. "Interesting about Petru. He finally turned on his master. We have to assume Dracul's dead. That's the one problem with our species—no body. We can't stick around, in any event. Willem is already ferrying Harry, Paz and Demi back to the ship, along with Dafydd and the baby."

Malcolm winced. "Och, I almost forgot about all that. What are we to do with the wee one anyway?"

"I'll take him and Dafydd, if he wants, back to Boston. Perhaps Harry and Lucien will be willing to foster him. Dafydd's done with fatherhood, apparently. That reminds me. There was no sign of the twins."

"Bugger me!"

"I know. This was a mostly successful effort. With Dracul's spawn still on the loose, and Petru, as well, we'll have to stay vigilant. I will, anyway. Your part in the war is over, Malcolm. For good this time." He came over and placed a firm hand on Malcolm's shoulder. "There would have been no doing this without you, my friend. I owe you everything."

"You owe me nothing, sir." Malcolm choked on his words. He needed to come clean once and for all. "All of this, the crash and being marooned, is my fault."

When Alex shook his head, he explained about his suspicions over his fellow navigator. "I knew he wasn't up to the job. I should have said something."

Alex closed his eyes briefly. "Oh God, Malcolm. I had no idea you felt this way." He gave him a pained look. "Do you think I didn't know his shortcomings? It was a political appointment. I had no choice about accepting him.

"I gave you all of the hard jumps. I thought he could handle this last one. I was wrong and we've all paid the price ever since."

Malcolm shook his head. In those few seconds, however, a weight lifted off his shoulders. He felt as if he could truly breathe for the first time since…forever. And he had something to look forward to. Brenin. His boy.

"Shit! I almost forgot. There was a boy with Dracul. Weird hair of black and white stripes, obviously changed and loyal enough to Dracul to attack me. He still doesn't deserve to die here."

"Go. We'll keep evacuating the others, but I'll have Logan hold off on the big boom until you're back."

Malcolm wasted no time running to Dracul's room. He entered cautiously and found it empty. Although he felt bad for the lad, it was not so much that he wanted to go searching the rest of the castle. It was time to go. He needed to see for himself that Brenin was safe and, God, he was tired. A month's worth of sleep wouldn't go amiss, as long as his boy slept by his side.

* * * *

Brenin paced and fretted, no matter what anyone else said. He wouldn't stop worrying until he saw Malcolm for himself. It was almost impossible to believe that the monster was dead. He'd seen too many horror movies to not expect some last-minute resurrection. Besides, the castle was big. Even with their speed, he didn't think Alex and the others had cleared every room.

A flash through the trees caught his attention. Then he was running toward it and into his man's arms. "Malcolm! You're safe."

Malcolm held him tightly. "Aye, laddie, we both are, and isn't that a grand thing?"

"I love you," Brenin said in a voice muffled by Malcolm's chest.

"And I you. Time for us to go home, heh?"

"To Rionnag?"

"Aye, if that is your will."

"It is. I want to live with you and Darling and Cook and get to know the rest of the village besides Doc McPhee."

Malcolm pulled away to take his hand. "Then that's what we'll do."

There was a loud rumble, then another and the ground shook. Logan laughed. They watched her push more buttons on her little black box. The woman was clearly in her element. She'd been a marine, Brenin had learned from the boys, and was damaged from the experience. That might be, but there was no denying she was having a hell of a time for herself.

Brenin looked back and saw the first plume of smoke. There went Dracul's domain. He should have had more satisfaction at this ending. Instead, he only felt kind of hollow inside. The good news, however, was that his love for Malcolm was already filling up that empty space. He had hope that soon all that would be left of this horrible experience was enduring love for his man and the life they would make together.

Getting back to the old trawler proved more complicated than the coming had been. There were now half a dozen pure humans and a couple of changed boys, one of whom had a pre-pubescent hybrid clinging to his arm. Brenin hated seeing them trussed up and gagged, but there was no telling what any of them might do. They'd lived under Dracul's rule for some period of time and might have even developed affection for one of the guards who'd been killed — either real or out of survival. Until they were back where they could be kept out of sight and under control, it was safer for everyone to keep them neutralized.

Brenin did his best, along with Mackie, Quinn and Jase, to help them all stay warm and calm, as they made their way down to the road. Val and Emil had commandeered a couple of the castle vehicles, which meant they could make it to the boat with only one trip. Good thing, too, given that dawn was breaking. They needed to be away before the inhabitants of the sleepy village started waking up. The smoke billowing out from the mountain wasn't going to make things any easier.

Brenin reluctantly parted from Malcolm's side the moment they boarded. While his man went to the pilot house, Brenin helped herd their 'guests' below into what constituted the crew's salon. They seated everybody as best they could. Brenin really wanted to start untying them, but he knew he had to wait for Alex's approval.

"It's okay," he said to the young hybrid as he put him next to his father on a padded bench. "You're safe. I promise."

The boy glared at him then sent a hardy kick right into Brenin's upper thigh. It missed his groin by millimeters. The boy's father grunted in alarm.

"Not to worry," he assured him. "No harm done." He moved to a safe distance nevertheless.

A bunch of squealing caught his attention. A hybrid had emerged from a cabin and Mackie had him in a choking embrace.

"Oh my God, Demi, you scared the crap out of me! Don't do that again," Mackie admonished. He pulled away and gave the other boy the once-over. "Are you all right?"

Demi rolled his eyes. "I'm fine." He glanced over his shoulder at Duncan, who'd also come out. "Trey saved me."

The cop scratched the back of his head. "Yeah, I don't know. It was more of a joint effort."

"Seriously?" Demi shook his head. "You..." He stopped, shook his head again and said, "You were great." Something more passed between Demi and Duncan. The boy's expression morphed into one not simply of love, but also of worship, maybe. The man's face reddened, although his eyes conveyed a poignancy that was almost painful to see. He broke the gaze first and moved away.

Demi shuddered visibly before turning back to Mackie. "I'm just glad it's over. Now I can come back to the club and save your awful choreography from itself." He gave Mackie a saucy grin.

"Oh!" Mackie glared at him for about two seconds before taking him into another hug.

The other boys, Quinn and Jase, joined in until there was something of an emotional scrum going on. Brenin didn't feel left out because he'd never been a part of their little group. Not really. And there was only one place he wanted to be anyway.

He left the salon and headed up to the pilot house. Malcolm sat at the helm, flanked by Willem and Alex. Brenin didn't hesitate to wind past them and up to Malcolm. With a welcoming grin, Malcolm pulled Brenin up onto his lap. Brenin placed his head against his hard chest and closed his eyes.

* * * *

The next thing he knew, they were pulling up to the dock of Castle Rionnag. There was Darling, Doc McPhee and little Annika, who was bouncing up and down. The moment the lines were secure, the parade of warriors, their boys and their unwilling guests started emerging from below. Someone had obviously filled the welcoming committee in, because the doctor and the majordomo were neither surprised nor reluctant to wade in and take charge.

Brenin stretched and hopped off Malcolm's lap to give him room to do what he needed. "What's going to happen to them?"

"That lot?" Malcolm gestured toward the dock. "Their my problem for now. Ours," he added. "I hope that's okay."

"It is. In a weird way, it gives me another avenue to heal from what the monster did. They're as much his victims as I was. We can help them build new lives."

Malcolm smiled and gave him a quick peck on the lips. "You're a fine one, make no mistake, Brenin Jones.

Not everyone who went through what you did would want to take on such a difficult task. You'd be well within your rights to demand they get out of your sight so that you could forget."

"There's no forgetting, is there? And I want to be useful."

"It won't be easy." He shut down the engines and took Brenin's hand. "The hybrid in particular will be a difficult thing to deal with."

"He's only a little boy."

"Not so young. We age differently than you do. He's older than he seems by human standards."

Brenin pulled up short and glared at him. "You're not to hurt him."

"Don't worry, my love. I won't. I might have to lock him in my dungeon at some point, but…"

"It won't come to that." Brenin resolved right then and there that he'd do what it took to alter any bad traits the boy might have picked up from his alien father.

As they left the boat, he watched how Lucien walked up the dock with Demi in his embrace and the two of them in Harry's. They were so obviously happy that Brenin found himself wishing for the same.

He gnawed at his lower lip before asking, "Do you want a son?"

Malcolm stumbled by the gangplank. It would have been comical if Brenin weren't so focused on his question. "I can't say as I've given that any thought."

"I'm asking you to consider it now, please."

"Och, Brenin, my bonny lad, that's entirely up to you. For my own selfish reasons, I want to feed you my blood to keep you with me for the rest of my life. It comes with changes, though, if we do it while you're young."

"How old would I have to be before it wouldn't work?"

"I can't say for certain." He led them down to the dock as they spoke. "Late twenties, early thirties, I guess. Harry would know best. It's a big step, make no mistake, and one I'd never ask of you. After all you've been through, I'll be that glad to have you in the way we've already been and not ask for more."

Brenin believed him. The only problem was, he didn't think that it would be enough for him. Dracul was dead. It was time to banish all traces of him. It wasn't the right moment to have this deep discussion, however. There was work to be done. The former slaves needed to be settled in and, if this was to become Brenin's home, he needed to get used to playing a major roll.

He tugged at Malcolm's hand and picked up his pace. "Come on. There's lots to do yet."

Laughing, Malcolm allowed himself to be led. "Whatever you say, laddie. I'm yours to command."

* * * *

Dafydd woke with a gasp. His head felt too heavy to lift, as did his whole body. There was a dull ache down where he'd once carried Dracul's son. The baby was gone. He could tell that much. Relief washed over him, as did confusion. He couldn't quite remember all that had happened and he had to blink a few times to see where he was. It was a bedroom, lovely and warm, but nothing he was familiar with.

"How are you feeling? Any pain?"

Dafydd jerked at the voice. It was gentle and he recognized it. Turning his head, he saw the young doctor coming out of the shadows. He looked down at Dafydd kindly and put his hand on Dafydd's brow.

"No fever. That's good."

"Is it?" Dafydd's voice was rusty and his throat hurt.

"You need water." The doctor poured a glass from a pitcher on the nightstand and helped Dafydd lift his head to drink.

It was coolly delicious and he was pathetically grateful for the kindness. "Thank you," he croaked out when he'd had enough. He still had some manners left in him.

Although no trust.

He eyed the doctor. "Do you own me now?"

The man was obviously startled by the question. He frowned. "No. Of course I don't. No one does. You're free. Don't you understand that's what happened when I arrived in your room?"

Dafydd shook his head slowly. "No. I… Dracul."

"Is dead."

The news hit him like a blunt instrument. He should have been elated, but all positive emotion had been beaten out of him long ago. The most he could muster was indifference. He lay there with nothing to say.

"Do you want to see your son?"

"No!" That was an easy answer. The thought of it made him sick. "I don't want that thing anywhere near me."

"He's your child."

"No. It's only ever been part of Dracul's master plans. It's a weapon of destruction."

The doctor seemed frustrated. "You know that's not how it has to be. You spent time with Demi. Do you understand what he risked to save your life?"

Dafydd shifted his gaze to the ceiling. There was a pretty pastoral scene painted there. "I told him not to bother. In any event, his father was different, so he is. That thing you cut out of me has evil in its veins."

The doctor sighed. "I'm sorry you feel that way. I don't, though. He's alive and well and is going to stay that way. Someone will bring him up if you don't want to."

"I don't. You waste your time and breath if you think you can change my mind on this. Kill me now if my answer doesn't please you."

"*Dafydd*, you know I'm not going to do that."

"You're not saying it right."

"I beg your pardon? Is there a better way for me to make my case to you?"

"I mean my name. You have an American accent."

"Because I'm from America. Boston, to be precise." Now there was amusement in the man's tone.

Dafydd glanced at him. "It doesn't matter. I don't care about any of that."

"Don't you?" The bed depressed as the doctor sat on the edge. Dafydd steeled himself to be touched but that didn't happen. "You have a chance to live a good life now. With Dracul dead, you can come to Boston, start over."

"Why would I do that?"

"Because you can. Look around you. This is what waits for you—comfort, safety, prosperity even. Alex and his family will take good care of you and ask nothing in return."

Dafydd snorted. "There is always a price."

"Not this time. Not anymore." The doctor was quiet for a while, sitting and not touching, not preaching. Then, "Would you like to name your son?"

"How many times do I have to tell you that I don't care about that thing." Maybe if he goaded the man sufficiently, he would end him. *I still want death, don't I?*

"So you've said. A baby needs a name, however. I'll call him Diego."

Dafydd couldn't help frowning. "That's stupid. He's not Spanish."

"True, although by your estimation, he's not Welsh, either."

Disgusted with himself for walking into the trap, he bit out, "Call him what you like, mun."

"At least you've upgraded the baby to a 'him' and not an 'it'. But your point is well taken. Just because I'm Hispanic doesn't mean I should choose something from my heritage. I'm not the boy's father, after all. What's a good Welsh name for a boy?"

"Idris." The moment the name passed his lips, Dafydd could have bitten his tongue. It must have been the pain meds he was on, making him fuzzy-headed and stupid with it.

"Oh, like the actor."

"No, like my da... Never mind." He turned away from the man. "I'm that tired and want to go back to sleep."

"Of course. I'll be right here if you need me. You're safe, Dafydd. Did I say it right that time?"

"No."

"I'll have to practice."

"Do as you please. It's nothing to me either way."

Closing his eyes, he ignored the man—or tried to. Even with his alien master dead and his rescue from his prison of so many centuries, he still felt trapped. This place was everything he'd never had—warm and inviting—and there'd likely be his fill of food, as well. It was a cage, nevertheless, and no amount of pretty words or creature comforts would change that.

Chapter Thirteen

"I thought I'd find you up here."

"It's a fine, clear night for stargazing."

Malcolm took his eye away from the lens to greet Brenin. The boy looked terribly fetching in his kilt and nothing else. Malcolm was the same, although he had a shirt on to hide the new scars on his body. He didn't want to alarm the boy or anyone else.

He tugged Brenin in for a long kiss. The boy melted into him and his tongue shyly met Malcolm's when it begged entrance into Brenin's mouth. Each time they touched, the boy's inhibitions fell away a wee bit more. Soon, Malcolm hoped they'd be gone for good, or at least as gone as would ever be possible.

"Hmm." Malcolm pulled back. "I thought you were sleeping."

"I tried, but I think my internal clock is still screwed up. I took a nap and feel refreshed, though. So much so I was hoping you'd give me a lesson about the planets and the stars." He let go of Malcolm and sauntered up to the telescope.

"If that's what you want, I'll be happy to." He'd give him the moon, if he could. "What do you want to see?" He lowered the scope to Brenin's height as he asked.

"Um." Brenin pursed his adorable lips. "How about we start with the basics? Venus?"

Malcolm adjusted the scope and stepped back. "Look there."

Putting his eye to the lens, Brenin made a humming noise. "Nice. Jupiter?"

Malcolm guided the scope with his hand, watching Brenin's reaction. "Here."

"Uh-huh. Mars?"

He moved it again. "Here."

"Sirius?"

"That's a star system. The brightest from our vantage point here on Earth. This is it."

"I think I'm beginning to see the distinctions. How about Cassiopeia?"

"That's a constellation." He moved the scope once more.

"You're going to have to teach me the difference between all of these things."

"Gladly, laddie. What do you want to see next?"

Brenin stopped looking through the scope and stared instead into Malcolm's eyes. "Show me how it can be between two men who love each other. All the way."

Malcolm's breath caught hearing that request. He had to make himself breathe and he thought maybe his heart had skipped a beat. "Are you sure? Brenin, you don't have to do this for me. I meant it when I said what we have is enough."

Brenin placed his palm against Malcolm's chest. "It's not for me. I want this." He moved in closer and stood on his toes. "I want you." He gave him a kiss, not a long, lingering one, but one that was firm. Certain.

Malcolm ran his hands up the boy's arms. "I will treat you with all the care in the world," he vowed. "And while I'll guide you, you have control. If anything makes you uncomfortable, you tell me and I'll stop. Agreed?"

Brenin nodded. "Yes."

"Come to my room, then." Taking his hand, he tried to lead him out.

"No." Brenin dug in his heels, figuratively and emotionally. "I want to do it here, under the stars and away from everyone else."

Malcolm frowned. "Seriously? There's no bed here and the rug isn't that padded."

"I'm sure." So saying, Brenin dropped his kilt and went down on his knees. As he'd worn nothing underneath, he was completely naked.

That was all the persuading Malcolm's cock needed. He went hard in an instant and, because he also hadn't bothered with his boxer-briefs, his arousal was visible.

Brenin smiled at it and crooked his finger. "Come join me."

"As if I could deny you anything." Malcolm took off his kilt and threw it aside. He hesitated a moment before doing the same with his shirt. If they were going to truly be lovers, Brenin needed to see him fully, warts and all. Brenin gasped and, when Malcolm knelt in from of him, it was the scars the boy touched, not the straining dick bobbing between them.

"These are new."

"Aye, from the tunnel."

"You got them saving me." There was moisture in the boy's eyes.

"Dinnae fash yourself on my account. They're a small price to pay."

"Won't they ever heal?"

"No. If someone had been there to close the wounds with saliva, you wouldn't see a thing. As it was, the skin turned to ash, as is our physiology, and it won't regenerate."

Brenin traced the scars lightly with his fingertips. The effect was to cause Malcolm's cock to go even harder and his balls tightened. "You're more vulnerable than I am in that way?"

"Aye."

"And your nose is crooked. You broke it?"

"I did. I can ask Doc McPhee to reset it if you'd like."

A smile flashed across Brenin's pretty face. "No, that's fine, then. I wouldn't want you to be too handsome, like. I might have to fight the other village boys over you. Besides, it makes you look more like my wild highlander."

"I'll always be that, laddie. I want to kiss you," he confessed in the next breath. "May I?"

"Always. I like kissing."

That was all the permission he needed. Taking Brenin's hands in his, he pulled him forward. Malcolm landed on his back and encouraged the boy to lie on top of him so that he could capture his lips without overwhelming him with his body.

Brenin didn't need much coaxing. He plastered himself on top of Malcolm and met his passion with equal fervor. They chased tongues from one mouth to the other. When they tired of that game, they took turns nibbling around each other's lips. Their position, meanwhile, caused their cocks to slide together skin to skin. Malcolm cupped Brenin's arse to press their bodies even closer. He thought he might come from this frottage alone.

The lad had other ideas. He broke the kiss and peppered Malcolm's chin and neck, before moving down his torso. Malcolm thought he would stop at the dick, knowing how he must have been forced to suck Dracul's cock.

No, don't think it. That's what Dracul wanted, to ruin it for both of us.

He banished the past and, flinging his arms out, let Brenin have his way. The first tentative licks along the weeping head caused Malcolm's hips to rear up. He forced them down, made himself lie flat. Brenin ran his fingers up the shaft, slid his thumb through the slit. Malcolm jerked and hissed.

"Do you like that?" Brenin either sounded genuinely curious or was messing about. Malcolm couldn't tell and didn't care.

"You're killing me. Don't stop." He closed his eyes and concentrated on the good things happening below his waist.

Brenin chuckled then returned with his lips. This time, he sucked the cockhead into his mouth. He didn't take much and didn't need to. The way he laved the bundle of nerves underneath with his tongue was more than sufficient to cause Malcolm's head to explode — the small one. He came with such speed that he didn't have time to issue a warning.

The boy gasped.

"Sorry, sorry. Damn." He tried to wiggle out of the way, even as his orgasm made him shudder.

"No, it's fine." Brenin slid the side of his finger up the shaft. "It will make for good lube."

"What?" Malcolm forced his eyes open. "No, don't!"

In the process of rubbing the cum around his hole, Brenin froze. "What? Did I do something wrong?"

"Never. I just don't want to hurt you, is all."

"You won't. I can take you dry if I have to."

The casual way in which Brenin accepted his brutality infuriated Malcolm as nothing had before. Did he really think this human could recover that quickly from his degradation? Malcolm had to assume that he knew nothing of how it should be between them.

"You asked me to show you what it's supposed to be like. Let me, then. Trust me."

"I do."

"Good lad. Come up here." He guided Brenin so that he straddled Malcolm's neck. "I want a taste of your sweet cock."

"You don't…" The boy's words dried on his tongue as Malcolm swallowed him in one big gulp.

"Oh." This was why men liked having their dicks sucked. Sure, on an intellectual level, he'd understood. But this? The exquisite feel of Malcolm's lips and tongue and throat working Brenin's shaft was beyond imagining. Malcolm acted as if this was a special treat for him. He moaned and his eyelids closed to half-mast.

Brenin held himself steady by planting both palms on the floor beside Malcolm's head. He couldn't keep his own eyes open. With his sight gone, he could concentrate on the amazing sensations. His balls tightened and they ached in a sweet way that was almost painful. His cock jerked when Malcolm sucked particularly hard, and his hole clenched. He was afraid he might come too soon.

Malcolm seemed to know how to pace himself, though. Just when Brenin was about to issue a warning, the man's efforts slowed. He pulled back on the cock and tickled the underneath with a wagging tongue. Brenin clawed at the floor and moaned. He wanted more. He just didn't know for sure what the more was.

Again, Malcolm knew. The man slid his hand up the back of Brenin's leg and cupped his arse. He slid a finger in between the cheeks and teased Brenin's hole. It spasmed at the attention but not enough to keep Malcolm from slipping inside. The bit of cum Brenin had massaged around it still lingered. And he knew how to relax, especially when Malcolm handily distracted him with more deep-throating.

"Yesss," he hissed, then moaned in case he hadn't made himself clear. "More, please."

Malcolm did as he asked, inserting his finger as far as it would go. He fucked Brenin with it, syncing the rhythm of his head bobbing up and down Brenin's cock. Brenin could feel his hole loosening, opening up to the gentle invasion. There was a sensation of fullness there, no pain, then a starburst of pleasure rocked him as Malcolm scraped along some inside part of him.

Brenin couldn't stay still. He rocked back onto the finger before reversing and sending his dick balls deep into Malcolm's mouth. His lover stayed with him, never faltering, giving him everything he demanded — and more than he knew how to ask.

Pulling off the cock, Malcolm said, "Scoot forward, laddie. Put your sweet arse against my mouth."

It was on the tip of Brenin's tongue to refuse. He couldn't do that, could he? Malcolm hadn't ceded control entirely, apparently, because he forced Brenin up. He parted the globes and stuck his tongue in where his finger so recently had been. The way he licked and teased Brenin's hole, it opened for him without complaint. When Brenin thought he'd go mad from the pleasure, Malcolm sent him heavenward by stabbing the tip of his tongue inside.

"Oh God, I'm going to come!" he wailed, desperate for it and yet not wanting it to end so soon.

"Stay with me, bonnie lad." Malcolm's breath bathed Brenin's wet hole, sending shivers through him.

When Malcolm urged him to slide down his torso again, Brenin fumbled to comply. Malcolm was there for him, using his strong hands to help him into position. Brenin understood what he wanted, felt ready to give it to him, and still Malcolm held him back. Instead of seating him on his once-more-erect cock, Malcolm milked it with his own hands. Pre-cum dribbled out to meet that which had already dried. Malcolm scooped it up and this time, it was he who used it as lube.

It was maddeningly slow, the way he inserted one coated finger then another to open Brenin. There was a burn with the wider insertion, but nothing like the pain he was used to. This was different. It held the promise of intense pleasure. Every pass of those fingers across his prostate sent his arousal higher. The ache in his balls became an incessant pressure.

"Malcolm, please."

He didn't wait for his lover's consent. Brenin was in control. That was the deal and what he wanted right now—what he needed—was Malcolm's cock inside him. He found the strength to push the man's arm aside and position himself so that the tip of Malcolm's dick was pressed against his loose, puckered hole.

"Brenin," Malcolm breathed the warning.

It was too late and, the moment the cock breached the hole, there were no more warnings. No more words, only the joining of their bodies. Brenin sat all the way down and waited with his eyes closed and his lungs heaving as he adjusted to the way the cock stretched him wide.

"Brenin?"

"It's all right. I'm bloody fine. Fuck me, for God's sake, Malcolm."

His lover gave him what he pleaded for. Grabbing Brenin by the hips, Malcolm fucked himself with Brenin's willing body. It was perfect, the experienced man leading the novice, yet in a way that didn't make him feel overwhelmed or trapped. All Brenin had to do was hang on for the ride.

And, oh, what a ride it was. He panted and curled his fingers against Malcolm's chest. He scrunched up his face and his toes, as well, and clenched his hole around the hard length embedded in him. Now that he was loose, he perversely missed the burn. He tried to bring it back, even as he held his release in check. He wanted them to come together.

The dick inside him swelled. He knew what that meant. "Come now, Malcolm."

"Are you with me, laddie?" the man gasped.

Brenin threw back his head. "Yes! No, wait!" Madness was upon him perhaps, but he needed more. If they were truly going to join, sex wasn't all there was. He had to give this last, other bit of himself to his man or they would never be the 'one' that he wanted for them.

He collapsed against him, crooking his head to one side, exposing his neck. "Bite me."

"No."

"Do it!" He screamed in his frustration.

It worked. Malcolm sank his fangs into Brenin's jugular. The pain was nothing compared to the intensity of the orgasm that claimed him a split-second later. He cried out and went limp. The tugging at his vein was joined by flooding inside his arse. Malcolm drawing in Brenin's blood while filling him with his cum.

It was perfect. It was peace and it was love.

* * * *

"You sure you're all right?" Malcolm tucked more of his kilt around Brenin as they sat by the fire he'd built after they'd made love.

Brenin leaned against his hard body. He felt so safe with all this strength at his beck and call. "You've got to stop asking me that or I'm going to feel as if I did it wrong."

Malcolm chuckled and kissed the top of his head. "You did everything perfectly. It's me I'm worried about."

"Well, stop. I'll remember this night forever and a day."

"That's all right, then." Malcolm sighed. "I want to give you everything. I only wish I could show you the stars from up there. You can't imagine how beautiful they are when you're in space."

"It could happen one day. You don't know. Technology is changing so fast and we'll live a lot more years. We may see a time when we can shoot up there for a holiday."

"That's true." Malcolm played with a lock of Brenin's hair. "Have you made up your mind, then, to take my blood?"

"Yes, I want that. I want to bear your sons, only not for a while yet. We have to get our guests settled and there's no telling how long that will take. I don't think I could handle pregnancy and a bunch of hurt boys."

"You wouldn't change that fast. It takes years, I believe. We'll ask Harry, to be sure."

"Oh, in that case, let's get started sooner rather than later. I want to become stronger, more like Mackie."

"So that you can feel safe?"

He turned so that he could face Malcolm. "No, you already make me feel that way. It's only that after what happened in the tunnel, I don't want you to have to put yourself in harm's way for me again."

Malcolm kissed the tip of his nose. "Sweet lad, the danger is over."

"Is it? Petru is still out there — and others. It's not truly over."

"It is for us. Alex has promised."

"But that's not fair. They may need us again and I, for one, want to help whenever I can."

"You put me to shame, Brenin. All I want is my Scotch, my salmon and you. Most of all, you."

Placing a hand on Malcolm's cheek, he kissed him. He tried to pour all of the feelings he had into that gesture. "I love you, no matter what."

Malcolm stared into the fire, saying nothing for a long while. "I think," he finally said, "the thing that bothered me the most was how easily eons of evolution got tossed aside in the span of a few hundred years. Our entire existence, our species, had been devoted to the one constant that the hive was everything."

He brought his gaze back to Brenin. "Dracul and the others should never have entertained the idea of mutiny. They turned on their hive brothers, Brenin. I can't tell you how utterly contrary that is to our nature.

"It scares me that they did it and I worry that if they could change so much, maybe I could, as well."

Brenin scoffed. "That's just silly. You could never be like them."

"No? I led my dear friend, Fergus, into the battle at Culloden. His father wanted his one remaining son to stay with him, safe. But I was loyal to Alex and once I got a taste for it, I was spoiling for a fight whenever I could. Fergus wouldn't leave my side.

"I got him killed when all was said and done," he added with a sorrowful look that broke Brenin's heart. "His father never forgave me, but he let me take his place and made me promise to look after his land and his people. I've been good to my word, so far."

"And brilliant at it, too, if your people—Darling, Cook, Doc McPhee—are any judge. The fact that an entire village keeps your secret says a lot about their love and loyalty."

Malcolm picked up Brenin's hand and kissed the knuckles. "When I see myself through your eyes, it makes me think better of myself." He pulled Brenin down on top of him. "I promise you that I will never turn my back on my hive. If Alex ever needs my help again, I'll go—and willingly. So long as I have you by my side, I know I'll never fail."

Brenin threw his arms around his lover's neck and hugged him tight. "I promise you'll always have that. Now, can I ask for another favor?"

"Anything."

"Can we do it again?"

"It?" Malcolm's eyes were guileless, except they'd already turned black and his cock had stiffened.

"Och, you do try a mun," Brenin said in his best imitation of a highland burr, which wasn't very good at all. "This time, I ride you all by myself."

And he did.

Epilogue

Dracul held on to the bit of rock inside the catch with his bleeding fingertips eroding with each passing second. He ignored that loss of his flesh, as well as the pain. Fury made him strong. The thirst for vengeance had him drawing on a well of strength he'd not known he had. It wasn't until the castle shook with an explosion that he finally lost his grip and plunged all the way down. The jagged stone shaft dug agonizing grooves along every part of his body.

He hit water and sank below. His lungs burned as he kicked his legs to bring him to the surface of the cistern. He gulped in a huge breath before sinking again. This time, he stayed longer, hiding from his enemies, in case they still searched for him.

More explosions reached his ears, telling him that they couldn't possibly have remained, with the destruction they'd wreaked. He pushed up again and swam to the edge. He caught the scent of the ones who'd brought him down — both of them, the boy and the navigator. He grinned at the vision of tearing them limb from limb. It would happen. He needed only to regain his strength, then he'd go after them all, including Petru, the traitorous dog.

With the last of his strength, he pulled himself onto the stone floor. Darkness claimed him, and when next he opened his eyes, mismatched ones stared down at him.

Relieved by the sight, he forced words past his ravaged lips. "Hello, slut."

The human smiled. "Master, I thought I'd lost you. I followed the other one and crept down here once they'd left."

As tiresome as it was, he smiled up at the boy and praised him. "How very clever of you. I will have to come up with a suitable reward when I'm back to my full strength."

The human's strange eyes lit up. "You're badly hurt, Master. I'll help you."

"Of course you will. Is there any danger of this collapsing on us?"

"I don't think so, Master. They blew your arsenal and there are fires, but the stone is holding."

"Good." He tried to rise and grunted in anger and frustration when he fell back again. At least he landed on the slut's lap and the boy was wearing one of Dracul's robes, so it was worthy of cushioning his head.

"I need blood to regain my strength."

"Master, please take mine."

"That was the plan." Dracul grinned. "I might drain you dry," he warned as a test of how devoted his new slave was.

"I trust you," the boy said, tilting his neck to expose his pale, slender neck.

"You shouldn't." With that warning issued, Dracul struck. He grabbed the boy's shoulder and yanked him in tightly at the same moment his fangs sank deep into the proffered flesh.

He tugged the healing blood in with deep pulls. It nourished his hurts and fanned the flames of revenge sparking inside his heart. He would kill every one of them...eventually. This time, he would be more patient. He would be patient as he'd never been before, scheme and wait for the perfect opportunities.

The only problem was deciding on the order. Such a delightful predicament to have. In the meantime, he would drink his fill, then he would fuck the boy raw. After that, he would have to access his stored wealth, find a new place to live and start all over again — damn it. Ah well, the best-laid plans and all that. He couldn't let this get him down. He was better than that.

He was better than all of them.

Want to see more from this author?
Here's a taster for you to enjoy!

Alien Slave Masters:
The Untamed Pet
Samantha Cayto

Excerpt

"Easy now. No need to be afraid."

Stuart couldn't help shying away from the touch of even gentle hands. This is what his short time with the other alien had done to him. Never a bold person, despite his wishes to the contrary, he had become a cowering, fearful creature that he despised almost as much as he did the Travians.

"Please don't hurt me." He cringed inwardly at his pathetic pleading, yet couldn't help himself. *"I won't fight you. I promise. I'll be good."* He was unable to control the tremors racking his body.

The alien loomed over him. Instead of the sneering, predatory look Stuart had come to fear, he saw kindness and concern – or maybe he only thought he did. He no longer trusted his own judgment in anything, not since he'd made the fatal decision to join Joel and the others in their harassment campaign. That fateful choice would be the death of him. He had no doubt of that now.

"Of course you'll be good," the alien all but crooned. *"And I will be good to you in turn."* A large hand, pale as death, loomed in the periphery of Stuart's vision. He shrank in on

himself, trained already to expect a blow. None came. Instead, the alien threaded his fingers through Stuart's thick, red hair. Once again, where Stuart expected pain, there was only gentleness. No tugging, merely stroking.

"Your hair is so pretty." The alien moved that same hand down to cup Stuart's chin then lifted it. Stuart didn't dare look anywhere other than the floor. "All of you is so lovely, small and delicate."

What was Stuart supposed to do with that observation? His former master had said much the same with a certain amount of sadistic glee, as if pleased with the ease in which he could brutalize his human pet. Stuart had always hated being short and thin compared to other boys. Travians, towering monsters that they were, hadn't made him feel much worse about his stature, just more of the same. That is, until he'd been hauled into the quarters of the first officer to claim him. He'd never known such agony, and he assumed that no matter what this one said, things would be the same. God, why couldn't the creature just get on with it?

His trembling increased and his breath came out in mounting pants. "Please," he begged again, although not sure what he wanted, other than to go home – back to New World Colony Seven. As inhospitable as that world had been, he'd come to appreciate the opportunity it had afforded him to grow into his own. And it was home, for no other reason than because his parents lived there. Guilt stabbed at him. He'd left them – not by choice, but by dint of his foolish need to fit in with the other boys. His poor parents hadn't known what he'd intended and they undoubtedly mourned his loss, thinking him dead. Better, maybe, that they thought that than know the truth.

"Hush. All will be well. This can go," the alien said, lifting the hated collar off Stuart's neck and tossing it aside. Not once had the Travian choked him with it, and that was something, he supposed. "What are you called, little one?"

Surprised by the question, Stuart blinked up at the creature for a second before lowering his gaze again. The other one hadn't asked that question, had merely called him 'pet' when not calling him something worse. "Stuart McKay," he managed to say through a throat clogged with fear.

"Stu-art-mac-kay." The Travian said the two names as if they were one, accenting the wrong syllables, not that Stuart would correct him. "Hmm. It's too strange on my tongue." The alien puffed out a breath, a form of alien laughing Stuart had come to learn at his own expense. "I will call you Mac." Another puff. "Yes, that is the perfect name for my pretty pet."

The alien placed his hands on Stuart's shoulders and turned him slowly around to face the bed. Stuart's breath hitched at the sight. He hated this! As much as he'd longed for a boyfriend back on Seven — or even just some kind of sexual experience — he'd never get used to this casual using of his body. Never mind the searing pain... It was the degradation that got to him the most. In these aliens' beds he became a thing — an object to be used — nothing more. It was far from the tender lovemaking he'd always envisioned with a tall, strong man who valued him. The ruination of his fantasy, more than anything, made him want to take a one-way trip out of an airlock.

"Up you go," the alien said with a soft push. "Lie down on your stomach. We must rid you of Garen's stench." This last bit was said with a hard edge that made Stuart tremble even more, as he scrambled to comply. Was that his former tormentor's name? He hadn't known or even cared. Just like it didn't matter to him what this one called himself. He only wanted to survive the night with as few injuries as possible. Maybe, just maybe, if he did as he was told, this time he wouldn't be beaten.

He lay down and closed his eyes, unwilling to watch the Travian shed his uniform. He curled his hands into fists, clutching the bedding to keep himself from vibrating too much. Part of that reaction came from being cold, but that would stop soon. When the larger creature covered him, the heat would be like a furnace. Tears slipped past the corners of his eyes, despite his efforts to be calm. When the bed dipped with the weight of the alien, a small whimper escaped his tight lips.

"Hush," the Travian admonished again, running his hand down Stuart's back. He pressed a knee between Stuart's legs, opening them.

Stuart made himself spread them wide, being the good boy he'd promised to be. He couldn't stop the jump, though, when the alien clasped his ass cheeks and spread them. More murmurs filled his ears and a soothing massage of his flesh accompanied slick strokes against his hole. This was it, the tearing agony of being breached and filled beyond capacity. He willed his body to relax, knowing being tense would only make the experience worse – except the brutal invasion didn't happen. Instead, there was teasing and stroking. Something much smaller than a Travian cock entered his ass, breaching it slowly, infusing him with something wet and slippery. The stroking of his channel continued, the speed and stretching increasing so gradually that when a dick finally replaced the fingers being used, it went in with surprising ease.

As he lay there being fucked at an ever greater pace, his body rocking back and forth, the breath wheezing out of his lungs, Stuart knew that his life had changed once again. This time, however, he might be able to survive.

Mac woke up with a start. Foggy with sleep, he had trouble remembering where he was. A transport ship, not Narith's quarters, although his master sat beside him, engrossed in something he was reading on the built-in tablet for his seat. The remnants of Mac's dream remained swimming around his head, and the effect was easy to see if one looked. He quickly placed his hands on his lap to hide his semi-hard cock. The soft, clingy clothing he wore certainly wouldn't do the trick.

He smiled a little to himself, thinking of how much his life had changed. He hadn't gotten hard that first night with Narith, but things were different now. He was different now.

It wasn't only that he looked different with his longer hair, braided away from his face, and his harder body. He thought of himself by a different name, the one Narith had given him. Gone was Stuart McKay, the shy, quiet boy who'd always hung on the periphery of everyone else's fun. He'd been replaced by Mac, Narith's beloved pet and a guy who didn't simply endure being fucked but participated in it — wildly and enthusiastically. He'd become bolder, too, in his dealings with the other boys. Whereas before he'd deferred to them and had gone along to get along, these days he'd started asserting himself. He spoke up and even argued when the occasion demanded it.

He couldn't resist pressing his hands onto his still-burgeoning erection. After spending much of his adolescence tamping down his sexuality for lack of an outlet other than his own hand, Narith's excellent tutelage had turned him into something of a sexual monster. It had been too long, while in this last leg of transit, since he and his master had had an opportunity for any kind of sexual release. His action caused a spike of pleasure to shoot up his groin. Suppressing a moan, he shifted his weight in response.

"Don't fidget," Narith ordered under his breath, without looking up from his tablet.

Mac instantly stilled, his body and mind well-trained already to do as this male commanded. He'd taken to his role as a pet easily, naturally. He'd long recognized his submissive nature and despaired of ever finding the kind of alpha male that he longed for. With a colony as small as Seven, he would have been lucky to find another man at all compatible with him, let alone one who embodied the dominating persona he'd envisioned. Once he'd realized he needn't fear the Travian, he'd been able to accept the creature's mastery.

He'd also fallen hopelessly in love with Narith.

Those feelings alone made Mac want to obey and not cause trouble. The transport officer had just about shit his pants with outrage when Narith had insisted that Mac sit with him on the flight and not be tied up somewhere in the cargo hold. So Mac was trying his best to blend into the background. The difficulty lay in the length of the journey and the weird way Travians had of remaining preternaturally still—at least by human standards—during the flight. Even if they moved, they did so with an economy of motion that Mac had no hope of emulating. His human 'fidgeting' seemed to annoy them as well, for some reason, earning him quick glares from the other passengers.

He didn't want to cause Narith any more stress. The poor guy was already grieving at the loss of his mate's first pregnancy. He didn't say it, of course, or really show it in a way someone who knew him less well would notice. Mac did. He'd come to know the Travian better than he'd ever known anyone, other than his parents. The expressions he wore and the set of his broad shoulders spoke volumes to Mac. And the closer they got to Travia Prime, the tenser the young officer became. Mac desperately wanted to help him. If for no other reason, he didn't want the guy to regret his decision to bring Mac with him, as opposed to giving him over to another of the ship's officers. Mac was under no illusion that the alien returned Mac's level of affection. The only reason for bringing his pet was to find comfort or distraction. If Mac turned into an inconvenience, Narith might send him back to Kell or hand him over to someone else on the planet. Mac didn't think he could stand either of those possibilities.

So, here he sat, being the good boy that he always promised to be. And he'd proved to be a great distraction in the earlier parts of their journey, if he said so himself. Fucking worked wonders for the both of them, he knew. He'd gladly allowed Narith to use his body as much as he wanted. They'd also fucked nonstop during Narith's last off-duty shift before leaving the ship. Mac understood, finally, about the scent marking, and he even reveled in the idea that he smelled like his master, even if he couldn't detect it himself. He loved how all of these Travian soldiers around them knew that he belonged to Narith, even beyond the collar and leash that he wore.

Something changed suddenly in the way the craft moved. Narith put his tablet away. "We are entering the atmosphere of Travia Prime." He gave a Mac a tight smile. "This will get a bit rough."

So saying, he reached over and clasped Mac's hand, just as the ship's trajectory became steeper and they picked up speed. Everything shimmied and shook alarmingly. Mac tightened his fingers around the larger hand. He'd never landed on a planet awake before. The colonists had all been in suspended animation for their journey until they'd touched down on their New World. To his inexperienced self, it was hard to tell at the moment if they were landing or crashing. He figured the former only because no one was screaming. Or maybe Travians would go calmly to their deaths. What the hell did he really know about the species?

But, no. With a thud and a bump and a grinding of something, they stopped moving. Mac let out a sigh of relief and shyly smiled over at his master. Narith didn't return the look. He merely let go of Mac's hand and stood up. They had no luggage, Narith needing to bring nothing and Mac having nothing to bring. The clothes he wore were the first since his capture, and they were intended to avoid offending females, not that he'd seen many. His clothes never seemed to require any cleaning, and Narith had assured him that once they reached their destination, others would be manufactured for him instantly anyway.

Their journey had been a long one, filled with interesting sights. It had taken them through four space stations, the first one housing Joel, giving Mac some time to catch up with the guy. He'd been afraid at first that Joel would sneer and berate him for his obvious obedience and affection for Narith. Mac had sometimes thought that Joel had come out of the womb with a 'fuck you' on his lips. He'd been surprised to find a relaxed and happy Joel, seemingly at peace with his life, perhaps for the first time ever. Mac still couldn't believe that the tough-seeming kid had settled into being the pet of the station's commander. The stations themselves had been eye-opening, filled with wondrous sights, including Travian females and other creatures. He and Narith had stayed mostly in the military parts of each station, however, giving Mac little opportunity to interact with Travian females.

That was about to change in a major way. Narith guided Mac by his leash, leading him out of the smallish shuttle and into the gigantic spaceport. Mac had thought he'd be inured to their large buildings because of the stations. He'd been wrong. Those spheres spinning in space were nothing compared to what they had dirtside. The place was huge, the ceiling barely visible to Mac's eyes, and it was teeming with Travians. Here the military mixed with the civilian, giving Mac his first real, prolonged experience with females in large numbers – and even children.

He'd known from what Wid and Joel had said – and from his own limited travels – that Travian females were like peacocks to the males' peahens, a complete reversal of Earth birds' plumage. Yet, how else could one think of it, the way the females adorned themselves in a riot of intricate color, while the males who weren't in uniform wore simple monotone clothing, much like his dark gray tunic and pants. His feet were bare, though, in stark contrast to everyone else. Despite Mac's rather timid protests to the contrary, Narith had remained firm on the matter. Apparently footwear – or lack thereof, of all things – set Mac apart as a pet and nothing more. His poor feet slapped against the cold floor with each step he took.

"Stay close to me, Mac," Narith said with an uncharacteristic tug of the leash that caused the collar to tighten uncomfortably.

Mac did as he was told to ease the choking and, frankly, because it made him feel safer to be tight against his master's side. He didn't like the stares he got, the downright leers of some males. As far as he could tell, he was the only non-Travian in sight – maybe within the whole spaceport. Narith had informed him that there would be other pets on the home world, just not other humans. Keeping subspecies as domesticated playthings was a common practice of Travians. Mac had tried not to bristle at the idea that he was a subspecies. Instead, he'd listened intently to Narith's instructions on what to expect when they arrived at Narith's home – his mate's home, actually, as Travian males didn't have homes of their own. They lived with mothers, then mates, or maybe with sisters or other female relatives. Or, barring any of that, they could live in military barracks.

Mac had found the concept strange and a bit fascinating, yet he hadn't asked more than the necessary questions. He didn't want to embarrass Narith, and that had to remain his main focus. The poor guy was too preoccupied not only with the loss of the much-anticipated first child of his mate, but also with the chilling fact that the female had already taken a second mate to conceive again. Although his master hadn't confided in him, Mac knew the young male had been devastated by the news. Still reeling from one blow, he'd had to deal with another. He'd gone so far as to explain to Mac that Narith's position as a mate of a high-born female was in jeopardy. He had to get back to her quickly to reconnect and strengthen their bond, even though it could damage his career to leave such an important post mid-deployment.

They entered some kind of moving enclosed sidewalk and were crammed into a corner away from the other passengers. Their efforts to be unobtrusive proved pointless. It seemed as if every pair of Travian eyes rested upon them. Mac wanted to cower and cling to Narith's arm. Then he remembered that while Stuart would have done so, Mac had more balls. He straightened up and held his gaze steady, if unfocused. He didn't intend to challenge anyone, just convey an air of pride. They were all likely looking at a human for the first time. It was important that they came away with the sense that humans were confident and brave, even if Mac's insides were quivering.

This next leg of the journey seemed interminable. As long as he'd lived with Travians, Mac still couldn't quite figure out Travian time. He just knew they had more stamina than he did, standing when he would have killed for a place to sit and staying alert when his eyelids drooped. Finally, the conveyance came to a stop. The females disembarked first, followed by the males. Narith allowed the others to leave before he guided Mac out. They headed toward an area in which Travians in twos and threes climbed into big, clear bubbles with seats and electronics. They turned out to be yet another mode of transportation, this one more private, and it became airborne.

Mac did grab hold of his master's arm when the thing lifted straight up in the air. Narith laughed – the first time he'd done so in forever, it seemed – and he glanced over at Mac. "You're perfectly safe, pet. This craft is self-operational and preprogrammed. We'll be home soon, not to worry."

But Mac did worry. Not about the flight. Having spent so much time in space, he wasn't afraid of a little terrestrial flying. Much. No, his angst focused on what would happen when they reached their destination. He wasn't convinced that Narith's mate would be as sanguine about having a human pet in her home and in her mate's bed as Narith seemed to think she would be. He wondered – not for the first time – if she'd make him sleep outside or something. He knew his master would be powerless to stop it. In this society, women ruled. Besides, even without the cultural differences of their species, Mac had lived for a while now in the single-sexed environment of a military ship. He worried he'd do something to offend a female of any type. He'd have to watch his every step, and knowing that was enough to make him very nervous.

He decided to shift his focus for the time being onto his surroundings, trying to adapt to flying through the air with a three-hundred-and-sixty-degree view of the world below them. Once his stomach settled and his brain accepted the fact that they weren't going to plummet a few hundred meters to their deaths, he actually enjoyed what he could see. This was only the second alien world he'd even been on, and it blew away Seven, that was for sure. Where Seven was a bland planet that grudgingly allowed things to grow, Travia Prime was a lush, colorful haven. It reminded him of make-believe places in his childhood stories, with rolling hills interrupted by thick forests of strange trees.

Or maybe they weren't trees. How could he know? Having chosen to work in the hydroponic gardens back on Seven, Mac's early interest in plants had grown, as it were, into a passion. He desperately wanted to ask Narith a million questions about what he saw as they raced along. He dared not. The alien's face was frozen now in a grim expression, and he held his body so rigid, Mac worried it might crack into a million pieces if he so much as tapped on one shoulder. So he sat quietly and took in everything he could, storing away his questions for a better time.

God, he hoped there would be a better time.

Narith knew he made a poor host, not that he owed his pet any particular courtesy. By the beliefs of his people, he had every right to expect his pet to cater to his whims, not the other way around. Yet, in the time that he'd spent with Mac, Narith had come to appreciate that the human was intelligent and had feelings just as sharp and genuine as any Travian's, perhaps more so. Out of the corner of his eye, he could see the boy craning his neck around as he took in the sights. Narith knew Mac liked botany and had found a useful place in the hydroponic gardens maintained for self-sufficiency on the ship. He bet the boy had a million questions, yet held his tongue for Narith's sake.

So empathetic and considerate, as always, and it made Narith want to be the same way in return.

He was too wrapped up in his own misery and apprehension to find even a modicum of space for Mac, however. As they neared Orianna's home, Narith's stress level ratcheted up exponentially. His skin seemed to tighten around his body, squeezing on every taut nerve and muscle, crushing his skull, pressing on his brain until he wanted to scream out his frustration and rage. In his younger days, he would have given in to the feelings. The Mother knew that he'd gotten into a plethora of trouble giving free rein to his impulses, not really considering the consequences. Propriety and decorum had often been ignored in favor of wildness and daring. The military had literally beaten a fair amount of that out of him. His mother and other female relatives had done the rest, molding him into a more useful tool for the family.

Now he sat rigidly under control, a master of his body, if not completely his mind. This hard-won discipline was how he'd climbed his way up to his rank and secured a coveted position as junior navigator on a deep-space ship. It was also how he'd caught the eye of a high-born first daughter. His transformation into an accommodating male, endlessly patient with female doings, had gotten him noticed at social gatherings. His looks, frankly, hadn't hurt, either. He'd caught the eye of males and females alike. But it was an advantageous mating that his family had hoped for, and he'd succeeded in giving it to them. He couldn't afford to lose his shit when it mattered most.

He sat unseeing and not appreciating the lovely view of his home world, a place he hadn't expected to return to so soon. His focus remained on what he'd find when he arrived. He could picture Orianna, her ethereal beauty still something that took his breath away and made him feel less worthy than his relatively low-caste birth already did. Mating with her had been a thrilling and frightening experience. Even his rebellious nature had never led him to fucking a female, and his experiences with other males hadn't prepared him for the wholly different feeling of coupling with a softer, more delicate bedmate.

But he couldn't work up excitement over seeing her again, and not merely because the sight of her would bring a fresh stab of grief over the loss of the child he'd proudly given her. It was because another male would be standing by her side — her second mate, his scent overpowering Narith's on her body by this time. He hated the thought of sharing her. Travian males weren't supposed to feel jealous, their more primitive sides having been wiped out by eons of evolution. That's what females believed anyway — or really, demanded. And maybe there were many males who were happy to share a female if that was what she wanted, her happiness being paramount.

But most males knew — and even dared confess to each other — that their baser sides remained. No matter how their species progressed, the scent marking remained as strong as ever. Nothing prodded a male's primitive instincts more than his own smell on another, whether a female, an offspring or even a pet. With a sideways glance, Narith inhaled deeply and Mac's smell, concentrated in the confined space, helped calm Narith's ever-more-frayed nerves just a bit. The human pet remained his and no one else's. Plus, Mac had proven to be an enticing bedmate, blending the parts of being with a female and a male that Narith enjoyed.

He really needed to pull himself together. The journey was nearly over, Orianna's grand home being not that far from the regional spaceport they'd arrived at. With another glance at his pet, he made a decision that bothered him on some level. He hated to interrupt his pet's pleasure, but the creature did exist at this point to serve his master, and Narith would make it up to him eventually in some way. He reached over and, cupping his palm around the back of the boy's neck, tugged him down to the floor. He felt a little resistance, just for a moment, and the human's gaze slid over to Narith before complying.

Such grace in the lithe body, the way he slipped to his knees and maneuvered between Narith's legs with little additional prompting. Clever boy. He understood Narith's needs so well now. With his quick and nimble fingers, Mac had Narith's fly open in a heartbeat and freed the cock that had already started to swell with anticipation. Narith leaned back against his chair and closed his eyes. He moved his hand to Mac's head, enjoying, as always, the feel of the thick, wavy hair so unlike his own. He sighed when his pet wrapped moist lips around the head of his dick. Tension bled out of him in an instant.

Mac brought Narith to full hardness with his clever tongue, laving the sensitive ridge below the glans. Narith took pride in knowing he had been the one to teach his pet how to give a proper blow job. The boy had had no sexual experience with anyone other than the hateful Garen, who had undoubtedly just face-fucked the poor thing until he'd gagged with it. Narith had no such intentions, couldn't even imagine why one would want to — not when the boy sucked and licked with obvious joy. The effort sent sparks of pleasure straight down to the root of Narith's cock, making his balls tingle as they tightened against his body.

Narith groaned through stuttering breath. He rolled his hips in an involuntary plea to have his pet take him farther into that delightfully tight, wet heat. He knew he was too big for the boy to swallow completely, but Narith still jerked with the tightness along his shaft. His release — already desperate to come out — pulsed through his dick. Mac stayed with him, taking every drop down with convulsive movements of his mouth and throat. Narith let his arms drop to his sides and he sighed again with the relief.

Moments later, with his pants refastened and his pet once more sitting beside him, the craft signaled that they were nearing their destination. The post-orgasm relaxation vanished in the face of his imminent arrival. Not even the beautiful vista of Orianna's vast land could distract him from his focus on the large house looming in his vision. He stared in the direction of the main entrance, long before he could actually see it. Having sent his itinerary ahead, he knew the family awaited his arrival, a fact confirmed when he saw the head female of the house, Salan, standing on the top of the staircase.

"We have arrived," he said quite unnecessarily as the craft hovered and landed with a soft bounce. "Remember what I told you."

"Yes, master." Mac waited for Narith to exit first, then followed.

Of course the human would remember all the things Narith had drilled him on about comportment. The boy was smart and eager to please. If anyone would fuck things up, it would be him. Playing by the rules didn't come naturally to him. He'd had to work hard to alter his demeanor, if not his attitude. He would have to be very clever indeed to hide his disappointment in the change of circumstances and dislike of the existence of his new house brother.

He strode up the steps of the great manse, as pleasant a look on his face as he could manage, yet nothing too cheery, given the solemn nature of his visit. "Salan, it is good of you to wait on me."

The older female sketched a simple bow. "Senior Sire Narith, welcome home. Our Lady awaits you with the junior sire." The female turned on her heel and headed back into the house.

Narith grimaced inwardly at being called senior sire instead of just sire. He had to get used to his new reality. With a quick swivel of his head, he confirmed that Mac trailed a few paces behind him, quiet and with his head down. That would have to be the last time he gave in to the urge to check on his pet. From this point forward, his total focus had to be on his mate. He saw her as soon as his eyes adjusted to the change in light. She sat at the back of the great hall, on her usual seat for entertaining visitors, the one that elevated her enough that she could look down on someone, even when they stood. Her exquisite beauty still had the power to stun him momentarily, making him clumsy in his steps. He wouldn't have cared about the stumble if not for the smirking male standing by her side.

Narith slid to his knees at the proper time and made the expected greeting. "Dearest mate, I have returned to you with a heavy heart at your loss, but with great joy at seeing you once more." He bowed at the neck.

Once he'd raised his head, Orianna graced him with a smile. "First mate, Narith. Although my heart is also heavy, I am overjoyed at having you home again." She gestured with one delicate hand at the male to her left. "I present to you your house brother, Rone."

Narith made himself shift his gaze to the male, keeping his pleasant expression in place. "Younger brother, I am gratified to meet you." Fucker.

Rone bent his neck a fraction before replying, "Elder brother, I am honored in return."

Narith read the lie in the male's expression. He was older than Narith somewhat, but social norms dictated that because Narith was the first mate, he was the elder brother. He took in the male's uniform, noting by his insignia that he was of a local regiment. Of course, this time Orianna had picked someone who would always be close at hand. Narith took some pleasure in noticing that the male stood a bit shorter than Narith's own tall frame, although the male filled out his uniform with greater muscle mass. He mentally shook himself. He really needed to fight the urge to compare them, or he might go mad from the effort. He tried to muster a more genuine interest in his new brother, but then the complex scent wafting off Orianna finally reached him full force. His mind took a moment to process the meaning of what he detected. Then a great emotion welled up inside him. Part rage, part despair, it swamped him.

Orianna hadn't simply mated again. She was already pregnant.

PUBLISHING

Sign up for our newsletter and find out about all our romance book releases, eBook sales and promotions, sneak peeks and FREE romance eBooks!

https://totallyentwinedgroup.us7.list-manage.com/subscribe/post

About the Author

Samantha Cayto is a Boston-area native who practices as a business lawyer by day while writing erotic romance at night—the steamier the better. She likes to push the envelope when it comes to writing about passion and is delighted other women agree that guy-on-guy sex is the hottest ever.

She lives a typical suburban life with her husband, three kids and four dogs. Her children don't understand why they can't read what she writes, but her husband is always willing to lend her a hand—and anything else—when she needs to choreograph a scene.

Samantha loves to hear from readers. You can find her contact information, website details and author profile page at http://www.pride-publishing.com